Bubba and the Zigzaggery Zombies

By

C.L. Bevill

Bubba and the Zigzaggery Zombies
©2013 by C.L. Bevill, LLC

Bubba and the Zigzaggery Zombies is a work of fiction. Names, characters, places, and incidents are the product of the author's imagination or are used fictitiously. Fictitiously used characters are utilized without intent to defame or denigrate.

Bubba and the Zigzaggery Zombies is intended as book 5 in the Bubba series. The series follows this order:

Bubba and the Dead Woman
Bubba and the 12 Deadly Days of Christmas
Bubba and the Missing Woman
Brownie and the Dame (3.5)
Bubba and the Mysterious Murder Note
The Ransom of Brownie (4.5)
Bubba and the Zigzaggery Zombies

It is best read in order.

Table of Contents

Chapter One

Bubba and the Zigzaggery Zombies

Friday, March 8th

It's a lovely day without corpses, Bubba Snoddy thought.

It *was* a lovely day. And there *weren't* any corpses within sight. Everything was win-win.

It was win-win although Bubba was sitting in a cemetery and was, in fact, leaning against a tombstone that said "Here lies Timothy Wake. He stepped on the gas instead of the brake." This was Bubba's very favorite tombstone. In Longtall Cemetery, which was a graveyard located on the, not ironically, tallest hill in Pegramville, the marker was the most humorous one. Bubba hadn't known Timothy Wake, nor did he know of any Wakes in Pegram County, but he liked the idea that one didn't have to go into the darkness without a smile. (Okay, there *were* corpses on this lovely day, but they were all buried and most of them had died of natural causes or at least causes that didn't call for the police to locate a rabid perpetrator holding a knife, gun, or possibly a handmade Taser.)

Bubba's mother, Miz Demetrice Snoddy, probably would have told Bubba that sitting on a grave was unlucky and rude and conceivably illegal. (The illegal part wouldn't have made a little mosquito-sized bump in his mother's conscience, but the other stuff would.) Bubba didn't think Timothy Wake would have minded. Besides the fact that he was dead, he'd had a decent wit, or he'd had a family who had felt the need to earmark his passing with good-natured absurdity. (Bubba couldn't argue about the

4

unlucky part given the situations he'd found himself embroiled within the last two years.)

Tim's stone didn't have dates on it, but it was in the oldest part of the cemetery. Bubba looked around and saw that some of the birthdates were from the 19th century and one particular gentleman had been a Civil War veteran. Sergeant David Stafford had served in the 1st Louisiana Cavalry Regiment and he had died after the war. His marker didn't indicate his date of death but the stone to his right had his daughter's name on it and she had been born in 1872. (He assumed that she had been the sergeant's daughter because there was an engraved notation saying "Daughter of David", but Bubba might have been incorrect.)

Bubba sighed. He'd been in the Army until he had caught his fiancée in his very own bed with their very own commanding officer. Bubba had been discharged after breaking their very own commanding officer's arm. There wasn't going to be a marker commemorating Bubba's military service, although he'd been a first rate mechanic at two separate Army posts in the United States and one in Germany. (Bubba had six framed letters awarding him various medals that said just that, but those had been awarded before the arm-breaking incident. The medals themselves were stuck in a barely singed, handmade oak box that had survived a fire set in the house in which he'd lived.)

Breaking the captain's arm hadn't been the smartest thing to do, but Bubba liked to think it had turned out well for his ex- fiancée. She had married the captain and lived in marital bliss. That was until she had been murdered by someone determined to frame Bubba.

Bubba frowned. It *hadn't* turned out well for his ex-fiancée and hadn't been so hot for Bubba, although it was difficult for him to feel sorry for himself when he was still breathing. The murder of Melissa Dearman had been more difficult for her husband and for her toddler son. The blonde-haired boy would probably never remember his mother. Melissa hadn't been a bad person, but she had always wanted more in her life. She had wanted Bubba to apply for Officer Candidate School and Bubba liked being enlisted just fine. Thus, she had moved onto someone she had deemed more fruitful. It hadn't meant that she deserved to be killed for it. It hadn't meant that a little boy should have to grow up without his mother.

Understanding exactly why Bubba's mind was on his ex-fiancée, he allowed his thoughts to drift to other less rancorous subjects.

Bubba moved his legs and brushed off some voracious ants intent on the bounty of his picnic basket. Mentally he catalogued his preparations. He had the checked blanket, the wicker basket, and a plump pillow in case a post-carbohydrate induced nap was needed after the meal. The Snoddy's housekeeper and dear friend, Miz Adelia Cedarbloom, had fried the chicken contained in the basket using a recipe that a certain Colonel had once tried to entice out of Miz Adelia's mother using means that are best left unmentioned. Miz Adelia had also made the potato salad inside a neat little Tupperware bowl sitting on one side of the basket. Bubba himself had put in the iced RC Colas and the moon pies, but the smell from the chicken was what was inducing the local fauna into surveying the area for possible snackage. A squirrel had made several forays into his vicinity, gazing hopefully at Bubba.

Clearly other people had fed the squirrels while paying homage to their deceased relatives and/or friends. Bubba threw the squirrel a handful of Cheez-its. (A big fella like

6

Bubba included all the basics in a picnic because he had to consume a lot of calories to keep up his transcendent physique.) The squirrel, ignorant of such human ideals, pounced on one small yellow-orange square and skittered away with it, chirruping happily as it went.

Bubba brought his knees up and rested his chin on one, considering the blissfully blue sky and its lack of clouds, trying to ignore the insidious twist of his guts. He shouldn't be nervous, but he was. He had everything taken care of. There was the picnic basket with actual food inside. The blanket was clean and spread out to show its checked glory. Bubba was wearing a clean white button down shirt and his best pair of jeans. He had shaved twice and only nicked himself three times. He had managed to get little squares of toilet paper on the cuts before the blood got on his white shirt. He had cleverly eluded his mother's unerring eye as he had collected the picnic basket from Miz Adelia earlier in the day. Miz Adelia wasn't surprised about the picnic. Having lunch in the cemetery was one of Bubba's favorite ways of spending time with the woman most on his mind at the moment.

Bubba supposed Miz Adelia might have been suspicious. Bubba knew that he might have been acting antsy. He had butterflies the size of armadillos in his stomach, but the housekeeper had handed him the basket with a curt, "Don't let that salad sit in the sun too long," which indicated she couldn't be bothered with his social goings-on.

Glowering, Bubba thought about it. His mother and Miz Adelia had been distracted lately. Certainly it was something to be considered. Miz Demetrice, the not-so-sainted matriarch of the Snoddy clan, was generally up to something most of the time. Many times Miz Adelia was gleefully helping in the process of whatever demented madness his mother was incurring. Thursday nights was Pokerama, or the illegal poker game that his mother ran. The regulars called it the Pegramville Women's Club activities, but it was still unlawful and, of course, highly sought after. The governor's wife played at least once a month and allegedly once Katie Couric had attended.

Both Miz Demetrice and Miz Adelia had been looking over their shoulders of late, and in a way that they didn't normally look over their shoulders. (Goodness knew they were both experts at over-the-shoulder-looking. His mother probably had the word paranoid tattooed on her tuckus.) It should have made Bubba highly suspicious but he had his mind on other things. Now that he was down to the wire, sitting in the cemetery, waiting for his date to arrive, listening to the thud of an active heart, his mind wandered freely, having an ersatz moment to consider all things Pegram County. In other words, he wanted to think about things not related to what was really on his mind, and his mother's dubious leanings were the first thing that popped in.

Miz Demetrice behaving shadily and Miz Adelia conducting in a chary manner equaled trouble. Not just trouble, but TROUBLE. Also ***TROUBLE*****!!! Bubba didn't know what kind of trouble, but he thought that it was possible all kinds of law enforcement would show up at the Snoddy Estate at the soonest inconvenient moment. After all, everyone else had been inside the mansion of late. Brownie Snoddy, Bubba's cousin's son, had been kidnapped the previous November, and all kinds of badges had wandered helter-skelter through the antebellum mansion. Although the feds had eventually disregarded the event as a falsehood Bubba knew better, and the pair of seedy individuals that he personally believed responsible for the act had pragmatically and rapidly fled the town, the county, and the state for parts unknown.

Brownie had stayed at the mansion until his baby sister had been born and returned to Louisiana to take part in the shared activities of changing poopy diapers. There had been several calls from the boy wondering if he was needed in assisting with any potential mysteries in the greater Pegramville area. Apparently his baby sister, already nicknamed Cookie, pooped prodigiously in her diapers. Hugely and repeatedly and with great zest. Cookie also did not sleep very well. Furthermore, Cookie had a set of lungs that would have made an opera singer jealous.

Bubba chuckled. He didn't exactly know all the details of babies, but there had been enough of them coming and going through Snoddy Mansion that he had learned the basics of infant care. Diapers, food, and loving were key. If any of the big three couldn't fix the problem then the best thing to do was to hand the baby back to Mama.

Babies. He sighed gustily. *One with green eyes just like…*

But back to Miz Demetrice. The eldest Snoddy was acting awfully cunning. She didn't have a lot of "tells," but Bubba was attuned to her shiftiness. It didn't bode well and made the hair at the back of his neck stand straight up. Bubba didn't have much to hide, but he didn't know if he wanted to be cannon fodder in whatever craziness his mother was planning.

His stomach growled. Bubba eyed the picnic basket. *She* was late and he only had an hour for lunch. However, he worked at Culpepper's Garage and Gideon Culpepper probably wouldn't care if Bubba was late. Bubba was rarely late and had only called in sick once in the last twelve months, so Gideon cut him some slack. Although

Gideon did tend to get nervous about bombs being mentioned in his presence. (There had only been one at Culpepper's and it had been a small one. It was the one at the courthouse that made Gideon really panicky. Bubba considered. It had been *two* bombs actually but only one had gone off.)

He looked at another tombstone in order to get his attention off the picnic basket and off of bombs. Hardin Long had been born in 1878 and died in 1948. Flowers and ivy ringed his plain little marker. It certainly wasn't as fancy as the angel atop a towering memorial on his left side. That one said "Dear Departed Dave." Then in smaller letters that Bubba had to squint to see it added, "He shouldn't have chased the bear into the cave."

Tim wasn't the only one with a sense of humor, Bubba determined. He supposed he shouldn't be thinking of death. It was like inviting fate to do her damnedest. He should have just spit into the wind and got it over with.

Bubba tossed a few more Cheez-its to the squirrel, who had returned with a companion. Then he ate the rest of the Cheez-its in the baggie he held.

"I'm hungry," he explained to the squirrels. The two squirrels picked up their booty and skedaddled for one of the large oak trees. It was possible that the two did a fist bump just before they bolted. "Hey, ya'll think I should be nervous?" he asked their retreating furrinesses.

Bubba's head came up when he heard a distant noise. Someone was driving up the hill. It sounded like a Bronco, the same kind of outdated Ford Bronco that the Pegram County Sheriff's Department used because they couldn't get enough money to buy something newer. He smiled as it pulled up to the gate to Longtall Cemetery. The Bronco parked next to his 1954 Chevy truck and the engine promptly shut down. Either he was going to be arrested for something he didn't know about or the woman he had been waiting for so anxiously had showed up.

She had.

The sun didn't need to come out from behind a cloud because there were only a few clouds about. The rays, however, seemed to settle on her figure as she exited the vehicle. She adjusted her Sam Browne belt and returned her baton to its holder. She couldn't sit in the Bronco with the baton in her belt because it was uncomfortable. The cans of mace on the other side of the belt didn't seem to bother her at all. Neither did her holstered gun. Bubba thought it was a Glock but he hadn't ever thought to ask.

His big heart hitched in his chest, missing a beat. Perhaps he should see a doctor about that pesky skipping heartbeat.

Willodean Gray wasn't the loveliest woman he'd ever seen, but she was definitely in the top ten. She had shoulder length black hair that he could wax poetically about. It didn't seem fair to compare it to a raven's wing because it was unfair to the bird. She wasn't that tall, but it didn't matter when he picked her up in order to kiss him. She didn't mind much either and her compact yet curvy form was a pure pleasure to hold. Finally it was a toss-up between whether he liked her eyes or her lips more. The eyes were bottle green, the color of an algae covered pond that he particularly liked fishing in. The lips were a shade of red that was similar to the shade of a Radio Flyer Wagon.

But it wasn't just the exterior of Willodean that had captured Bubba. She was good, kind to children and dogs, and she could shoot the flea off the ear of a raccoon at a hundred yards. Left or right. *And Lordy, just put a can of mace in that woman's hand and throw her in with a group of disgruntled criminals. It's a wondrous sight to behold.*

11

Bubba put his hand over his heart. *Thank you, God, for putting Willodean on Earth.*

Willodean smiled as she climbed up the hill toward him. She followed a path that mourning feet had pressed into the earth. The grass and the weeds had given up their determined duty and let the path stay untouched from the local flora.

Bubba watched enthusiastically. The squirrels squealed and went back up the tree, evidently unimpressed about the presence of the interloper.

When Willodean reached Bubba's side, she said, "Sorry I'm late."

"It's all right," Bubba said because there wasn't anything else to say. "Do you need to hurry?"

"Only if the dispatcher calls," Willodean grinned. "Do I smell Miz Adelia's chicken?"

Bubba nodded.

"I just drooled on my uniform. That's just sad."

Bubba threw open the lid to the basket and pulled out two Chinet plates. He smiled nervously as he served up the food, only asking, "White or dark meat?"

"Are there two drumsticks?"

"Yep."

"One of those. Oh, potato salad. I'm going to have to loosen my belt."

Bubba watched her out of the corner of his eye as he dished out salad. Willodean took off her Sam Browne belt and hung it over the side of Tim's gravestone. He supposed his mother would have something to say about that, too, but Bubba wouldn't tell her. Nor would he tell Tim. She settled down on the blanket beside him and lifted her face for a kiss. And Bubba couldn't say no to a kiss. Still holding a plate and a serving spoon he kissed her and he was pretty certain that both of them could feel the tingling all the way down to their toes.

Bubba had thought about this event for weeks. Finally he reluctantly pulled away from Willodean and she sighed beautifully. Pretty much everything Willodean did was beautiful. She even used a set of heavy iron manacles beautifully. *She had.* He had seen it. *Well, I felt it anyway.*

Oh, Willodean wasn't perfect. She was crabby first thing in the morning. She didn't like being criticized by men in her department. God forbid that Bubba should act protective, although he was certain that he couldn't not be protective around Willodean. And finally, she couldn't cook. To be precise she *could* cook, but what she cooked wasn't good.

That was okay. Bubba had a cast iron stomach, with the exception of this particular day. He handed her the plate in his hand and tried to will the muscles in that hand not to tremble.

Willodean balanced the plate on her lap and immediately started on the drumstick, not bothering with the plastic fork. (Who could cut chicken with a plastic utensil?) She sighed again and chewed with gusto. Once she swallowed she said, "I tried to get this recipe out of Miz Adelia but she said something about that being as likely as an Icee staying slushy in hell."

It was an opportune moment to say nothing at all. Bubba took a bite of the breast he'd served himself. Miz Adelia could cook. Willodean would probably burn chicken to a crisp or something worse. The poor chicken would likely come back from the dead to protest its wretched treatment.

But still, Willodean was about as perfect as a woman could come. Bubba even liked her family although most of

13

them could shoot as well as she could. (The fact that they had aimed weapons at him upon a singular occasion should have deterred him, but it did not.)

"Kids?"

Bubba swallowed the bite of chicken whole. His eyes began to water as the bite got stuck in his esophagus. He coughed once and put the plate down. He choked and hit his chest with a fist. Willodean put her plate down and slapped his back. He choked again and she hit him again.

"Sorry," she said. She whaled on him a third time, putting her whole hundred pounds and change behind it. The chicken flew out of his mouth.

Bubba watched the piece fly through the air and took in a gasping breath of air. This wasn't going the way he'd wanted it to go. It was actually going the opposite of how he had wanted it to go. Maybe he should have hired the sky writer plane. His eyebrows came together in a frown as he remembered why he had choked. Willodean had said, "Kids?"

"What about kids?" Bubba asked carefully.

"I want to have children one day," she said, patting his back but not as hard as she had done before. "I'd like two, but I wouldn't say no to three. What about you?"

"Um," he said because he had precipitously gone stupid in the head. This seemed like a test that Bubba couldn't help but fail. If he said he didn't want kids he was hosed. If he said he wanted more than three or less than two, he was hoist on his own petard. The damnable thing about it was that he didn't know what a petard was. "I want kids," he said.

"I don't mean right now," Willodean said forcefully. "I'm just thinking about the future, you know?"

Bubba eyed Willodean doubtfully. Had his mother and Miz Adelia picked up on something and spoken to the

14

beauteous sheriff's deputy? Had someone said something about his visit to the jewelry store two towns over? Had all of Lloyd Goshorn's (the town's biggest slack jaw and handyman) gossip about multiple bride's maids and groomsmen finally gotten to Willodean? Where was a Magic 8 Ball when he really needed one?

He caught himself thinking quickly. This was a good thing, right? The woman of his dreams was asking him about children. That meant she was interested in more than being boyfriend/girlfriend, right? *God, maybe this would be a good time for a sign from you?*

There was a loud moaning.

Willodean blinked and looked over her shoulder. "Did you hear that?"

Bubba heard the squirrels making little squirrel noises. He looked and saw them pounce on the chicken bite and drag it off. They chittered anxiously at each other and suddenly their heads came up. They looked and then they vanished.

Another moan echoed through the cemetery. Bubba thought that someone must be in one of the higher sections mourning in a loud manner. There was another parking lot on the opposite side ot the cemetery and people visited it often.

"Oh, jeez," Willodean said, still looking over her shoulder. "I don't believe this."

Bubba said, "It isn't what you think. Well, it *is* what you think. I don't know who told you but I dint want it to be this way. I wanted it to be special and look—" Bubba pulled a bouquet of red roses from behind Dave's gravestone "—flowers, for you."

Willodean looked back at Bubba and then at the flowers.

A third moan resonated across the cemetery. Then the sun unexpectedly went behind the clouds. Although it was spring and the temperature was in the seventies, it felt like there was an icy wind tickling their spines.

"Pretty, but you shouldn't steal from the graves," Willodean said.

"I didn't steal this," Bubba protested immediately.

Willodean took the flowers and sniffed. "Sorry. Of course, you didn't."

"I um-well-look-I—"

A fourth moan sounded from behind them and Bubba finally steeled his shoulders and turned to look to see what was making the noise.

It was a zombie.

Bubba had watched *Night of the Living Dead* at least thirteen times. He knew a zombie when he saw one. There was the telltale shuffle, the gray skin, the ripped clothing stained with earth and what appeared to be blood. The zombie's eyes were completely bluish white and his black mouth opened up wide and he moaned, "Braiiiiinnnnnssssss."

Bubba looked behind the zombie and saw that the rest of the cemetery was covered in zombies. There were dozens of them, all shambling in zigzag patterns toward Willodean and Bubba as if the pair was the main entrée of the day.

There was only one thing to say, so Bubba said it, "Don't that put lumps in the gravy?"

Chapter Two

Bubba and the Fetid Filmmakers

Friday, March 8th

"CUT! For the love of God and all that's Frank Capra, CUT! CUT! CUUUUUT!" someone yelled. A man wearing riding pants, a short wool coat, and a felt beret came striding out of the tombstones. He also wore tall leather boots and held a megaphone up to his face. He stared at the army of zombies and loudly asked, "By Cecil B. DeMille's ghost, there's no sheriff's deputy in this shot, is there?"

"No, Kristoph," a young woman with a clipboard answered promptly, appearing from another stand of towering markers. "'Scene XXVII - Zombies moaning as they move through the cemetery,'" she read from the clipboard. "This is just stock footage for the cemetery scenes. You!" she yelled at Bubba and Willodean. "Yes, I mean you two with the picnic basket! Who said for the costume people to bring a frigging picnic basket?"

Willodean looked at Bubba. "I can shoot them, right?"

"You're the deputy," Bubba said, "and I would say I dint see nothing."

The zombie nearest them moaned. Two men with large camera sets fiddled with their equipment and one lowered the gear to the ground with a deep breath.

"And did *anyone* tell the zombies to moan, 'Braiiiiinnnnnssssss!'?" Kristoph demanded irately. He waved the megaphone around imperiously. "Really. Braiiiiinnnnnssssss. How Avant-guard. Do you see George Romero hiding in the shadows around here?"

"Sorry, dude," the zombie said. "It was just the look on the guy's face." The zombie giggled as he gestured at Bubba. "He thought we were real. Braiiiiinnnnnsssss."

"I did not." Bubba frowned. There had been a brief moment. A very brief moment. Perhaps a nanosecond or less. He would never admit it. In fact, it would be like he had suddenly caught a case of selective amnesia.

"He probably sharted!" the zombie added.

Bubba hadn't sharted. He didn't know what sharted meant and he wasn't going to ask.

"Seriously, Bubba, you didn't know?" Willodean said. "It's been all over town about the filming. They went in the sheriff's department. Sheriff John nearly had apoplexy. The director over there—," she pointed at Kristoph and they both watched as he managed to flip his shoulder length silver hair over his shoulder without losing his beret in the process,"—wanted John to play the gruff yet golden hearted sheriff in the movie. You can probably guess what John said about that."

"I kin guess," Bubba admitted. Sheriff John didn't like any kind of media, even the mundane kind. Threats of bodily harm had probably taken place. Bubba was just sorry he hadn't gotten to hear all the minute details.

The girl with the clipboard trip-trip-trapped up to them. "I was talking to you," she said to Bubba and Willodean. "You're totally in the wrong place. This kind of ineptitude costs the film thousands of dollars. You're just getting paid scale and you don't even have a line. So can you just toe the line?"

Bubba glanced at the half-eaten plate of food. Then he looked at the picnic basket. He should have gotten the sky writer. Zombies couldn't have messed that up. Neither could Hollywood types.

Willodean got up and slung her Sam Browne belt around her waist. "We don't work for you," Willodean said slowly to the clipboard girl, as if she was speaking to someone with a mental deficiency, which was possible considering that the girl was working in the film industry.

"I'll have you fired," the girl threatened. "That uniform just sucks anyway. It looks about as real as a meter maid's. A Sam Browne belt and a police baton. Please. What's in the mace cans anyway? Spray cheese? Don't the costume designers do any research?" She peered closer at Willodean. "Green contacts, really? We're *totally* not going to need you today."

Bubba saw Willodean's hand twitch toward the mace on her belt and his eyes widened. He clambered to his feet, ready to prevent an incident.

"*Not* in your movie," Willodean gritted. "Do you not speak English? And I *am* a sheriff's deputy."

The clipboard girl poked Willodean in the sternum. Willodean's shoulders straightened as the girl said, "We've got permits to film in the cemetery today, and we don't need the hired help ruining our takes." Clipboard Girl looked heavenward. "And people wonder why we want to shoot on a soundstage."

Bubba stepped up and put a hand on Willodean's shoulder. "Ifin I had known the cemetery was booked, we wouldn't have come here. It was an honest mistake."

Clipboard Girl looked at Bubba derogatorily. Then she looked back at Willodean and poked the deputy again as she started to say, "And I'll tell you another—" A moment later Clipboard Girl was on her knees and Willodean was gripping the other woman's index finger so that it was twisted at an awkward angle. She had the younger girl's whole arm bent behind her and was only touching the finger with her fist. It had looked practically effortless. Willodean wasn't even breathing heavy.

The very sight made Bubba very nearly blurt out the words he'd practicing blurting all week long. But it wasn't right and it most certainly wasn't the right time. No, if he did, Willodean would probably do that to *his* finger and she wouldn't talk to him anymore and he would sit on the ground and cry and eat dirt. That would be bad for everyone.

"That's felony assault on a law enforcement officer," Willodean informed the girl in a voice that sounded gentle but really wasn't, "but I'll let it go today on account that you're *un*informed. Regrettably woefully *uninformed*."

"Uninformed," Clipboard Girl agreed. Sadly, she had dropped her clipboard.

The scene had instantly made everyone else in the area go silent. Even the zombies had ceased their moaning.

Kristoph swept his hair over his shoulder and came closer. "Her name is McGeorge," he said regally. "She doesn't understand about honest mistakes." He made a motion with his megaphone that indicated that the whole sorry affair would be swept under the rug, or in this case, under the gravestones. He looked down at Clipboard Girl, AKA McGeorge. "McGeorge, you should go get some lattes. You know how I like mine. Take your clipboard." He wiggled his fingers in the direction all the zombies had originally come from. "Shoo, fly."

Willodean paused significantly before letting go of McGeorge's index finger. McGeorge snatched up her clipboard and cradled it to her chest and walked jerkily away, muttering under her breath.

Kristoph turned his attention to Willodean and the man smiled winningly at the deputy. (The man's teeth glinted. Really they did.) Bubba growled. Kristoph turned toward Bubba and brightened. He tucked the megaphone under one arm and made a frame with his hands, centering it on Bubba's face. "Square jaw. Muscles upon muscles. Broad corn fed shoulders. Button down shirt. Levi's. Lord have mercy, are those real cowboy boots?" His eyes traveled back up to Bubba's face. "And *blue* eyes, oh my." The director smirked at Bubba in a way that made Bubba shudder inwardly. "How would *you* like to be in a movie?" The question was asked in the same manner that a questionable individual would ask a child if they wanted some candy.

Willodean shook her head just as they all clearly heard her radio go off with a request for deputies for a domestic dispute. "Got to go, Bubba," she said. "Try not to succumb to *them*." She jerked her head at the director. The zombies and the two cameramen milled about. One of the zombies picked idly at loose skin on his forehead and another one said, "Don't pick on that. It's going to all fall off and then you're hosed, dude."

Willodean pressed a kiss on the side of Bubba's mouth, which made him sigh wistfully and he watched her trot to the Bronco. Abruptly he realized that all the men in the immediate neighborhood were watching her trot, as well.

"I never got arrested by anyone who looked like that," one zombie said.

Bubba began to pack up the picnic.

"Everyone take five," Kristoph announced. The first zombie took a pack of cigarettes out and inserted one in between his rotted lips. He lit it with a disposable lighter and drew in the first lungful with obvious pleasure.

21

Kristoph adjusted the megaphone and looked at Bubba. "Seriously, a big good looking fellow like you could make a few bucks and impress a few girls."

Bubba snorted. He put the chicken back in the Tupperware box and popped the lid in place. He was still hungry, but he didn't think he was going to be able to eat with all the fake dead people around. Wasn't that just like the Pegramville Murder Mystery Festival, except they were still walking around, pretending to be dead? *God, I know I asked for a sign, but this isn't funny. Mebe it's funny to you, God, and I accept that, really I do, but couldn't you have given me a few more minutes? I was almost...*

Wait. Did that man say something about money? Bubba wasn't impressed with the movie making business in general. He didn't want to be a star. In fact, he didn't care for the publicity he'd received in the recent past at all. If put into a film, he would doubtless do something awful like knock over an entire movie set by accident, but there was a little rule that had been bouncing around his head of late. The owner of the jewelry store had said, "The standard is two months' pay." But two months' pay for Bubba wasn't all that much. Roscoe Stinedurf was his next door neighbor and since he had more than one of what Bubba wanted, Bubba had asked his opinion on the matter. Roscoe said, "The standard of two months' pay is somethin' done writ by jewelry companies. Besides you got to go to the horse's mouth." Since Roscoe hadn't been more forthcoming, nothing else had been added. The brief words hadn't been particularly helpful.

Kristoph smiled fetchingly at Bubba and turned away to bum a cigarette from the zombie. They immediately began talking about "aerial shots" and "cinema verite" and something about "David O. Selznick." Bubba stood up and flapped the checked blanket, dislodging the last of the hopeful ants. He checked his watch before he began to fold the blanket.

Someone said, "Hey, Bubba," and Bubba turned to see a zombie with blonde dreadlocks standing beside him. The dreadlocks were askew and sticks and leaves protruded from them. Bubba jerked backward at the sight of the hazy, solid white-blue eyes staring interestedly at him.

"Kiki?" he asked.

Kiki Rutkowski was a college student who lived next door to Willodean. She had helped Bubba on several occasions with information on the various evil whatnots that had happened in Pegram County. She had even helped Bubba when Willodean had mysteriously vanished. She liked to wear t-shirts with names of rock bands on them and sometimes she didn't like to wear underwear, but Bubba thought she was a good person.

Brushing some dreads over her shoulder, she smiled at Bubba, showing a mouthful of black and red teeth. Bubba winced as he took in her ripped t-shirt (Rolling Stones) and begrimed capris. Even her pink Crocs were splattered with dried blood.

"I always wanted to be in a movie," Kiki said. "We haven't had this much fun since the Murder Festival." She reconsidered. "Well, some of it was fun, except for that guy who really got murdered. I guess he didn't have a good time. I've never seen so many people with knives and weapons before. Are we going to do it again this year?"

Another zombie shambled up and Bubba determined it was Dougie, who was Kiki's roommate and, Bubba thought, her boyfriend. It was kind of hard to say since Dougie didn't say a lot.

"Mrgenvennopd," Dougie said.

23

"Don't mind him," Kiki said. "They've got the thing on his face so that it looks like his jaw is falling off from decomposition, so he can't talk."

"Derph," Dougie agreed. Bubba eyed his face and silently agreed that it looked like his jaw was about to fall off from decomposition. It looked realistic enough that Bubba almost expected the man to smell bad, but all Bubba could smell was Givenchy. His aunt Caressa had given him a bottle of toilette water the previous Christmas.

"So how long has all this nonsense bin goin' on?" Bubba asked, folding the blanket three times.

"The last week or so," Kiki said. "Kristoph Thaddeus rode in with all the vans and a meager cast, ready to throw money at the town. The mayor was so happy he nearly tinkled. The Red Door Inn is completely booked. They've got people staying all over the town. Folks rented rooms to the crew. They're shooting on a budget and should be finished in about three weeks. They're filming all over town. In fact, they're shooting—"

"Mrdut," Dougie said.

"Oh, yeah," Kiki nodded at Dougie. "Kristoph shot *Mutant Vampire Zombies* a few years ago. He's won a Saturn award for...what was it?"

"Rwqurt mna Zippels," Dougie said.

"I don't remember that one," Kiki said. "This makeup itches like a sonuva...oh, hey, there's the assistant director. He's been nominated for an Oscar. Back in the nineties. His name is Risley Risto. Doesn't that sound made up, dude?"

Bubba wasn't sure if he was actually supposed to answer or not. He'd heard worse names.

"That girl who was poking Wills is Kristoph's go-to girl. Her name is Liz McGeorge. She comes from some old

Hollywood family. Used to work in special effects before she became his executive assistant. She thinks her kaka doesn't smell. I suspect it does smell. Nevertheless, I wouldn't be poking Wills. Wills practically broke the McGeorge's finger. I would break the McGeorge's finger if I had the chance. You know she is *the* McGeorge, don't you?"

Dougie chuckled but it didn't exactly sound like a chuckle. Then he said, "Lapprew."

"You should totally go get a latte, Dougie," Kiki said. "You can drink it with a straw. I've got to hit the porta-potty before Kristoph calls action again." She shrugged at Bubba. "He says five minutes but that's really like thirty minutes in Hollywood time."

"Okay," Bubba said agreeably. The pair shambled off, clearly still partially in character.

The man that Kiki said was Risley Risto spoke briefly to Kristoph and then Kristoph pointed at Bubba. Bubba gathered up basket and blanket and hoped he hadn't broken any laws. He was tired of going to jail. At the very worst there were dead people around who weren't really dead, unless one counted the ones already in the ground.

He trudged toward his truck, trying not to shuffle, although it was hard not to.

"Hey, fella," someone called and Risley Risto caught up to him. "Kristoph loves your look."

Bubba looked at Risley. It did sound like a made up name. Risley was about five feet ten inches and in his mid-fifties. His hairline was receding and what was left was pure salt and pepper. He had earnest brown eyes that observed Bubba intently. Bubba didn't know what an Oscar nominee looked like so he observed back.

"Okay," Bubba said because there didn't seem to be an appropriate man response to the statement.

"If we advertised for actors, we'd get a flipping slew, and that would be *such* a headache," Risley went on. "Literally thousands of people would flock here just to have a walk-on part and the town would probably throw us out so fast our mothers' butts would spin. It's the whole *zombie* thing." He did the finger quotation marks when he said the word, zombie. "So snapping up local talent is much better. Easier, too. It wouldn't be a great role, but you can talk like a redneck, right?"

"I kin do that," Bubba said dryly.

Risley clapped his hands together and laughed. "Yes. Just like that. Great. Be on set tomorrow early. Five a.m. Makeup starts then. It'll be a long day but you'll get paid scale plus scale and a half for having a few lines."

Bubba said, "How much is scale?"

"Oh, details," Risley said. "I don't remember exactly. It'll be about 700 dollars plus another 700, plus the half, so maybe 1800 bucks for a full day of work. Look, yea or nay. I've got to get a few more people, too."

"Yea," Bubba said promptly.

Risley smiled and handed Bubba a card. "Everything's done on scene tomorrow. This is the address. Don't be late."

Bubba glanced at the address, looked up at the assistant director, and then down at the card again. "Oh, carp."

"What? You should see this place," Risley said. "What am I thinking of? You live here. You know the place, am I right?"

"Yep. I reckon I do," Bubba said.

Risley clapped. "That's priceless. Ah reckon you do, too. Ohh-kay?" His fake accent made Bubba's ears hurt. "Kristoph loves to look over the really weird places and loves to use them in the film even more. He has a problem keeping out of them as a matter of fact. It's gotten him in trouble with locals before." He sighed. "Anyway, tomorrow's Saturday and we may film on Sunday if we can wrangle things out. If you do a good job we'll find some more lines for you but I do not promise anything."

Bubba nodded.

"Toodles." Risley turned toward the zombies. "Kristoph, you're not supposed to smoke on account of your heart condition. You know your wife has threatened me if you keep smoking and she knows everything. Billy, stop giving him your cigs or I'll fire you or shove the cigs so far up your butt that you'll have to swallow a lighter to smoke them."

●

Bubba went back to work, repaired a Chevy transmission, replaced a battery in a Chrysler, and attempted to figure out the wiring schematic of a 1978 Dodge Magnum. His boss, Gideon Culpepper, didn't say anything about him being late, so Bubba didn't complain when Gideon asked him to work late on the Dodge.

An hour past his usual end of day, Bubba found the wire under the dash that had been worn completely through. Thus repaired, the car started again. It didn't sound wonderful but it ran.

Bubba drove to his home with a heavy heart. Sure he'd repaired the nearly antiquated car, but he hadn't done what he'd really wanted to do. He pulled around the mansion and eyed the caretaker's house. It wasn't really the caretaker's house anymore. The woman who had murdered Bubba's ex-fiancée had tried to burn it down. It hadn't been burned badly but certain load-bearing walls were affected enough for the local inspector to declare it history. It also hadn't been insured, but Bubba had managed, through horse-trading, finagling, and other means nefarious and not-so-nefarious, to get it rebuilt. The original had once been a stable. Bubba's grandfather had it converted to a house after WWII to house soldiers from nearby Fort Dimson. It had been transformed into an oddball residence, into which Bubba had moved when he'd returned from the Army. Now it was a trim two story house that superficially resembled its predecessor. It was on the small side but once the trim was painted and the stickers taken off the windows, it was all but finished, paid for, and even had a few meager possessions within it.

Bubba parked the truck and rested his head against the steering wheel. All of his debts had been paid off. Some of them he had paid off. Some of them had been paid off by fundraising done by Willodean. (She might not be able to cook, but that didn't mean she wasn't worth her weight in gold.) As of the last month, Bubba was officially in the black again. It was a mark of something good to come. He'd taken it as a sign and had started to move along, but zombies had come up and bitten him on the metaphorical buttocks.

An intense howl made Bubba's head spring up. His dog, a Basset hound named Precious, barreled out of the mansion and charged toward the truck, baying all the way. She was so happy that he was home. She knew the sound of his truck and she was ready to get her lovings.

She abruptly stopped, raised her nose to the air and turned around, plunking her long posterior on the ground. Clearly, being excited to see her master was being too easy. She knew she couldn't go to work with Bubba, but that didn't mean she wouldn't play hard to get when he came home.

Bubba smiled and climbed out of the truck. He'd saved some of the chicken for Precious and put it in the refrigerator at work. He'd even remembered to bring it home for the pernicious pooch. He pulled the Tupperware container out of the picnic basket inside the cab. Precious's head twitched, but she didn't turn toward him.

"Yum," Bubba said vociferously as he popped the lid open.

Precious's ears fluttered but she didn't budge.

"A fella's got to work, you know," he said. He blew over the top of the container in the direction of Precious. He did it three times before Precious's nose trembled and convulsed.

"All this chicken done gone to waste," Bubba said prosaically. "Mebe them big koi in the pond would like some of it. They et chicken, you know. That's what Miz Adelia said happened to those hens and roosters she tried to keep last year." Privately Bubba thought it was coyotes but the koi in the pond *were* awfully large.

He took a single step before Precious turned rapidly and came for him. Her tail wagged frenetically and she jumped up on him, reaching her paws up his body, while her body shuddered in glee. Whether the canine was happiest to see Bubba or the chicken became a moot point.

Chapter Three

Bubba and the Mendacious Mama

Friday, March 8th – Saturday, March 9th

"Ma," Bubba said. It was a single word and a single syllable that denoted all kinds of meaning within its simple two letter structure. Warning, dismay, irritation, and a plea for normalcy were all contained within it.

"Ididn'tdoit," Miz Demetrice said straightaway. She paused to consider what she had said and added, "Oh, dear Lord, Brownie rubbed off on me."

They were sitting at the dining room table. Miz Adelia had just served creamed chipped beef over Texas toast. Bubba passed the platter of cornbread around to his mother and he paused to appreciate the mouthwatering scent of southern cooking. Specifically, he appreciated the scent of *Miz Adelia's* southern cooking. "Smells rightly good, Miz Adelia," he said.

"What didn't I do?" his mother asked as she served herself a square of cornbread. After she put the cornbread on her plate, she smoothed some her white hair back away from her face. Cornflower blue eyes, the same shade as his own, steadily regarded him. If there was one thing in the world that his mother was good at it was bluffing, however the problem was that she was good at a great many things. Furthermore, she knew that she was good at them. Miz Demetrice was not the Titanic backing up to hit the iceberg again.

Miz Adelia sat down next to Bubba and he handed her the dish of creamed chipped beef without hesitation. She took a deep breath and stared at the food she had just prepared. It wasn't a typical look. Both women seemed a little on edge.

"Is there *something* you need to tell me?" Bubba asked his mother. Something was going on. He didn't need to be a rocket scientist to figure it out. Everyone was acting flaky and it was a matter of putting the pieces together.

Miz Demetrice had transferred her gaze to the food, but upon Bubba's words, her head shot right up. Bubba saw Miz Adelia replicate the movement out of the corner of his eye.

Up To Something could be the name of a Broadway musical. Something, as the pundits would say, was fishy as a barrelful of largemouth bass.

"Ma, that butterfly flew all 'round the perty flowers and then done landed on a cow pie," he remarked. Bubba didn't know exactly what it meant but it was something along the line of someone making a poor decision. His mother had been known to make a poor decision or two, but then she usually covered it up with cow patties or something else. Sometimes she had even shoved an unknowing soul in front of it as a ritual sacrifice to the gods of him-first-lord. Bubba might have been the unwilling and unknowledgeable recipient of that shove once or twice.

Miz Adelia served herself a spoonful of creamed chipped beef. She skipped the toast. Then she carefully picked up a fork and put it on the plate. She spread out her napkin and put it on her lap. It was a calculated process determined to stall the conversation. She picked up the fork and served a forkful into her mouth.

Bubba tapped his fingers on the table. "I was in the cemetery today."

"That's nice, dearest," his mother said.

"There were zombies there."

Miz Adelia choked on the creamed chipped beef. The subsequent swallow sounded like a sink hole swallowing an RV in Florida.

"*The movie,*" Miz Demetrice said understandingly. Bubba's eyes returned to her and it seemed to him as though his mother was relieved. She took a deep breath and her shoulders relaxed. *Really, really relieved.*

"Yes, the movie. I dint catch the name," Bubba said. "Pass the green beans, please." *Should I tell Ma I'm in the movie or should I figure out what she's about? Oh, these wretched decisions.*

"*The Deadly Dead,*" Miz Demetrice said helpfully.

"The deadly what?"

"*The Deadly Dead,*" she repeated. "I know it's not the best of movie titles, but I didn't make it up, dearest."

Bubba stared at his mother. Then he looked at Miz Adelia. Miz Adelia had composed herself. She hadn't needed a sheriff's deputy to whale the blockage out of her esophagus. Her dark hair spilled over her shoulders and her dark eyes were focused on the meal.

Bubba stabbed a green bean viciously. He couldn't very well stab his mother or Miz Adelia. Precious bumped his leg from under the table. Clearly, the canine was sensitive to undercurrents. She nosed his ankle and rested her head across his foot.

"The film company is coming tomorrow to film here." Bubba waved the green bean around in order to emphasize his words.

Miz Demetrice nodded. "They're paying fairly well. It seemed lucrative and timely."

"I'll say," Miz Adelia muttered.

The green bean froze in space. "Why? Do you need money, Ma?"

"I wouldn't say that. The economy's a little slow. Do I need to repeat what I usually say about the idjits in Washington D.C.?" Miz Demetrice pushed her plate away. "It smells delightful, Adelia dearest, but I'm feeling down in the tummy."

Miz Adelia pushed a chunk of creamed chipped beef to the part on her plate farthest away from her. "I understand."

"The economy's bin slow for the last few years," Bubba said. "Damned shame."

"People don't always want to spend money on seeing an old wreck of a house, no matter who tromped through it in the past century and a half. The stories about the Civil War gold are dying down, too."

"Thank the Lord," Bubba said fervently. "Precious fell in the same hole as that federal agent did who broke her leg. I need to get a backhoe to fill that in. I think there might have bin bats down there." He ate the green bean. "We should be grateful she dint sue us."

Miz Adelia and Miz Demetrice looked at the ceiling, at the floor, and at the sideboard. They looked anywhere but at Bubba.

He swallowed the vegetable and then asked conversationally, "Is there anything else you need to tell me?"

"I've often wondered why McDonalds doesn't sell hotdogs," Miz Demetrice said. "They could call them McWeenies."

"If it's square why do they still call them crop circles?" Miz Adelia asked.

"I've always wanted to know what would happen if you blow a bubble in space?" Miz Demetrice said. "Perhaps we could call John Glenn."

"I'll never understand why Ginger had so many different outfits on *Gilligan's Island* when it was only a three-hour tour," Miz Adelia commented. "Mebe she had OCD."

"Or why was it *Gilligan's* island? Why wasn't it the Skipper's island? Or Mary Ann's island?" Miz Demetrice smiled at Bubba. "These things do boggle the mind, dearest."

Bubba's mind boggled all right. "Is someone going to get murdered? Are you trying to tell me that you done kilt someone and dumped the body in the swamp?"

"I would never dump a body in the swamp again," Miz Demetrice avowed fervently. "When I killed your father I tried to put chains on his corpse and put it in the swamp but it kept floating to the surface." She waved a genial hand across her face and added sotto voce, "All that gas, you know. Your daddy loved beans. Pintos. Limas. Great northerns. Kidneys, too."

"Pa's in the family cemetery, Ma," Bubba said.

"Well, he is *now*."

"And he died of a heart attack."

"That's what it says on the death certificate."

"What have you done, Ma?"

"Nothing too terrible," Miz Demetrice said. "Finish your dinner. We're expecting company."

"Jack the Ripper? Adolph Hitler? Richard Nixon?"

"Don't be silly, dear," his mother said. "Jack the Ripper has probably been dead eight or nine decades."

"That's if he was about thirty years old when he done killed all those women," Miz Adelia added obligingly. "Or if *she* was about thirty years old."

"Jill the Ripper," Miz Demetrice chortled. "I like that."

Bubba proceeded to ignore the two and got to eating. He wasn't a growing boy anymore, but he was a big man and he needed his calories. When they were done, Bubba even helped carry the dirty plates into the kitchen.

He was drying the last plate when they heard the sound of a vehicle coming down the lane. Bubba tilted his head. "Don't sound like the po-lice. Could be some kind of mass murderer, I reckon."

Precious barked once and Miz Demetrice hushed her. Precious knew better than to disobey Miz Demetrice. After all, Miz Demetrice had been known to put perfume on the dog. Once she had even put a rhinestone collar on the hound and pink ribbons around her ears. It had been positively dreadful. It had taken the dog ten minutes to get the ribbons off and another five to bury them under the oleander bushes around back. It was a deplorable record for Basset hounds.

Miz Demetrice grimaced at Bubba and went to open the kitchen's door. "Wonderful," she pronounced. "They're here."

Miz Adelia whipped her apron off. "I cain't wait to see the little chillen."

"It's not Fudge and Virtna with Brownie and Cookie, is it?" Bubba asked suspiciously. A sneaky Miz Demetrice, a close-mouthed Miz Adelia, a dodgy Willodean, zombies, and Brownie. It would be purely chaos. It might cause WWIII.

"No, that little baby's only sleeping half the night and they're plumb tuckered out," Miz Adelia said. "They ain't going away from Monroe in a month of Sundays, or until that chile gives them a break."

Miz Demetrice went outside followed closely by their housekeeper.

Bubba put the last plate away and debated whether he should escape out a window or not. Before he could make a move, his mother and Miz Adelia ushered a couple into the kitchen. Each of the couple was carrying a small child in their arms.

Bubba smiled tentatively when the man winced upon seeing the big man. The man was in his early forties and Hispanic by descent. He wore a workman's shirt and worn khakis with work boots. He adjusted the child in his arms and glanced at Miz Demetrice. Clearly he was silently asking about Bubba's presence.

The woman was a similar age with gray-shot brown hair and deep brown eyes. She tugged at the scarf around her head and shuffled to the side of the kitchen with her own precious burden.

Both children were obviously asleep; their little heads pillowed against the parents' chests.

"Alfonzo," Miz Demetrice said, "this is my son, Bubba. Bubba's a good sort, although not the most knowledgeable." There was enough of an emphasis on the word knowledgeable that Bubba knew his mother was sending some sort of message to the other man. "Bubba, this is Alfonzo Garcia."

"Meetcha," Bubba said.

"*Buenas noches nos dé Dios*," Alfonzo said. He tilted his head toward the lady who had entered with him. "This is my wife, Pilar."

Pilar nodded. Bubba smiled gently at her. The woman was petite and thin, as if a strong wind would blow her away. Her clothing was comparable to her husband's. It was well-used but clean and serviceable.

"Our children, Blanca," Alfonzo said, nodding at the child he held, and then at the one his wife held, "and Carlotta. It's been a long trip." Although he had a slight accent, Bubba had an idea that Alfonzo had been raised first generation American citizen.

"We have cribs upstairs or toddler beds if you think they'd be more comfortable with those," Miz Demetrice said.

"*Las niñas* need to sleep in the same room with us," Pilar said immediately. "They're a little upset with the trip." Even Bubba could hear the urgency contained in her voice. He frowned as he realized that Pilar was frightened of something. He wasn't sure of what it was. She wasn't comfortable with him in the room or with being in a strange house or perhaps it was that she was in a *huge* strange house.

"I've got some supper ready," Miz Adelia said eagerly. "Ya'll can take turns with the showers and I'll bring a tray up. A good night's sleep will do the trick."

"*Si*," Alfonzo agreed. "I think they're so tired they won't wake up if we put them down. Then Pilar can shower while I eat, or would you like to eat first, *mi dulce*?"

"Shower," Pilar said gratefully. "The girls can take baths in the morning, *si*?"

"Of course they can," Miz Demetrice said. "Our house is your house. If you get hungry in the night, you should come down and help yourselves. Miz Adelia has left cookies in the jar and there are cold cuts in the cooler. Those little ones will probably wake up starving."

"Ma," Bubba said, "don't forget about the zombies in the morning."

Alfonzo's face crinkled with confusion. Pilar said something in Spanish. Then Miz Demetrice said something else in Spanish. Bubba's Spanish was very rusty. He thought he might be able to ask for a shot of tequila and possibly where the bathroom was located.

"A movie set?" Alfonzo said in English in response to what Miz Demetrice said.

Miz Adelia took down a tray and got some plates out. She made herself busy as Bubba watched the expressions on his mother's face and on the faces of their guests.

"Wouldn't want the kids to be scared," Bubba explained.

"No," Miz Demetrice said. "I'll show you upstairs. And we've got a box of toys for the girls. Diapers, too. I'll show you where the television is. I have some movies for children with dubbed Spanish. *Toy Story, Wall-E,* and *Cinderella.* We might have to keep them inside tomorrow."

"Is that a minivan I heard?" Bubba asked Alfonzo.

Alfonzo nodded slowly.

"It sounded like it could use a little work," Bubba said. "I'll look it over when I've got a chance. Ifin you leave the keys I kin take care of it."

"Bubba's a very good mechanic," Miz Demetrice said as she directed the couple with their children out into the long hallway. Alfonzo paused to toss the keys to Bubba.

"I'll leave the keys on the kitchen table," Bubba called. He waited until he was sure that his mother had the four people halfway up the stairs. He heard Pilar say something about the chandelier. After all, it was the size of a VW Beetle hanging in a two-story open foyer and one could hardly not notice it. Miz Adelia cleaned it once a year and everyone had to help. All the crystals on it took forever to wipe off.

"Adelia Cedarbloom," he said softly.

Miz Adelia's shoulders stiffened, but she didn't turn around.

"What in tarnation is going on around here?"

•

Bubba found it difficult to sleep. He stayed awake thinking about Willodean Gray, his mother, Miz Adelia, and the worried expression on Pilar's face. He wasn't stupid and if his mother was doing something illegal with the Garcias, then she almost certainly had a good and moral reason for doing so. If Bubba could count on any one thing in life, it was that Miz Demetrice would run the road of good and moral, until she could no longer do so. His mother would have been the first fake Indian on the boat at the Boston Tea Party.

He finally dozed off about two a.m. and woke up at four. He got up, fed Precious and let her out, and dressed. After washing his face and brushing his teeth, he went out to see if he could do anything with Alfonzo's minivan. It was a first generation Dodge Caravan with a bunch of miles on it, but it was a solid vehicle. He used a shop light to see while he cleaned the battery leads and gapped the spark plugs. He changed the oil and the oil filter. (Bubba had a collection of automobile filters he used for all kinds of friends and relatives and one was just the right size for the Caravan.) He was just finishing with the air filter when other vehicles started pulling into the area in front of the mansion.

The sun wasn't going to come out for another hour and a half and everyone was ready to work.

Alfonzo came out with two cups of coffee and handed one to Bubba.

Bubba took it gratefully and watched the film crew get to work. They began setting up tents to one side and unloading equipment.

"Tires are getting a mite lean," Bubba said.

"I'll replace them as soon as I can," Alfonzo said. "*Gracias.*"

"I kin get you a deal at the local tire place. I get a discount because I work for the garage." Bubba named a price. "Ain't sure about it but I can prolly get Virgil to give you another ten percent off. He worships the ground Ma walks on ever since she raised money for his sister's surgery."

"*Si.* I think we have enough cash for that." Alfonzo took a drink of coffee and motioned at the film crew. "Is this place always like this?"

"Sometimes it's much worse," Bubba smiled around the mug he held to his face.

Both men watched the scurrying of people as they did incomprehensible acts. They heard such phrases as "follow-shot," "pull-back," and "vorkapich."

"Are they speaking English?" Alfonzo asked.

"Ain't sure," Bubba responded. "I don't think so."

Precious attempted to eat one of the film crew's legs until Bubba called for her to heel. It was a little too busy for the Basset hound on her home turf and she was unmistakably discombobulated enough to want to bite someone.

"Good looking hound," Alfonzo said. "I've always liked hounds."

Precious nosed his leg, obviously recognizing a kindred spirit. Alfonzo bent to scratch her in the correct spot behind her jowls.

Bubba wanted to say something complicated and complicated would indicate that he understood that Alfonzo and Pilar were involved in some sort of intricate fix that could only be assisted by someone such as Miz Demetrice Snoddy. He wanted to wax prolifically about how he would back his mother up, and by proxy he would have Alfonzo and Pilar's backs, so that the couple could lose their pinched facades that plainly expected some authoritative figure to descend upon them with hobnailed boots. Oh, he wanted to, but it wasn't the way that his speech processes worked, as evidenced by his colossal failure in speaking to Willodean Gray the day before. Instead he said, "Yep."

And it became further clear that Alfonzo tended toward the same manly limit to human speech. Their conversation was something along the lines of:

"Nice outside."

"Yep. Kids up?"

"*Si*. Woke with the birds."

"What do you do?"

"Construction. Handy work."

"For Ma?"

"*Si*."

"Breakfast?"

"Certainly."

"Pancakes."

"*Bueno*."

"Go on in. I've got to do some more stuff out here," Bubba said. He watched Alfonzo wander in and thought that the other man was observably more relaxed. It was amazing what a simple conversation could yield.

Chapter Four

Bubba and the Maladroit Movie-Makers

Saturday, March 9th

It wasn't long before one of the film's crew nearly attacked Bubba. She shoved herself into his face with chaotic energy and an urgency that he simply couldn't replicate even if he'd had a thousand cups of Miz Adelia's coffee. "You're the guy that Risley hired!" she shrieked into Bubba's face. "Right? Right! We need you! Now! Now! Now!"

Bubba jerked backward involuntarily and Precious growled lowly.

The film crew girl was a redhead in her twenties with a black t-shirt that proclaimed, "The Deadly Dead RISES!" The word "RISES!" was dripping with blood. She looked him over. "I knew it had to be you! Good jaw line!" she said loudly. "Nice contour on the shoulders!" She touched his collarbone. "We've got just the thing for you!" She tugged on his arm. "Come on! Did you go potty?"

"Yep," Bubba said because he didn't know how else to answer that. His mother had taught him that bathroom humor was never de rigueur. His grandmother had taught him what the meaning of de rigueur was. Bubba was almost never de rigueur but it had never bothered him. It wasn't bothering him now.

"Good, because you'll be sitting in a chair for three hours!" the redhead said. "THREE HOURS!"

Bubba called to Precious, "Heel, girl."

Precious trotted behind them as they threaded through the tents.

They eventually ended up in a tent that had chairs in front of tables covered with bottles, jars, brushes, picks, and things Bubba didn't even want to try to identify. One chair already had a young man in it with a purple-haired man lurking over him, saying, "—white base with a green tint. One missing eyeball. Black hole it. I mean so black that Stephen Hawking would go, 'Whoa.'"

The redhead left as Bubba was directed to the chair next to the young man with the impending black holedityness. The purple-haired man turned to him, looking him up and down in a way that made Bubba feel like a cut of beef. "Jesus, they grow them big out here." He turned to one side and yelled, "Simone! Get your cute little butt over here. He needs the full facial implement. You know, shotgun in the face. Let's make the NRA have second thoughts!" He adjusted the black scarf around his neck and threw the thin ends over his shoulder.

Precious ducked under Bubba's chair. Presumably she thought it was safe there.

The purple-haired man caught sight of Precious. "Oh, my God, a zombie dog. And even better, a zombie Basset hound. How adorable. Kristoph will *die*. Will she sit still for makeup?"

"If food is involved," Bubba said, thinking it was a joke.

"I must have my special case!" the purple-haired man bellowed in Bubba's ear. "The very special case! I must work!"

Another girl with long blonde hair started on Bubba who he assumed was Simone. She had him change into a ragged set of jeans and a plain but shredded t-shirt. When he returned to the chair, she positioned his head with her

43

two tiny hands and said, "Don't move. Don't breathe. Don't move or breathe. If you have to move or breathe, raise your hand. You're Zombie #14/Farmboy. If you hear someone yelling for Zombie#14/Farmboy then that is *you*. You will answer to the name of Zombie #14/Farmboy. You will have dreams tonight of being Zombie #14/Farmboy. You get a line tomorrow when you do your scenes then, so be happy."

"How kin I get a line tomorrow ifin I'm a zombie?" Bubba couldn't help but asking. "I always thought that zombies ain't the chatty type. Right?"

The blonde girl, who Bubba still assumed was Simone, rolled her eyes. Bubba thought it might hurt. "We're not shooting in sequence, duh. Must be a local." She tilted her head at Snoddy Mansion and said, "You probably live in the big antebellum dump with your sister. And a pig named McGoo."

"My mother," Bubba said, "and a Basset hound named Precious. "Ain't no need to be rude."

Simone's eyes widened. "I was joking. Really, you live here?"

"In the other house," Bubba said. "It just got rebuilt from when a murderer tried to burn it down."

Simone sighed. "I'm just not going to ask. Okay, don't move. Don't breathe. Did you go pee already?"

Bubba had to move and breathe to answer, so he said, "I did."

Simone rubbed her hands together. "Let's make magic," she said energetically.

●

It turned out that the movie making business, especially the zombie movie making business, was more complicated than Bubba could have imagined. Just in the little section he sat in was a squadron of people doing makeup. Simone informed him that this was logical since it was a makeup heavy movie. There were full facial jobs and full body jobs that took up to eight hours to apply. Only some of the actors had a little amount done, like the leads in the movie. They got to be a little dirty but still extraordinarily beautiful.

"Tandy North," Simone said, "is the lead actress." Using sure and coordinated movements, Simone smoothed over some kind of glue on the lower part of Bubba's face. He wasn't sure if he could move or breathe voluntarily anymore, even if he had wanted to. "She's a classic beauty. She really doesn't need makeup but if you don't have a base on, the camera reflects the skin. It looks like she's a shiny pink ball if she doesn't have something on. Did you see her in *Bubble People*? It was an amazing film. I loved the wardrobe."

It also turned out that Simone loved to talk to people who couldn't talk back. It was like listening to a perky blonde radio with a permanent ongoing talk show.

"And Alex Luis, well he's just a six foot edible morsel that begs to be covered up with chocolate," Simone continued. "Sex on two legs. He's got the creamiest skin. It seems like a shame to cover it up. And nice, too. I think he might be gay, although he does have a girlfriend. She's his cover. Too bad for me, but too lucky for some boy."

Bubba wanted to fill in the pauses with "Uh-huh"s and "Um-huh"s but his jaw had been glued in place. Simone placed a glop of bloody plastic over part of his mouth and jaw and surveyed it critically.

"Of course, you're not bad, with that whole redneck, county boy, farminess going on." Simone patted his hand. "A girl could be happy for a few days out here in the sticks. But how do you not have a Starbucks around here?"

Bubba didn't know. He'd never been to a Starbucks. At least, he hadn't been that he could recall.

"You've met the director, right? Kristoph is so wonderful and cool, too. He doesn't hit on all the girls, either. He loves his wife. They've been married for three years. That's practically their diamond anniversary in Hollywood time." Simone smoothed something wet over Bubba's brow. "And Risley is pretty neat, too. You know he was irritable last week and suddenly he got all loosy-goosy. We think he got laid, but we all don't know with whom. There's a bet whether he's AC or DC or AC/DC, but no one's got an inside tract. Did you know the producer is Kristoph's wife, Marquita? She's not really Spanish but she took a stage name. I mean I like Simone but my last name is Sheats. Do you know how many jokes I hear about that?"

Bubba could imagine. He'd heard a few jokes about both Bubba and Snoddy. *How much money am I making for this? Is this really worth it?*

"Schuler is our head makeup artist," she said, moving the gossip train to a new stop. "He's the one with purple hair doing the work on the dog. He loves to wear a scarf, so we call him Scarfie, but not when he's listening. I didn't know we were going to have a zombie dog."

After a while he tuned Simone completely out. Then he was turned so she could work on another side of him and he could watch as Schuler plied Precious with bits of bacon. Bubba was still sitting in the chair with Simone fluttering over him when Schuler led Precious away. Lights came on in the form of portable flood lamps and someone yelled, "Action!"

"That's Risley shooting your dog," Simone said and Bubba jerked. Abruptly he realized Simone meant that they were *filming* Precious. *Good luck with that. She might et the camera.*

Risley must have gotten what he wanted because Precious came back with Schuler ten minutes later. Schuler carefully removed the blood and brains from the canine even while he fed her a bite of bacon. (This was a purple-haired man who had owned dogs before and probably still did.) Precious knew a good thing when she had it because she didn't even struggle. The bacon might get away.

The last thing that Simone did was to carefully put some contact lens in Bubba's eyes. She followed up with some eye drops. "You're a kickass Z," she pronounced staring at his features with critical regard. "I would totally squeal if I saw you in a graveyard."

I had a girl in a graveyard yesterday and she dint squeal. She was supposed to squeal but then the zombies showed up. I hate zombies. I really do.

When Bubba was finally completed, he was led away by the first redhead. She spoke rapidly to him. "You're a zombie. That's your motivation. You like brains, brains, and more brains. Anything that's not brains is poo-poo. Basically you're wandering through some woods looking for brains. You can do that, right? Those clothes look good on you. This is exactly what modern day zombies wear while chasing down brains."

Bubba would have glanced down at his shredded t-shirt and ragged jeans but he couldn't really reposition his head, in addition to not being able to move or breathe. It seemed pointless to protest.

He glanced over to the side of the circus and saw Alfonzo observing the hullaballoo with Miz Demetrice also looking. Each of them held a child and all four were avidly

47

watching the action. Bubba didn't know what the toddlers got out of it. Maybe all the bright lights were exciting.

Bubba saw his mother watching him. He had a feeling that she didn't actually recognize him. After about thirty seconds Miz Demetrice blinked and her mouth opened in seeming amazement. He was too far away to hear the words, but he could read her lips as she said, "That *cain't* be Bubba."

"When Risley yells action, you start here," the redhead pointed at an x scraped into the ground, "and stumble over to there." She pointed out another x. "Drag a leg or something. Remember you took a shotgun hit to the face and some of your vertebra may be broken. You have to get to those brains. Right?"

Right. Shotgun to the face. Broken vertebra. Brains. I think I need to pee.

•

The film making business abruptly seemed less complicated. Bubba staggered from one x to another x. He grunted because he couldn't open his mouth. He dragged one leg and almost did the pee pee dance because he hadn't realized he'd been sitting in the makeup chair for nearly three hours.

Kristoph had shown up, wearing another variation of what Bubba called the Silent-Movie-Director ensemble. The beret, boots, and megaphone might have been the same as the previous days. The riding pants and wool coat were different colors of brown and gray.

Kristoph briefly called aside Bubba and the three other zombies in the scene and repeated the redhead's motivational speech. It was unpretentious and Bubba simplified it further in his head. "Groan, moan, and shuffle. Try not to breathe. Act. Personify. Brains."

Bubba wasn't impressed.

They did three takes, which Bubba thought was excessive and then he managed to indicate by hand gestures that he needed to use the facilities. He went inside the mansion and managed to frighten Pilar and saying sorry with his face all gummed up was difficult, but she finally realized it was Bubba.

Once Bubba had taken care of nature, he'd come out to the kitchen and found a mug of coffee and appropriated a straw. There was a little hole in the corner of the jaw apparatus so that he could get a little fluid. It was used appropriately while Miz Adelia stared at him from the opposite of the kitchen. It dawned on him that she hadn't immediately recognized him either.

The housekeeper was probably grateful that Bubba couldn't speak. It was, after all, a long time before she could speak because she was laughing so much. When she had recovered she took several pictures of him with her cell phone. "I'm sharing this on Facebook," she said. "This is funny as all get out."

Bubba moaned at her.

"I think they're calling for you." Miz Adelia waved toward the outside.

Bubba saw the redhead running across the lawn and a second later he heard, "Zombie #14! We've got a composition shot! ZOMBIE FRICKING #14! WHERE ARE YOU? GET YOUR SHUFFLING, BRAIN-CONSUMING ASS OUT HERE, RIGHT NOW!"

Bubba shrugged.

Miz Adelia said, "I'll find your dog and keep her inside so she doesn't get into too much trouble."

Bubba shambled outside where the redhead was nearly shaking with extreme anxiety. She was like one of those little dogs that shake when it's cold, or when someone looks at it, or when it's hungry, tired, anxious, or generally when it's awake. She led him back to where Kristoph was having a furious discussion with Risley.

Oh, these madcap Hollywood people, Bubba thought. Then he wondered when he could get the thing off his face because Miz Adelia still had a few pancakes leftover. Precious nosed his leg and he bent to scratch behind one of her long ears. He could have Miz Adelia puree the pancakes and sip them through a straw. This had worked when his jaw had been wired shut after Willodean had hit him with a set of manacles. (The manacles hadn't broken his mandible, but when he had fallen and hit the stone stair step with his jaw, that had done the trick.) And regardless of popular thought, not everything tasted good pureed.

The redhead corralled the zombies like a seasoned cowboy while Kristoph said, "I'm going to do it my way, Risley!"

"You always do it your way!" Risley yelled back.

"And they say actors are prissy little uptight poopbags!" Kristoph bellowed. "That's nothing on the executive staff!"

"At least I don't have a corncob that needs to be surgically removed!" Risley yelled.

"These riding pants don't have room for a corncob!"

"That's because the corncob is already shoved far enough up—"

"What, not again!" a tall woman with waist length brown hair yelled as she waded into the morass. She was taller than Risley and Kristoph and her brown eyes flashed with disdain. "Does this have to happen every time you get together?"

"Marquita, honey pookums," Kristoph said.

Bubba blinked. The tall woman didn't really seem liked a honey pookums. *But wait, dint Simone say that*

Kristoph is married to a Marquita? So the tall woman is his wife. They didn't seem to go together. Marquita might have been in her fifties and was taller than her husband. (Bubba took note of the four inch heels.) But she possessed an eternal beauty that would carry with her until she died. (Just like Willodean Gray.)

"Mar," Risley said immediately after Kristoph spoke.

Marquita stamped her four- inch heel.

"Love Moschino boots," said the redhead. "God, I love those."

"He wants to do an artsy-fartsy shot," Kristoph said. "We're on a budget." He tapped his watch. "And we're three days behind. The studio is going to come down on my head like a pile of bricks."

"Do you want to do a half-rate, bloody gore fest or do you want to do something that can grab attention?" Risley asked.

"I want to get through this so I can do the indie film I really want to do," Kristoph snapped back.

"Always in a hurry, always rushing around." Risley rolled his eyes. "Not looking at the bigger picture."

"Haha. That gets funnier every time you repeat it."

Do they always fight like this? Bubba wanted to ask but he remembered that he had a thing on his jaw and he couldn't actually speak.

"They always fight like this," the redhead said. "Just keep your zombified head down and it'll all be over in a few minutes."

"Better to beg forgiveness than ask for permission!" Risley shouted.

"And where is the money coming from?" Kristoph bellowed.

Marquita stamped her foot again. "Stop this before I snatch you both a new hole!"

Kristoph scuffed his feet on the ground. "He started it."

Risley threw his hands in the air. "I'd already be done if the little man-boy would just let the megaphone go for a minute."

Marquita slapped her husband in the back of the head and knocked the beret off. Then she didn't hesitate as she did the same thing to Risley. He didn't have a beret, but it did muss his receding salt and pepper hairline. "Ris, shoot your shot before I change my mind," Marquita said. "Kris," she added, "have you had too much caffeine this morning?"

"The lady inside the mansion makes the best cup of coffee," Kristoph protested. "It would have been a crime not to drink it."

The redhead sighed. "Kristoph becomes a monster when he's had too much caffeine."

Marquita gently shooed her husband off the set and waved frantically at Risley as she prodded Kristoph along. "You just need some organic juice," she said. "I picked up a bag of oranges at the local farmer's market."

What local farmer's market? Bubba would have frowned but he was actually prevented from doing so. He hoped that Marquita wasn't talking about the limited amount of produce provided at Bufford's Gas and Grocery. There was every chance that any fresh food there had been stolen from orphans or picked out of the CDC's testing waste.

Bubba would have sighed but he couldn't do that either. He just needed to get through the day and figure out what his mother and Miz Adelia were up to and how it was going to impact him and then he would need to figure out how to get Willodean alone again sans zombies or anything else that would keep him from saying four little words to her.

There. That wouldn't be so hard.

Right.

Chapter Five

Bubba and Pernicious Problems

Saturday, March 9th

The shot really didn't take long. Risley's direction involved Bubba and the other zombies looking pensive. Then they were directed to look contemplative. Risley then asked Bubba to brood. He didn't know exactly how to make his face broody when he couldn't move it, but he did his best. The assistant director looked happy enough with the end result.

After the shoot ended, the redhead said to Bubba, "All right, Zombie #14, you can go home now. Go by makeup and have Simone take the prosthesis off. Don't forget about the contacts." She handed him a sheet of paper. "This is where you need to be tomorrow. Make sure you have the same clothing. Simone will mark the clothing and bag it, but be our good bud and make certain it's the same when you put it on tomorrow in the wardrobe/makeup tent."

Bubba moaned. It was a real moan. This whole thing had taken hours and he was starving. Also he had a headache. He stumbled over to the makeup tent and Simone got right to work on him. Fortunately it didn't take that long to get the gory fake jaw off his face. It took a lot longer to get the glue and plastic off the other parts of his skin.

Bubba rubbed his jaw in appreciation of its newfound freedom. Then Simone rapidly and efficiently popped the lens out of his eyes, putting them in a special case.

"There you go," Simone said. "Try Noxzema to get the rest off tonight, although I'm going to cover it all up again tomorrow so don't peel your skin off." She directed him back to a changing room with a plastic bag. "Put your wardrobe in the bag. See, it's marked Zombie #14/Farmboy."

Bubba grunted. It was a little difficult to move his jaw. He didn't know if it was because it had been closed for hours or because it had been broken. It didn't matter much.

Bubba almost tripped over McGeorge, the assistant who had been irritated with them the day before in the cemetery. She pushed him to one side, muttering, "I hate directors. Give them one stupid award and they think they're Spike Jones and Orson Welles' love child." She stopped to glare at Bubba. "You. From the cemetery. What are you doing here?"

Simone laughed. "He just finished his scenes, McGeorge. What crawled up your ass?"

"I'm looking for her grace, the star of the film," McGeorge snarled. "The royal RV is empty."

"Toking up behind the barn with the best boys," Simone said.

Bubba moaned again. It was really hard to get his mouth open.

"Bubba?"

Bubba's head shot up. The glorious sparkle of the light moment of sun's light just before it set scattered into a thousand iridescent beams of brilliance, touching everything in its path with a glimmer of warmth.

Willodean smiled crookedly at him.

"Bubba?" McGeorge repeated. "His name can't really be...Bubba. That's like naming a Dalmatian dog...Spot." She shook her head, eying the sheriff's department patch on Willodean's shoulder and absently rubbing the index finger that Willodean had bent backward. "Simone was joking about the toking. Hey, I made a rhyme. I'll go find Tandy. I'm sure it's nothing."

"Better bring the eye drops," Simone called after her as McGeorge strode off, nearly skipping as she hurried along.

Bubba waved at Simone and offered an arm to Willodean. She took it with another one of her lustrous smiles.

Willodean looked at him. "A zombie? Really?"

Bubba shrugged. He rubbed his jaw and said, "Majawstug."

"I didn't get that."

"Ma jaw eh stug."

"Is that makeup on your face?"

"Um."

"You know," Willodean said as they threaded their way through tents and stepped across electrical cables, "I might have been a little, oh, pushy yesterday. When I said something about kids."

Bubba tripped on an errant bloody arm. A film crew member snatched it up and glared at him as if Bubba had done it on purpose.

"I kind of sprung it on you," Willodean added quickly, completely ignoring the errant bloody arm and the crew member cradling it in his own arms. "I wasn't trying to push you into anything. I suppose children have been on my mind lately. But it's not like my biological clock is ticking and ticking and about to explode, or something like that."

"Mmm?"

"I'm not sure how to explain it," Willodean went on.

"Urmg?"

"We've been dating and I was just curious what you thought about children." Willodean looked away and appeared to study a skeletal zombie sipping Coca Cola from a straw struck in the can. Her free hand sketched a nervous pattern in the air. "With Brownie being around and sometimes Janie, although they're not exactly children, are they? More like some sort of warped offspring of karma or the like. I'm just blathering on and on. I mean, you choked on your chicken when I said it and I feel just awful about it. I should just shut up now." She closed her perfectly formed mouth and Bubba was dumbstruck for a moment.

Speak. Say something, dumbie. Quick. She's goin' to get away.

"Eh nah tha," Bubba said, unpleasantly surprised that he couldn't speak when he desperately wanted to. He looked around as if that would somehow miraculously aid him. Two zombies were playing volleyball in the front yard. Miz Demetrice was on the veranda chatting with Marquita Thaddeus. She held one of Alfonzo and Pilar's children and Marquita was tickling the toddler's stomach. Another pair of zombies was smoking by the line of vans. *Not toking. Smoking cigarettes.*

Here was a prime opportunity. Bubba knew he should take advantage of it but it was impossible because the words wouldn't come out of his mouth and he couldn't make them come out of his mouth no matter how hard he tried. "Wahdee, woo oo mah meh?"

There. He had said it! HE HAD SAID IT! But hellfire and damnation, it didn't sound like he'd said it. He could be asking about the weather, or whether she'd like to go to Taco Bell for lunch, or whether she thought he wore boxers or briefs.

Willodean glanced at him anxiously. "Your jaw is a little swollen, Bubba. Did that stuff they put on you do something? Or...oh, God, was it from when I broke your jaw?" She jerked her hand out of his arm and touched her face. It appeared as though she was afraid to touch his, in case it exploded or something equally awful. "Maybe we should take you to Doc Goodjoint?"

Bubba shook his head. "Ehh wa tha mahut," he tried to tell her.

Willodean appeared horrified. She took a step away from him. "Is this some sort of weird rejection? You're afraid to tell me that I pushed a little too hard?"

Bubba shook his head frantically. *How could this have gone so wrong, so quickly? Oh, that is a stupid question. This is my life.* Just when things were going well, something came around and slapped him right upside the face. "Na tha," he said urgently. "Na tha!"

Willodean didn't look too convinced. "I'm going to talk to your mother now. We can talk later when you *can* talk."

Bubba watched her walk away with a miserable feeling deep in his soul. She hadn't even paused to kiss him on a cheek or given him a chance to buss her on hers. He silently said a few swear words. Then he laid his head against the side of one of the vans and thought seriously about banging it a few times just to see if that would make a difference. Unconsciousness might help him considerably.

When Bubba raised his head, he saw his mother talking to Willodean on the veranda. Willodean had clearly put Bubba in the back of her mind and she stood facing away from him. Miz Demetrice still held one of the toddlers. He couldn't tell if it was Blanca or Carlotta, but the baby was waving arms and legs keenly. His mother put the child down and she stood on her two feet with her tiny little arms wrapped around Miz Demetrice's legs.

Willodean knelt next to the child and clucked the little girl on the chin. The child moved around to the back of Miz Demetrice's legs, clearly apprehensive of Willodean. Maybe it was the uniform.

Bubba frowned and then didn't frown because he couldn't frown. Alfonzo and Pilar spoke like they had lived in the United States for a long time. It might mean they were here legally, (Both Alfonzo and Pilar sounded like folks who had grown up in Southern Texas along the border of Mexico.) but their association with Miz Demetrice and Miz Adelia meant something was afoot. They might not like being around figures of authority because they had been ill-treated by them. Even the baby cottoned to that.

Kids. Bubba mentally frowned harder. *Are kids on Willodean's mind because she's in the whatever game that's happening with Ma and Miz Adelia?* That would be something that Miz Demetrice was more than capable of doing. After all, Willodean was involved in the Pegramville Women's Club's activities, and Willodean had helped his mother out before. They had illegally searched the sheriff's office once because Miz Demetrice suspected that there was an important clue there. Willodean had been the one to let them into the sheriff's department. It was part of the reason he liked Willodean so much. When the going got tough, she didn't pull out a rule book and quote verbatim. Instead, she was more likely to shriek, "To hell with the rule book!"

Bubba eyed the side of the van. It wasn't too late to pound his head against it. If there was a dent in the van that resulted then he knew just the right people to fix it.

He'd actually said the words (garbled the words was more like it) and Willodean hadn't understood him.

Damn.

Ignoring the two zombies who watched him, Bubba stumbled back to the makeup tent. Simone was cleaning up and repackaging multicolored tubes of everything a happy little cosmetologist could want.

"Bubba," she said and giggled. "I can't get over that. Did you mother really name you Bubba? I mean, does it say that on your birth certificate?"

Bubba pointed at his jaw and asked, "Wha uh ooh ta ma yah?"

Simone stopped smiling. "Oh, it's a little numb?"

He nodded.

"That'll wear off in a few hours. We use a glue that has an analgesic in it so people won't mess with the prostheses too much." She touched his jaw. "I see a little swelling. Remind me not to use that glue on you tomorrow." She turned away and dug in a portable refrigerator. "Water. Water. Hey, who hid my Red Bull in here?" Simone made a triumphant noise. "There we go. A gel pack." She stood up and handed it to him. "You *can* still breathe, right?"

Bubba took the compact gel pack and put it against his jaw. Since it had been in her little fridge, it was icy and felt good. He nodded shortly. *I kin still breathe. That's got to be a good thing.*

Simone grimaced. "Some people have a little reaction to the glue. I've seen it before. It'll wear off in a few hours. I've got some antihistamines around here."

Bubba shook his head and waved at her. What he really wanted was a beer. A nice cool bottle of beer. Some kind of lager that he hid in the back of his fridge for a special occasion. He wouldn't be able to drink that if he took an antihistamine. Also he needed to let Precious outside and play with her awhile. It would make both of them feel better.

Simone waved back.

When Bubba walked around the last van that was parked nearest to the mansion, he saw that the sheriff's department Bronco was gone. It made him want to hit the van with his head again.

●

Miraculously Bubba had lost his appetite. He drank from an ice cold bottle of Rogue Juniper Pale Ale. It was made in Oregon and a gift from Willodean. It had taken him three months to drink all six and the last one was held in his hand, with condensation dripping over his fist.

While the reds, blues, and oranges faded from the western skies, he'd drug out a ball and tossed it for Precious until she collapsed on her side, heaving with well-earned exertion. After retrieving the isolated beer from his fridge, he'd sat on a lawn chair and batted at mosquitos while watching the film crew pack up and leave. Then he'd witnessed Miz Demetrice and Miz Adelia sneaking Alfonso and Pilar out the side door and tucking them in Alfonso's minivan. The babies went with them, belted safely in little carriers and covered with blankets to keep the night air away. Bubba could see this because his mother and the housekeeper both carried Maglites and pretty much showed everything.

Bubba placed the bottle of ale next to his jaw. As it was still cold, it helped a little. He wondered if workman's comp would cover that little issue and decided it didn't impact his mechanicking skills so it probably wouldn't.

Figures. He looked up at the skies. An array of brilliant stars glittered across a sea of darkest velvet. *If all were going to the way it typically went, then a comet*

61

should streak in and demolish my truck. Or...there should be a dead body on it.

Bubba nodded to himself. *A dead alien body from a comet. Mysteriously kilt by someone else and put on a comet headed for Pegram County, Texas. Then I git blamed for it. Some alien from a distant galaxy takes me away because they think I done did it and then he locks me up in an alien jail. Then I have to eat glow-in-the-dark grubs because they don't make human food there. Yep.*

The minivan backed out of the parking place and slowly turned around, all the while not turning on its lights. The two older women armed with Maglites waved as the dark shape of the van moved away.

Bubba would have checked his watch for the time but he wasn't wearing a watch. He had an idea that it was after midnight. The day had slid away. Four a.m. had him up and fixing a Dodge Caravan. Five a.m. had him sitting down and being zombified. The remainder of the day had skated away from him, right up until the moment he'd seen Willodean at sunset.

And then I surely crapped on that like a hundred pigeons on a big statue in a park.

Screwing up his features, Bubba realized he could move his jaw a little more. It hadn't been a good time to say anything to Willodean. She was nervous because of what she had said and there were zombies and his mother everywhere. To be perfectly precise, it had been a horrible time to say it. No woman in her right mind would have responded favorably asked at a time like that.

Mebe, just mebe, it had been blessed serendipity. Bubba should be relieved. He'd have another shot. *Probably.*

Suppressing a yawn, Bubba meandered over to where his mother and Miz Adelia were talking quietly to each other.

"—think they're suspicious," Miz Adelia said.

"Of what?" Miz Demetrice whispered back. "It's not like it's obvious."

"We should be more careful. We need to get all the shipments through," Miz Adelia said.

"What shipments?" Bubba asked and was pleased to see the two women jump. It was the little things in life that brought pure enjoyment.

"Bubba!" Miz Demetrice yelled. She fluttered a hand in front of her chest, nearly hitting herself in the face with the larger Maglite. "You nearly gave me a bad case of the all-overs!"

"Ma, the day that you're nervous is the day I should go to Tahiti and live on the beach," Bubba said.

"Did you see Bubba as a zombie?" Miz Adelia asked swiftly. She was nearly as adept at changing the subject as Miz Demetrice. In fact, she had probably learned the skill from the older woman.

"I almost didn't recognize the boy," Miz Demetrice said. "Shall we go to bed? I'd like to get a good night's sleep."

"Hard to sleep when you're driving around," Bubba remarked, "like a couple with two little kids."

"That's the best way to get a baby to go to sleep," Miz Adelia said promptly. "A car ride is just the thing."

"Uh-huh," Bubba said. It was challenging to quash the suspicion from his tone.

"Shouldn't you be getting some shut eye?" his mother asked pointedly.

Precious trotted up and nosed his leg. She was just as tired as she could be. She had been up with Bubba from the beginning and had only had five naps since that time. A dog could only go so far.

"I reckon," Bubba said, thinking he should give Precious a break. "I'm working tomorrow, too. They're filming something downtown. I'll be gone most of the morning. Them movie people coming back here?"

"Not tomorrow," Miz Demetrice said evasively. "However did they get you to agree to be in the movie?"

"I'm not exactly sure of that," Bubba admitted. "Ya'll in trouble, Ma? Is there something I should know about?" His mother was the queen of trouble-making. She didn't wait for trouble to come to her; she went looking for it. In fact, she was the expert's expert of locating inconvenience, danger, and affairs of woe. Bubba had gotten to be quite the professional of avoiding his mother's more disorderly undertakings. However, sometimes they had a habit of sneaking up and biting him on the butt.

"Oh, it's nothing to worry about," his mother soothed him.

"That's the part where it usually becomes the most worrisome," Bubba said. He leaned over and kissed Miz Adelia on the cheek and repeated it with his mother. "Get some rest, because I reckon ya'll are going to need it, being up to whatever it is that you're up to."

Miz Adelia shrugged and went to her car. Bubba watched as his mother went inside and watched as Miz Adelia started her vehicle up and drove down the lane. She turned on her headlights to do so. Alfonzo hadn't turned on his and probably hadn't until he had reached the main road.

Bubba shook his head and winced when he yawned. His jaw still wouldn't quite work correctly.

Chapter Six

Bubba and the Distressed Director

Sunday, March 10th

Bubba did manage to go to sleep and when he woke up he could use his jaw again. He wasn't looking forward to more of the same pain on this day so he took an antihistamine. He scrounged around his clothing from the previous day and found the piece of paper he'd been given and saw that he was supposed to be on Main Street at eight a.m. He would be just yards away from the Pegram County Sheriff's Department and one never knew when a suitable opening might present itself. Things might be changing for the better.

A positive attitude, he told himself. He glanced at Precious, who was doing the Dog-Has-To-Go-Outside-Now dance. "A positive attitude, girl."

Precious whined apprehensively and did a little twirl. Her tail waggled questioningly.

Bubba lurched downstairs and let his dog outside. He took care of his personal business and even shaved without cutting himself once. He let his dog back inside and fed her. She ate while he poured himself a large mug of coffee. The mug was one of a set of six matched, oversized cups and had been a housewarming gift from Willodean's parents, Celestine and Evan Gray. Apparently, locating one of their daughters who had been kidnapped by the brother of a murderer went a long way in their estimation. However, since Precious had been more instrumental in finding Willodean, the canine had gotten a Bone Bone Gift Basket from Doggies R Us. (An actual basket with a large red ribbon that Precious tried to chew to little bits before Bubba had taken it away.) Included had been carob treats, as well as organic, soy free snacks, and an assortment of chew toys. Precious's present had been bigger than Bubba's and Bubba had a sneaking suspicion that Celestine liked his dog better than she liked him.

It don't matter. It's what Willodean thinks about me that really counts. Bubba needed to hang onto that positive attitude. It was a bright, fresh new day with golden opportunity around every corner. There was lots to be done. And hey, he got to be in a movie. Willodean didn't seem impressed by the movie itself, but maybe she would appreciate his can-do attitude. *Is it possible that Willodean likes my dog better than me? Naw.*

When Bubba walked outside he tried to shoo Precious away from his truck, but she was having none of it. She had been left behind one too many times and she was ready to ride. He had an idea that she knew exactly what day of the week it was and why she should be permitted to join him.

"I have to work, girl," he told his dog.

Precious tilted her head.

"Ifin you come, you've got to stay out of trouble."

She tilted her head the other way. Big brown eyes stared at him. Liquid brown eyes full of pleading and wistful longing looked at him. Looked...at...him. Until...he...folded.

"Mebe you kin stay with Willodean," he said hopefully. It certainly gave him an excuse. He knew she had a short shift on Sunday and she would be around the department later in the day. Bubba brightened. *Sometimes a fella has to make an opportunity for himself.* "I'm goin' to be on it like ants on a honey bun," he swore.

Precious woofed expectantly. She knew a chance when she saw one and clambered up into the truck when Bubba opened the door for her. He had to give her derriere a helping hand, but she kept on eagerly pushing with her less than long legs. She scrambled to the passenger side of the bench seat and stuck her head out of the already opened window. She barked once at Alfonzo, who was already about and scraping some of the chipped paint from the columns in the front of Snoddy Mansion. Alfonzo waved leisurely with the scraper.

Bubba actually got to the downtown area of Pegramville without further ado. He parked well down the street from where the film crew was setting up. The streets were cordoned off with plastic sawhorses and yellow tape. Local police officers roamed around to ensure complicity. He paused to wave at Officers Smithson and Haynes, one of whom might have once kicked him in the head with a steel tipped boot. They didn't look happy when the redheaded girl appeared and ushered Bubba inside the lines.

"He's in the movie," she called to Smithson.

"As what? The village idiot?" Smithson asked.

The redhead flipped him off.

Bubba was mildly surprised. He didn't usually get immediate support from strangers.

She said, "He tried to grope Tandy North this morning. If it were up to me he'd be guarding a missile silo in the Arctic, but I suppose we can't make the local police do that." The redhead-Bubba wished he knew her name-guided him to a tent set up on City Hall's lawn. Precious followed with her nose held close to the ground lest she miss any particularly inviting aromas. "Wait here. I'll have Simone call you in when she's ready."

Bubba was also surprised to see several people he knew. Lloyd Goshorn was being turned into an emaciated zombie with one of his lungs dangling from his chest. He gestured halfheartedly at Bubba, a lackluster acknowledgement. Lloyd had been less than friendly since Bubba had almost run him down with a car. (Bubba *had* been trying to save someone's life in the process and he *had* missed Lloyd by a country mile, but Lloyd tended to forget both of those parts.)

Kiki Rutkowski and Dougie, both back in zombie uniform, grunted at each other in zombiese. Dougie pointed at Bubba and said, "Braaaaaiiiiinnnnns."

Kiki grinned at Bubba showing black and gray teeth.

Bubba waved.

Foot Johnson was also an extra and apparently not a zombie as evidenced by the lack of gore or wounds on his person. When he wasn't hanging out around Main Street, he was usually a janitor for the city buildings. He also cleaned up in the sheriff's department. He talked to Stanley Boomer while his children scuffed their feet in impatience. The Boomer farm was where the Christ Tree was located and where fainting goats were kept. Lissa Boomer, the youngest Boomer child, had a stuffed animal swiped by Precious when the hound had been stealing various items in preparation for parenthood.

Mary Jo Treadwell and Arlette Formica were decked out in authentic zombie gear, leaving one to wonder who was manning the desk at the sheriff's department. Filbert Turberville, the principal of the local elementary school, chatted with Wilma Rabsitt, who allegedly cheated at the weekly poker games that Miz Demetrice held. The principal inexpertly twirled a shotgun while Wilma held a machete that was likely longer than she was tall.

It was a good crowd. Bubba hadn't seen so many people together and covered with blood since the 1st Annual Pegramville Murder Mystery Festival. That had gone over so well it was expected there might not be a 2nd Annual Pegramville Murder Mystery Festival.

Willodean, Bubba was sorry to note, was not present. She was probably manning the receptionist's desk and answering the 9-1-1 line. *I should send her flowers.*

For what?

Because I didn't mind that she asked me about wanting kids. Because I couldn't talk to her when I wanted to talk to her. Because I messed up the first time I said you-know-what.

Bubba answered himself. *But Willodean don't know that you asked you-know-what. In fact, she's kind of freaked out that she said something about kids.* It was like she had gone out of order in the rule book of dating. First, casual dating. Second, more serious dating. Third, total monogamy and a commitment to dating exclusivity. Fourth, discussion about family and/or moving in. Fifth, moving in together. Sixth, engagement. Seventh, marriage.

Scowling, Bubba realized he was screwing up the order, too. But he knew he was old enough to know his own mind. He'd given the matter a lot of thought; however he had second thoughts after the debacle at the cemetery.

Bubba looked around for the van to bump his head against. Instead he found a man standing five feet away staring at him. He was about five feet ten inches and wore thick black framed glasses. He was in his forties and wore a sappy smile as he studied Bubba. "Hey," he said because one *should* say something to a person who was staring at you thusly, even if it was "Do I have boogers hanging?"

"Bubba," the man said.

It certainly seemed as though Bubba should know the man. He looked familiar. Bubba couldn't quite place it. Perhaps if he spoke some more.

"It's quite a thing," the man said waving at the varied crowd of zombies and non-zombies.

Bubba scratched the side of his head. It was too late to pretend that he knew the man. Bubba tilted his head to one side like Precious. It worked for the canine so perhaps it would work for him. It didn't work with him. Finally it popped into Bubba's head. All the man needed was a pipe or a purple mask or a pirate's scarf over fake dreadlocks.

"David," Bubba said, grateful that he hadn't had to ask. David Beathard was one of the mental patients from The Dogley Institute for Mental Well-Being who had been one of the Christmas Killer's patients. (It was a whole convoluted thing. You had to be there. There was a reason for revenge. There was a killer. There was a kid with a homemade Taser. Blah. Blah. Blah.) In any case, David had an interesting habit of developing new personas. Psychiatrists, super heroes, pirates, who knew what he was going to be next? (Hadn't there been a President's wife in there somewhere? He thought it was Michelle Obama but possibly it had been Barbara Bush.) However, he had been very helpful to Bubba in a thinking-outside-of-the-check-here-for-mental-disability-box way. It was even possible that he was Bubba's friend.

David smiled widely. "I know. I don't look like I usually do. I'm taking a break from the whole schizophrenic personality disorder thing."

"Okay," Bubba said equably. David didn't look like he usually did. He looked normal. It was rather disconcerting. "You in the movie?"

70

"I'm in the movie theater scene," David said. "I have explosive blood packs strapped to my chest. It'll be very exciting when they blow up. I'm supposed to be drenched with fake blood, but it's washable, so it's all gravy." He touched his mouth. "Red colored gravy, but still gravy."

Bubba's eyes slipped to David's chest. He was wearing the same kind of button-down cardigan he used to wear when he was David the Psychotrist. (Or had it been psychiatrist? Psychologist? Something like that.) The cardigan didn't seem poufy or anything, but some of the special effects the film company were producing seemed very realistic. (There had been that split second in the cemetery when Bubba believed that the zombies were real, no matter what he knew deep inside, not that he would ever admit it aloud.)

"There's a movie theater scene?"

"The scene is that people are inside watching the classic, *The Shrieking Horror From Above*, which is an inside joke, and zombies come in and eat the popcorn clerks. Cue the blood splattered popcorn. Of course, then the clerks go zombie-city on the patrons and chaos ensues. They're using the old theater on Walter Street."

"I thought that place went out of business years ago."

"They sell water beds now. Also they rent to the movie makers as a set."

"So what happens to you in the scene?"

"I think a zombie reaches through my back and explodes through my breast bone," David said confidentially. "I don't think a rotting corpse could really do that, but I'm not writing the movie script." He appeared contemplative. "Maybe I need to write a movie. I could do that. I have lots of good ideas." He dismissed it with a wave. "The Graphology and Reading shop isn't doing so well. I should have rethought the need for such a service in a small town. My only customer last week was the mayor, who wanted to know if the lines on his hand indicated something very personal about his more intimate characteristics. I won't repeat what it specified." David shuddered.

"That would be good," Bubba said.

David leaned closer. "So no mysteries to solve lately? No notes in car parts or the like? Irish Travellers or seven-foot-tall Buddhists? Disappearing or reappearing bodies?"

"No!" Bubba glanced around apprehensively and said it again, "No, and I'll thank you not to bring it up. You'll jinx me or something."

"Bubba, I hate to break it to you, but—" David paused and added the rest slowly and in half a whisper as if saying it faster and louder would cause the fates to toss anvils down on their heads "—there...are...corpses...everywhere...today."

"They're not real."

"It's probably a sign," David insisted.

"They're all actors, and in some cases, they're people you know." Bubba crossed his arms over his chest. "Yesterday *I* was a zombie."

"No."

"On account of this thing this gal attached to my face, I couldn't talk for nigh on eight hours."

"How could anyone tell the difference?"

Had David just made a joke? Bubba wasn't used to that. Maybe David the Psychotrist was now David the Comedian. Bubba's eyes narrowed.

The redhead called Bubba over and he said to David, "See you later."

"Be sure not to take any wooden corpses," David opined gravely.

Bubba grimaced.

Simone waited beside the redhead.   Simone got Bubba to change his clothing while the redhead disappeared to do filmy types of things he wouldn't begin to comprehend. When he returned wearing clothes from yesterday, she started on his face and hair. She even took time to take Polaroids of him so she could replicate the effort. She handed him a clipboard and said, "There are your lines. You need to memorize them."

"'It shore ain't a pink elephant,'" he read inexpressively.

The cosmetic brush Simone was using to apply some kind of powder to Bubba's face stopped momentarily. "Say it like this," she advised, "'It shore ain't a pink elephant!'" Her rendition was acute and full of expression.

"Why?"

"Because you're *acting*," Simone said. "Kristoph's going to have a fit when he hears you say it like that. Of course, he can always dub it with someone else's voice."

"'It shore ain't a pink elephant!'" Bubba said obediently.

"Better," Simone said and it was clear from her tone that it wasn't much better. "Imagine that you see something really weird and cool at the same time."

"Like a tricked out AC Cobra?"

"What is that, a car?"

"Yeah," Bubba sighed wistfully. It was the kind of car that reminded him of Willodean. It had lovely wondrous curves and was all business under the hood.   There weren't many of them and the ones that were left were to be worshipped.

"Are you...a *mechanic*...named Bubba?"

"Yep."

"Of course you are."

●

"'It shore ain't a pink elephant!'" Bubba emoted. Emote was his word for the day. Kristoph had the three involved actors practice. This technically included Bubba, although he was fairly certain he couldn't, in fact, act and wasn't entitled to be called an actor. Kristoph used the word emote thirteen times in his impassioned Braveheart-inspired speech. It might have been more like fifteen or sixteen times because Bubba hadn't started counted after he'd heard it three or four times.

Bubba emoted. (Emoting unfortunately could be compared to being constipated.) The lead actress, Tandy North, emoted. The lead actor, Alex Luis, emoted. The zombies emoted. It was emotiful.

"Cut," Kristoph said in a tone that could have shattered glass. "Bubba, a word with you."

Bubba trudged over to the director. He had decided that he didn't really like the director. Kristoph wore his Silent-Movie-Director ensemble again. Again the boots, hat, and megaphone were the same with the pants and the wool coat changed for effect. He also wore his What-the-hell-do-I-do-with-them? smile. He wasn't a very sincere person and Bubba suspected that Kristoph would have tried to cheat orphans out of their only piece of candy if they wouldn't emote.

"Just imagine," Kristoph said to Bubba, "that you're seeing something extraordinary and creepy and fantastical at the same time." He extended his arm and all the fingers of the hand were spaced apart as he slowly moved it across the length of his personal horizon, showing Bubba its limitless possibilities. "It's surprising you. It's scaring you. It's going to eat you and you know it. But you...can't...look...away."

Bubba glanced at Tandy. She stood at the side of the set and puffed a cigarette. It was a regular one. Alex reached over and nabbed the butt from her to draw on it.

The redhead snapped, "Don't encourage him, Tandy. He's supposed to have quit last week. It said so in *Tiger Beat*."

"What am I seeing anyway?" Bubba asked Kristoph, because he couldn't not ask.

"It's the super zombie, the target beast that has caused the apocalypse, and it's scary, mega-scary. It will make you pee in your manties."

"Then I wouldn't be saying, 'It shore ain't a pink elephant!'" Bubba pursed his lips and added, "I'd be shrieking like a little kid."

"Bubba, just say the line like you mean it," Kristoph said and his eyes were cold.

Bubba didn't really want to tick off the director. He hadn't been paid yet. He was directed back to his spot and Tandy and Alex joined him.

A kid with a bald head and piercings through both eyebrows held the clapboard with the scene's number and takes on it. They were up to ten and Bubba had a good idea that he was precariously balanced on the edge of two bad things: elimination or replacement.

Tandy took a last hit on her cigarette and flicked the butt to the side. It hit the head of the redhead and she glared at Tandy. "Sorry," Tandy said insincerely.

Bubba said to himself, "Time to cowboy up, ya'll."

"That's the spirit," Alex said and winked at Bubba.

Kristoph said, "Roll film." The cameramen got busy. The bald kid clicked the clapboard and vanished. "Action," Kristoph added softly.

Tandy immediately became all seriousness. Her eyes stared over the shoulder of the director. Her hair drifted a little in a light breeze and her lips parted in shock. If Bubba hadn't known, he would have thought she was genuinely frightened of something.

"Oh, my god," she said. "What is that? What in hell *is* that?"

Bubba looked toward the director. His mouth opened and he saw Willodean standing in the crowd behind Kristoph. She smiled tentatively at Bubba. Sheriff John stood beside her with his great arms crossed over his chest and a doubtful expression on his face. Bubba registered it peripherally because Willodean had almost 99 percent of his undivided attention. The one percent was focused on...

"'It shore ain't a pink elephant!'" Bubba said sincerely.

"Run!" Alex yelled.

The three turned to run and Kristoph yelled, "Cut!" He clasped his hands together and looked heavenward. "Perfect! Thank god, perfect! Finally, Bubba! You finally got it! Thank god for Bubbas!"

That was the moment that Precious heard the word "Bubba!" one time too many. She abruptly decided to see what was happening, to see if canine assistance was warranted, and in her uncontrolled struggle to reach her master, tripped the cameraman. The cameraman tottered as the dog attempted to decide which was up. Her ears flapped in the air as she slid to one side. Her back legs scrambled for purchase. The camera flipped out of the man's hands and he threw himself toward it trying to catch it before it hit the ground. Instead, he hit the side of Kristoph's director's chair and crashed against Kristoph's elbow. Kristoph was holding a cup of coffee with the hand that connected to that elbow and it was knocked over. It spilled all over Kristoph's riding pants and made the man screech like a little girl as the hot liquid made contact with his flesh. Everyone within a radius of a hundred yards froze at the sound.

It was similar to what would have happened to a group of people if they had suddenly heard the frenzied roar of a real live Tyrannosaurus Rex.

Precious promptly hid behind Bubba's legs with her tail down.

Bubba put a soothing hand on the canine's back.

The redhead appeared from nowhere and attempted to staunch the flow of coffee with a wad of paper towels she had instantaneously managed to find. Kristoph knocked her hand aside and his eyes settled on Precious and then Bubba.

Kristoph glanced at the pieces of the camera strewn on the asphalt. The cameraman was endeavoring to hide in plain sight. Bubba didn't have that luxury. The crowd of people had split apart like warm string cheese, to reveal Bubba at the other end, with Precious slinking behind his legs.

For a long moment silence ensued. The fart of a flea could have been discerned, if a flea had happened to be flatulent at that particular moment. Then Kristoph leapt to his feet and sound exploded viscerally out of him, filling the void with a noise that overpowered everything else.

"GET THE BLEEP OFF MY SET WITH THAT BLEEPING DOG!" Kristoph screamed at Bubba, except he didn't use the words "BLEEP" or "BLEEPING." "NOW! NOW! NOW!"

Now that's emoting, Bubba thought. *Totally has me convinced. Am I getting paid?*

Chapter Seven

Bubba and the Cryptic Corpse

Sunday, March 10th

Bubba did get paid. The redhead made sure of that. In fact, he got paid for Precious being in the movie, too. Two security guards in *The Deadly Dead RISES!* T-shirts helpfully facilitated his exit from the set, too. They even stopped at the wardrobe and make up tent to make sure he changed into his own clothing and said something about him not taking souvenirs.

Sticking the folded check into his pocket, Bubba said, "What am I going to take? Fake blood or a fake shotgun hole?"

The two taciturn men escorted Bubba right to the yellow tape strung between two plastic sawhorses and lifted it while he ducked under. Precious followed with her head down and her tail drooping. She knew she had done something wrong.

A few people stopped to ask Bubba what was going on or to shoot the breeze with him, so he didn't make it very far past the tape.

One was Doris Cambliss, the owner of the Red Door Inn. The Inn used to be a not-so-cleverly concealed brothel, but Doris had gone legit. She said, "Don't you pay that director no never mind, Bubba." She reached down to scratch Precious's head but it appeared the canine could hardly bring herself to enjoy the uncharacteristic stroke.

"I got paid," Bubba said woodenly, although the director had said something about insurance and suing him for the cost of the camera that had been broken. With his luck the cost to replace the equipment would be proportional to three times the amount he had been paid. Things that were broken always cost more than what one had in one's pocket.

"And you got to be in a movie," Doris said cheerfully. She had dyed black hair and always dressed in the finest clothing. Looking to be fifteen to twenty years younger than her actual age, she could have been a movie star herself. "That's something to cross off your bucket list."

"I don't have a bucket list," Bubba said. "Pardon me, Miz Cambliss, but I aim to go home before someone thinks to arrest me for doing something or other."

Doris nodded. "Been there. Done that. I've got the t-shirt." She considered. "Not that I'd ever wear a t-shirt." She waved and meandered off, stopping to chat with Rosa Granado, who was George Bufford's secretary when she wasn't being his mistress. George Bufford was the proud and cheap proprietor of Bufford's Gas and Grocery. Bubba had once worked for him and been fired for having been suspected of murdering his ex-fiancée.

Bubba glanced around for Willodean, but she wasn't anywhere to be found. That made him feel a little more dejected. In his moment of greatest infamy, he needed…but then he tended to have several of those moments and she had been there before. She probably had been called to a scene of something or other. (The subject of greatest infamy made him want to write an actual list of his top ten offenses. 1) Breaking the arm of his commanding officer while catching him in bed with his fiancée. 2) Discovering the body of his ex-fiancée on the family property with little to no alibi and practically having a smoking gun in his hand. Oh, Bubba could go on and on.

79

There was likely a lot more than ten. *Mebe twenty. Oh, hell make it the top hundred.*)

"'It shore ain't a pink elephant,'" someone half cackled at him with a gravelly voice.

"After you say it about a dozen times, it don't sound proper anymore," Bubba said to Sheriff John. "And it starts sounding like it don't mean nothing at all. Kind of like a congressman."

Sheriff John was one of the few men in the county who was taller than Bubba. He was also older, heavier, and was gray-haired and gray-eyed. His full name was Johnathon Headrick but Sheriff John had stuck in the days of his first election to public office. His trademark battleship gray colors were part of the man. He wouldn't have looked the same if he had brown hair. (No Just For Men for that fine figure of Orwellian authority.)

Bubba rapidly scanned the area again, hoping that Willodean was hiding behind the sheriff. She wasn't. "You send Willodean out on a call?"

"She needed to talk to someone," Sheriff John rasped. His voice had never recovered from being nearly strangled by a rope around his neck. He still had the scars there as well the remnants of a tracheotomy. Bubba ought to know; he'd been right on the spot to save Sheriff John's bacon. The older man had treated him somewhat more deferentially after that incident, but it didn't mean he couldn't tease him. "Must have been a hot date."

Another perfectly sane and pleasant day in Pegram County, Bubba thought inanely. "You arresting me for something?"

"For what? Bad acting?"

"The director said I had a square jaw," Bubba said.

"Did you get to talk to Tandy North?" Sheriff John asked. "Don't tell Darla, but she's a hot little piece of

Hollywood starlet." He considered. "Not that the wife isn't. But the wife isn't twentysomething anymore with a tushie as tight as a snare drum." He shrugged.

"Tandy might have said a few words to me," Bubba said. The words had been something like "Your mark is over there, dumbass," but they *had* been a few words. Bubba was rapidly coming to the conclusion that the Hollywood business was distasteful and most of the people were unfriendly.

Bubba noticed something in the distance as the crowd was dispersing. "Is that my mother with her new handy people?"

"Miz Demetrice has got new handy people?" Sheriff John asked curiously. He craned his neck. "What is she going to do with handy people?"

"I saw the fella scraping paint this morning."

"The mansion is a mite deficient in paint."

"I bin meaning to get around to that."

Sheriff John laughed. "With all the extra things you've bin doing for money, I don't see how you could have time. Everyone's engines are purring thanks to you. The City of Dallas prolly bought three boots for what you had to pay them. And the plasma place has a glut of product thanks to your donations."

"I only got dizzy once last week," Bubba said defensively, "and I finally paid the last bit to the hospital."

"From which visit?"

"I don't recollect. They lumped them all together. No pun intended." Bubba watched Alfonzo speaking with Miz Demetrice and Pilar. Looking like a jackass on a movie set was pushed to the background as he thought about what the trio was up to. (It was easier not to think of the movie or of Willodean.) Alfonzo held one of his daughters while Pilar held the other one. Miz Demetrice was nodding and

Alfonzo was nodding back. A few hours before he had been scraping the paint off one of the columns. Now they were mingling in a light crowd.

Then Willodean appeared next to them and she spoke to Alfonzo, who nodded. She clucked the chin of the child in the man's grasp. The baby eagerly held her arms out toward Willodean and Willodean instantly complied, cradling the child close to her body. That was funny. One baby didn't like Willodean and the other one did. And the sight made Bubba go weak in the knees, forcing him to go back to what he was thinking about instead of what darted into his beleaguered brain.

Willodean held the child like an expert. Kids had been on her mind lately. *Why is that? Because she's been around Alfonzo and Pilar and their two daughters.* It wasn't surprising to Bubba because he'd already surmised that Willodean was involved in whatever his mother and Miz Adelia were up to.

But what is it that they're up to and how much trouble is it going to cause?

"You ain't met Alfonzo and Pilar?" Bubba asked, trying to be innocent about it. *Do you know them, John? Are you in on it, too? Hmm?*

"I have not," Sheriff John said. "You'll have to tell me if they're any good because the missus wants some things done around the house. Lloyd Goshorn does some of it, but he's bin on a bender of late. Last night he was as fried as a corn pone. Tried to et all the pickled eggs out of the jar at the Dew Drop Inn. He went one cotton-picking egg too far and they had to call an ambulance to take him in. Boy swore he won't touch another egg in his life."

"You can et those eggs in the big jar?" Bubba grimaced but he kept his eye on Willodean. *Guess John ain't in on it.* "I thought they was just for show. Beg

82

pardon, John but I got to see a lady about a horse. Precious, heel."

Sheriff John glanced over his shoulder and at Willodean, then simply shrugged.

Bubba waded through a last rush of folks. He had to sidestep Mary Jean Holmgreen, who seemed to think he liked her flirting with him for some reason, but she was eighty if she was a day, and he didn't know how to tell her politely he wasn't really her type. She did manage to pinch his gluteus maximus in a way that made him jump a foot into the air. "Miz Holmgreen!" he protested as he sidled away.

Mary Jean winked salaciously.

By the time Bubba reached where Willodean and his mother had been, they were gone and Alfonzo was tucking one of his daughters into a car seat. Pilar took care of the other one.

"Say, Alfonzo," Bubba said, "did you happen to see which way the sheriff's deputy went?"

"*Qué?*"

"Little lady about yea high, has a gun, big green eyes," Bubba explained.

"*La policía,*" Pilar said to Alfonzo.

Alfonzo nodded at his wife. "She said something about a call on her radio."

Bubba's shoulders slumped and he put his head down, but not before he saw Alfonzo grin at his wife. Bubba made himself look away and studied the daughter that Alfonzo was buckling into place. *Wow. It's true what they say about children. They grow quick. Kid must have gained three inches since Friday.*

"Ya'll going to church or such?" Bubba asked politely. Whatever they were doing, it suddenly didn't interest him. The weekend couldn't get much worse.

Oh, that's not true, said a little voice inside him. *It could get much worse. There could be* real *zombies.*

●

Bubba decided to take his check, his truck, his dog, and his self to his home where he could lick his wounds in private and pretend that it was a normal Sunday. If Willodean wanted to avoid him, then he would let her go for the moment. Furthermore, he couldn't do anything about his mother's machinations but ruminate, and the movie business had been a complete but short bust.

Instead Bubba watched the Stars play the Blackhawks on his tiny, yardsale television. Occasionally he got up to eat something or to change the laundry. He folded his clothes as the game progressed. Later, out of the window, he saw the Dodge Caravan pull up to the Mansion, but didn't bother to look to see what they were doing. He also heard his mother's Cadillac pull into its regular parking place and focused on the game instead of wasting time and energy with what his mother was doing.

And that fella just lost some teeth, he thought as he folded a pair of boxers. Hockey wasn't as good as football, but it was better than the cooking show on the other channel. Since he wasn't hooked up to cable for the moment, hockey was the best choice he had and it wasn't bad.

Precious asked to be let out by putting her paw on the front door and whining inquisitively. As Bubba let her outside, he saw Alfonzo was scraping around the back of the Mansion. Bubba went into one of the outbuildings to find another scraper. He didn't really want to work but he couldn't sit inside knowing someone else was working without assistance.

Alfonzo, regardless of his involvement with Miz Demetrice's most recent master plan, was Bubba's kind of guy. Communication was generally limited to grunts and sentences of less than three words.

"Missed a spot."

"Yep."

"Those Stars."

"Uh-huh."

"Drink?"

"Shore. RCs?"

"*Bueno*."

They heard the babies before they came around the corner of the Mansion with their mother. Pilar carried one and the other one toddled behind. Bubba couldn't tell them apart, but he thought that Carlotta was the one toddling.

Pilar smiled at her husband and said something rapidly in Spanish that Bubba couldn't even begin to hope to follow, even if he remembered part of his high school Spanish.

Since it was a nice day, Bubba pulled the wading pool out of the barn and cleaned it with a scrub brush and a hose. Then he filled it a few inches so the two little ones could wade or splash. Pilar went to get towels while Carlotta stuck a tentative hand in the water. She jerked it back and said, "*Frío!*"

"It'll warm up soon," Bubba told the little girl. Liquid brown eyes stared up at him uncertainly.

Precious came to nose the wading pool and stuck a paw in the water. It was, after all, her wading pool, but most likely she didn't mind sharing with smallish humans. Both children were enthralled with the Basset hound.

Bubba went back to scraping the section he'd been working on, while Alfonzo sat with his daughters waiting on Pilar's return.

Pilar reappeared with towels. Later Miz Demetrice came around with lemonade and a few camp chairs. The conversation was limited to Pilar speaking quietly to the girls as they splashed in the water. Little diapers became engorged with water and Bubba wondered why they didn't just take them off.

It wasn't long before the two girls tired of the water and Precious decided it was her turn. She jumped in and splashed everyone within a certain radius. The two toddlers thought it was endlessly hilarious and Precious knew when she had a captive audience.

Bubba and Alfonzo kept scraping until they had worked their way around the other side of the house. Pilar took the girls inside to change their diapers and their clothing, probably in that exact order.

Then someone drove up. Several someones. Tires clunked to a halt. Brakes squealed protestingly. Doors slammed. People spoke to each other but not loudly enough for Bubba to hear what they were saying.

Bubba glanced at the heavens above. *Now what, God?* Several someones suspiciously sounded like the arrival of official law enforcement vehicles. He climbed down from the ladder and went around the side. It wasn't the police come to arrest his mother for her latest transgression. It was worse.

The film company had returned.

Risley Risto waved at Bubba and gestured for his team to get busy. The crew fanned out. Van doors were pulled out. Boxes were extracted. They got to work.

They wouldn't have brought the whole team to get the check back, Bubba reasoned. *Therefore they got more filming to do here. Some kind of evening or night shot. Ah. This is the big rotten cherry on top of a big poopy sundae.*

Bubba recommenced with the scraping. He didn't want to talk to them. It was a long time later when he climbed down the ladder and Alfonzo was rubbing his wrists.

Risley ambled up to Bubba. "You know, Kristoph will calm down later and he'll feel just awful about you and your dog. After all, it was just an accident." Precious came up behind Bubba and abruptly shook herself. Cold, doggy smelling water flew everywhere. Bubba didn't mind but Risley winced.

I care, Bubba thought. *Not.*

"You've still got one more line in the movie," Risley enticed. "How many people get to be in the movies?"

One too many.

"I remember when I was in my prime," Risley said, "twenty—" he looked Bubba over quickly "—oh, eight?" He waited for a response but Bubba didn't bite. So Risley went on, "Ready to take on the world. Kissing the pretty girls. Climbing mountains and kicking butt. Life was a lot more fun then." His voice became wistful. He glanced at Precious. "A man and his dog." He knelt, holding his hand out to Precious. Precious sniffed the fingers offered to her and then tilted her head for a pet. Risley obliged.

"'If it weren't for that dagnammed sprocket,'" Bubba quoted. "Ain't much of a line. Seems to me that you wouldn't miss me ifin I dint say it. You could have some cute little zombie say it."

"It's an integral line," Risley protested. "The second part of the middle of the film hinges on it."

"Have someone else say it," Bubba said, thinking of Willodean staring at him while the director yelled at him and his dog. Normally Bubba wouldn't be bothered with such things. It didn't matter in the least what Kristoph thought of him, or what he thought of Precious, but he'd dinged Bubba's pride at just the right time. *Or just at the wrong time*, depending on how one looked at it.

"Come on, think about it," Risley said and with a last scratch behind Precious's ear, he stood up and walked back to the vans. He began directing people to where they needed to be.

"You should think about it," said someone and Bubba jumped. It was the redhead. He still didn't know her name. She was the executive assistant of executive assistants. "The plot has a big hole in it without that line."

"Seriously," Bubba said doubtfully, looking at her face to see if she was joking.

The redhead shrugged. "Is there a swamp around here?"

Bubba pointed toward the back acreage. "Watch out for the koi pond. The koi are really big."

It was the redhead's turn to look at him doubtfully.

"Better bring a flashlight," Bubba advised as she walked away, "it'll be dark in an hour or two."

The next person was Schuler, the head of the makeup department. He flipped the ends of his scarf over his shoulder and said, "Really, you should come back. It's just that Kristoph hates dogs. Really hates dogs. That's why I put your dog in the film. Just to mess with him. It'll *kill* him." Then he wandered off.

Bubba helped with the scraping for another hour, while keeping an eye on the film crew. He saw the redhead return and was only mildly grateful that the koi hadn't eaten her alive, regardless of the fact that she hadn't done anything to him.

"Dude," someone said from the foot of the ladder.

Alfonzo was frozen still with the scraper pressed against the side of the Mansion. Then he muttered in a tone of awe, "*It's Tandy North*, Bubba."

Bubba shrugged and kept scraping. He glanced down at Tandy and saw Alfonzo staring at her with a gaping mouth.

"Just come say the damned line," Tandy said. She puffed on a cigarette and blew a large circle. Then she blew a smaller circle that went through the larger one. "Kristoph is going to blow a cork and if he dies, we might lose funding."

"Can I have your autograph, Miss North?" Alfonzo asked politely.

"Sure," she said.

Alfonzo found a receipt in his pocket from Piggly Wiggly and a chewed up Bic pen. "One of my daughters is teething," he said apologetically.

"It's okay," Tandy said, signing the receipt. She handed both items back to Alfonzo and he looked as if he had won the lottery.

"I've got to show my wife," Alfonzo muttered. "She loved *Bubble People*." He zipped around the corner of the house.

"So," Tandy said. She puffed expectantly.

"I'll think about it."

"Kristoph won't apologize," she warned.

Bubba shrugged.

"Whatever," she said and wandered off.

It cain't be that dang important, Bubba thought.

When Marquita Thaddeus came to talk to Bubba a half hour later, Bubba gave up. No one was going to leave him alone and there were more people wandering around the Snoddy Estate than a bank on payday. He got his scraper, his RC cola, and his dog, and he trudged the hundred yards to his house. Maybe if he left the light out, no one would think he was home.

It was a wishful thought. However, when he went inside, he found that someone was waiting for him.

And someone was dead. Very dead. Not even close to zombie dead, but real life dead.

Chapter Eight

Bubba and the Licentious Law

Sunday, March 10th

Bubba looked heavenward. *Really, God? Really? Seriously?* This was, of course, immediately followed by a gush of guilty remorse because he had been thinking only of himself.

With a blustery sigh, he put the RC cola down on a side table and looked at the body, because it was pretty much the entire focus of the room at the moment.

The corpse was face down in the middle of his meager living room. The person had obviously walked in, been accosted by person or persons unknown, and fell where they had stood.

Bubba didn't even have to roll the person over to tell who it had been. The riding pants, short wool jacket, and riding boots gave it away. The beret had finally parted ways with the man's silver-topped head and lay almost three feet away from him, an isolated testament to the aberration of the situation. Shockingly, there wasn't a megaphone present.

Yes, it was Kristoph, the director of the movie. The same man who'd fired Bubba in such an open public event. Even Willodean had seen it happen. Everyone had seen it happen. And if any one person had missed it, then the word had likely already gotten around. Mike Holmgreen, who was the arson-committing grandson of Mary Jean Holmgreen, probably got it on his iPhone and immediately posted it online.

Bubba supposed he should check the man's pulse to see if he was genuinely dead. After all, Bubba had been fooled before. But there was a problem with that. The knife in Kristoph's back was the same bayonet that Bubba's father, Elgin, had appropriated from the military during his time in Southeast Asia. Not inconveniently, Elgin had also appropriated a M1911 Colt .45 pistol from the same military and it had been used as the murder weapon in the attempt to frame Bubba for his ex-fiancée's murder. In any case, the knife was forcefully inserted into the area of Kristoph's back, dead center on the shoulder blades.

The last time Bubba had seen the bayonet it had been in his bedroom upstairs, in a box of items that his mother had brought over from the Mansion after the house had been finished. Although her memories of her late husband were less than stellar, she wished her only child to have some mementos of Elgin Snoddy. Remembering his father's true persona, Bubba had been of a mind to toss them all into his garbage can but he'd restrained himself on his mother's account. Elgin was long since dead and could no longer hurt anyone. Certainly his possessions should have been less than lethal. Ironically, the bayonet was not less than lethal.

The director, who had once won a Saturn award for a movie Bubba had never seen, was dead. He was very dead. He was so dead that Elvis Presley would have said, "Whoa."

Furthermore, Kristoph was dead in Bubba's living room with Bubba's knife in his back. Bubba would have groaned, but he suspected he would have sounded like a zombie, which was one of the last things he wanted. (The very last thing he really wanted was to have a dead person in his living room, and it was about as welcome as hair in a biscuit, but it was done.)

And he didn't know exactly what to do next. Coming up with a handy list seemed appropriate, so he cogitated.

A). Bubba could call the police. That was what he was supposed to do. The Pegram County Sheriff's Department would come. Snoddy Mansion was located in Pegram County, outside of Pegramville proper, and the sheriff's department had jurisdiction. Bubba thought he shouldn't know that fact automatically, but he had learned some things over the past few years that regular folks don't always know. (Willodean would probably show up and look beautifully pensive, but that wasn't the best reason to call the police.)

B). Bubba could pretend the body wasn't there. He could flip an area rug over it and say it was just a lot of dust bunnies under there. (Two hundred pounds of dust bunnies? Maybe.) Certainly there would be a big smelly lump in the middle of his living room, but who would really notice?

C). Bubba could call his mother. Miz Demetrice had considerable criminal experience, depending on her given circumstances. She would know what to do.

D). Bubba could dispose of the body himself. There was, after all, that swamp out back and they all talked about it. What else could one do with a swamp? Folks had been dumping bodies in swamps for millennia. (Bog bodies were an apt example.)

E). Bubba could call Lawyer Petrie. Lawyer Petrie was their family lawyer. Normally he only did family law but he'd gained significant knowledge with the onslaught of Bubba's so-called felonious exploits. Lawyers would know what to do with a corpse. They probably took special

93

classes on what to do with errant dead bodies. (Doing the Dead 101?)

F). Bubba could go to bed. It was a little early but his head was aching and a little shuteye would do him a world of good. The body would still be in his living room in the morning. (Probably would be, but one dead person Bubba had discovered had gone missing before)

Bubba thought about letter A). How many times had he actually called the police himself? The first time he'd encountered a body, Neal Ledbetter had called them. The second time the police had found him with the corpse. No calling had been necessary. The third time he had yelled across city hall's lawn. After all, the sheriff's department was right there. No phoning had been required. The fourth time was when his mother had found the body and she had called. The fifth time he *had* called. He had borrowed a cell phone to call. And voila, the body vanished. Of course, there had been boocoodle bodies around at that time, most of them significantly not dead. (Not zombies, but "victims" of the 1st Annual Pegramville Murder Mystery Festival.) And did Bubba need to remind himself that the other bodies had been long, long dead at that time and he hadn't even come close to finding them? No, he did not.

So Bubba *had* actually called the actual police one actual time. There was a precedent. Precedents meant he could do it. Hooray. A decision had been made.

He was reaching for the phone when someone screamed. It was a long and loud scream as screams usually are. It was also the kind that would have shattered a wine glass if one had been close enough to shatter. It certainly filled the room and made the hair on the back of Bubba's neck stand up.

Precious began to bark at the intruder and the screamer stopped screaming for a moment.

I guess I left the door open, Bubba thought and stared at McGeorge who was the screamer in question. The executive assistant, AKA Clipboard Girl, stood in the entrance to the living room and stared down at Kristoph's body. Plainly, she also had immediately known who it was. Furthermore, she obviously had a good idea that he was definitively dead. She paused to draw breath and screeched again, clearly going for a record of some sort. *Someone call Guinness.*

Bubba heard people moving around outside when McGeorge paused for breath. Phone in hand, he considered his options. Finally, he punched 9-1-1 because there still needed to be a police presence and it was better that he called them.

McGeorge had just paused for the second time when two of the film crew burst in behind her. Precious continued barking as the two men determined that McGeorge wasn't in need of immediate saving and peered over her shoulders at the corpse.

One patted McGeorge's shoulder and her scream cut off immediately.

"What the hell happened?" one demanded.

"Shut that dog up!" the other one said.

"Precious!" Bubba snapped. Precious whined then sat beside Bubba.

"HE DID IT!" McGeorge shrieked suddenly, shoving the index finger toward an unsuspecting target. Bubba looked to see where she was pointing. It was in his direction. He looked over his shoulder to see who she was indicating and then abruptly realized it was he that her finger was directed toward. He glanced down at himself. He was wearing the same worn clothing with nary a blood stain or splash to be found. There certainly wasn't a neon sign blinking "Murderer HERE!" with accompanying arrows.

"9-1-1 operator," a voice said on the other end of the line, "what's your emergency?"

Bubba thought it was Arlette Formica speaking. "Arlette, is that you?"

"Bubba," Arlette said amicably, "how're you?"

"Will ya'll send the po-lice over to the house?"

"Your house or the mansion?"

"Mine."

"Okay. What for?"

"Dead body."

"What? Again?"

"Again."

"Hedidit! Hedidit! Hedidit!" McGeorge squealed.

"Shore someone is dead?" Arlette asked. "Sounds pretty perky to me."

"She's a little hysterical," Bubba said, "but she ain't dead. The other one is dead."

"Hmm. I reckon you could slap her," Arlette suggested.

"I don't think so," Bubba said and backed into the wall. *Hit a woman? Oh, hell no.* Besides even at McGeorge's short stature and diminutive size, she looked as though she could take Bubba.

"Are you sure he's dead?" one of the crew asked.

"Could be a fake knife," the other one said. "Kristoph? Pretty funny, dude. Get on up before the real police arrive."

They all stared at Kristoph's body for a long moment. He didn't move. He didn't giggle. He didn't breath.

Of course he dint move. He's dead, Bubba thought. "Better hurry," he said to Arlette.

"I've already dispatched the sheriff," Arlette said. "So I heard that you and Willodean broke up."

"I-uh? What?" Bubba said.

"I would have liked to be invited to the wedding," Arlette said. "Did you hear that Billybob got his bachelor's degree? Liberal arts. First in the family to do it. I don't know what he's goin' to do with it, but he's got it."

"That's...good," Bubba said. "I'll talk to you later, Arlette, okay?"

"Okay," Arlette said companionably.

"Who told you about Willodean and me?" Bubba couldn't help but asking.

"Ah-ha," Arlette said triumphantly. "So it is true!"

"It ain't true!" Bubba protested. "There's a dead fella in my living room! That's the part that's true!" He hung up before anything else could be said.

Then he carefully went past McGeorge, collecting his RC cola along the way, and trudged around the two film crew members before anything else could be said.

"Where you going?" asked one of the men.

"To sit on my porch," Bubba said. "Precious," he added, "come on."

●

The law arrived with a flurry of flashing dome lights and the crunch of tires on gravel. Bubba immediately noticed Sheriff John and Deputy Steve Simms but Willodean was conspicuously absent. His shoulders slumped. That wasn't a good sign. *If a lady knows that her boyfriend is in need, wouldn't she show up? Yes, unless the lady is ticked off with her boyfriend.*

Various film crew gathered outside Bubba's house and he could hear their mutterings as word got out about Kristoph. Cumbersome whispers spread like wildfire as people asked the inevitable questions that follow such an event. Bubba sat in his chair, on his little porch, and listened to the chatter. It wasn't so much that most of them were upset that *Kristoph* had died, but that Kristoph had *died*. It was a whole job security issue. There were a lot of "What will happen to the film?"s repeated.

McGeorge sat in the front of one of the vans crying her little guts out even while the redhead awkwardly patted her shoulder through the open door. Basically everyone milled. It was the idea that something so dreadful had occurred. He heard the words, "murdered," "knife," and "killed." Several of the gathered crew cast baleful looks upon Bubba as if he had already been tried and found guilty.

It was an unpleasant spot of déjà vu.

Sheriff John climbed out of a Bronco. Simms came out of the passenger side.

"What, again?" Sheriff John asked as the crew parted before him. His unerring gaze settled upon Bubba.

Bubba winced. He jerked a thumb over his shoulder.

Sheriff John stopped and appeared to be pondering the situation. "Have we had a dead guy *in* Bubba's house before, Simms?"

"*In* his house?" Simms repeated. His gut swelled over the Sam Browne belt. He was definitely eating too many donuts lately. Bubba had heard that Simms was seeing Penny Sillen, which said volumes about her taste. However, she was alleged to be a very good cook, as evidenced by Simms' growing abdomen. "In the yard. Not in the house. At least not before this time."

Sheriff John and Simms stepped inside to see for themselves. After a few minutes the pair came back outside. Sheriff John studied Bubba thoughtfully and then launched into a series of instructions for Simms. "Cordon off the drive way. Make a list of everyone here. Better grab that camera from the back of the vehicle and start taking pictures of the crowd before someone slips away."

"All righty, then," Simms boomed. "No one is leaving!" This had the opposite effect in that several people tried to leave, which had the effect of Simms going after them.

Sheriff John turned to Bubba. He then eyed Precious who sat under Bubba's chair. "Is that your knife in the man's back, Bubba?"

Bubba thought about the answer. Honesty might not be the best policy, but it was the policy he had always been taught to apply to a given situation. "Yes, it's my knife," Bubba said. "Pa brought it back from the war."

"Bayonet, right?" Sheriff John didn't wait for an answer. "Prolly for an M-16. What about the necktie?"

"What necktie?"

Sheriff John tilted his head as he regarded Bubba with avid curiosity.

"Hedidit! Hedidit! Hedidit!" McGeorge shrieked from the van. The redhead shushed her.

"I did not," Bubba said solemnly. "I came in and found him just like that."

"Fella was a peckerwood," Sheriff John remarked. "Everyone and their cousin saw what he did to you today."

"I reckon."

"BUBBA!" someone else screamed. It was his mother. Miz Demetrice had been alerted to the problem. Bubba sank down in the chair and Precious whined like someone was trying to saw off her tail. "DID HE READ YOU YOUR RIGHTS?"

"Now hold on, Miz Demetrice," Sheriff John said reasonably. "I'm just gathering facts. Ain't no reason to get your panties in a twist."

Bubba's mother burst out of the crowd and grasped Bubba's hand across the porch railing. "Don't say a word, darling! I'll call Lawyer Petrie! You're being railroaded! Fight the good fight! Zip it, don't lip it!" She dug in the deep pocket of her pink flowered dress and produced her cell phone. It was evident that Miz Demetrice thrived on such situations; she was always trying to cause trouble in some way.

"Can you tell me what happened before you found the fella, Bubba?" Sheriff John asked politely.

"I got fired," Bubba said and instantly wished he hadn't. "Let's see. Fired, home to watch the Stars play the Blackhawks. Pretty sure a fella lost two front teeth in the third period but it's a little hard to tell on account of the fact that I got such a small TV. Helped the handyman with the scraping. Got the pool out for the kids." He pointed at the wading pool. The sun was starting to go down and they could barely see across the yard.

"Hold on, Bubba," Sheriff John said. "Simms! Let's get some lights out here!" He turned back to Bubba. "Go ahead."

"The film crew showed up. A couple of them talked to me about finishing my little bit. Said Kristoph would feel sorry about what he did. I got tired of that malarkey and went inside." Bubba pointed toward his front door. "There he was. Dead."

"How'd did you know he was dead?" Sheriff John asked. "Take his pulse? Touch him?"

"He looked dead." Bubba had seen a few dead people so it was nearly conclusive.

"So did Lloyd Goshorn," Sheriff John said, referring to a time where Bubba had mistaken Lloyd for a real live, er, dead corpse.

100

"So did Justin Thyme," Bubba snapped, referring to another dead body that had vanished and no one had believed that Bubba had actually seen it.

Miz Demetrice finished her call. "Stop talking, Bubba," she said. "They twist your words."

"It's John, Ma," Bubba said motioning at the sheriff.

"HEDIDIT!" McGeorge shrieked.

"Why does she keep saying that?" Sheriff John asked.

"I was about to call the po-lice when she came in and saw Kristoph all dead-like," Bubba explained. "It wasn't like I had my hand on the knife."

"What knife?" Miz Demetrice asked.

"Pa's bayonet," Bubba said.

"Oh, crap," Miz Demetrice said. "I mean, oh snap, I mean, snort. I mean, not again. Oh I don't know what I mean."

Sheriff John heaved a profound sigh. "So that gal who's screaming, 'Hedidit!' thinks you did it?"

"I reckon so," Bubba said. "But I ain't got any blood on me. You can turn on the porch light to see."

Sheriff John took his flashlight out of his belt and clicked it. He slowly examined Bubba's shirt and then examined his hands. Bubba had a few scratches from scraping the paint and his hands were still dirty, but there wasn't blood dripping from his fingers. *See. Completely innocent.*

"Okay," Sheriff John said. "Let me go talk to that gal. You stay here."

"You're not going to handcuff him?" a crew member yelled. "He killed Kristoph! Probably!"

"Oh, calm down," Sheriff John told the man. "I ain't got all the facts yet. Bubba ain't goin' nowhere." He approached the van where McGeorge sat and the redhead stood beside.

Bubba was going nowhere. Miz Demetrice anxiously chattered about keeping his mouth shut and paying for a lawyer and possibly escaping to Argentina until Bubba patted her hand.

"We'll get it all straightened out," Bubba said to his mother.

After a little while Sheriff John returned, put Bubba into handcuffs, and stuck him in the back of the Bronco.

Of course.

That was when Marquita Thaddeus rushed over and threw herself across the hood of the Bronco while cameras flashed in complete synchronicity. She wailed like a banshee while Bubba wondered who had really murdered her eccentric husband, the film director.

Chapter Nine

Bubba and the Jurisprudential Jail

Sunday, March 10th

"Hey, Tee," Bubba said to the Pegram County Jailor. His name was Tee Gearheart and he was a genial, big fellow with a good reputation. If an individual *had* to be arrested in Pegram County then Tee's jail was the one to go to. Furthermore, Tee was so well acquainted with Bubba and Miz Demetrice that Miz Demetrice was one of Tee's son's honorary godmothers. (The youngest Gearheart had four because his parents believed in covering their bases.) "How's Little Tee?" Bubba asked.

Sheriff John held Bubba's right arm while Tee got the paperwork straightened out. Tee was a big, big, big man weighing in excess of 350 pounds and it took him a little time to get things just the way he wanted them to be. One had to be patient when Tee was doing the work. It was simply going to take him a while to get it settled.

"Hey, Bubba," Tee said. "Little Tee's fine. Poppiann's potty training him now. We put a target on the bottom of the toilet. The little guy hasn't gotten dead center yet, but he's working on it."

"A target in the toilet," Bubba guffawed.

"Empty your pockets, Bubba," Tee said, "you know you have to."

Bubba pulled out a pocketknife, his truck keys, a package of Bubblicious Gum (Strawberry Splash), three lead sinkers, a rusty bolt with an equally rusty nut, and a lotto ticket. He dug a little farther in his left pocket and

103

found a wadded up twenty dollar bill. "Hey, I was looking for that," he said mildly.

He added it to his wallet which had been extracted from the back pocket.

"You wearing boots today, Bubba?" Tee asked.

"My Tony Lama's," Bubba answered. "No laces today."

Tee chuckled. "You could prolly do my job."

Sheriff John sighed pointedly.

"Okay, okay," Tee said. He wrote a description of the items and looked over it. "You print him and all, yet?"

"Picture, prints, processed," Sheriff John said. "I got a crime scene to get back to."

"That girl dint see me stab that fella," Bubba declared. "And can you ask Ma to feed Precious?"

"Uh-huh," Sheriff John said.

"On account that I dint stab Kristoph," Bubba had to add.

"The movie director got stabbed?" Tee asked. "Well, poop on a stick, Poppiann's goin' to be a mite put out. She had her heart set on Little Tee bein' in the film." He grinned broadly. "He's goin' to be a zombie baby. What's goin' to happen to the movie?"

"Don't know what's goin' to happen with the movie," Sheriff John said. It was evident that he was getting tired of that particular question. In the time that he had brought Bubba to the sheriff's department and booked him, the sheriff had been asked about the outcome of the movie no less than twelve times. Various town members were concerned about the impact of yet another murder in their town and furthermore, they were concerned about the loss of revenue from the film company, seeing as the film's director had been the victim.

104

"Is he dead?" Tee asked, pushing a paper across to Bubba. "Here, sign this, Bubba."

Bubba signed the form.

"Of course he's dead," Sheriff John snapped. "He had a big knife sticking in his heart amongst other things. I kin say it was likely a fatal case of steel poisoning."

"Your *new* house?" Tee asked Bubba. "Dang. Guess someone had to die in it first. Hope that fella don't haunt it."

"Should have bin of natural causes," Bubba said aggrievedly.

"Well, his heart did stop beating naturally," Tee acknowledged. "Ifin you dint kill the fella, Bubba, then who did?"

"I don't know, but I aim to find out," Bubba avowed. "Ma said she'd be by to picket the jail later, so you might want to blockade the doors. She was breaking out the signs when we drove out of the estate."

Tee brightened. "I love talking to Miz Demetrice. You think she'll bring some of that coffee that Miz Adelia makes specially?"

"Prolly."

"Bubba," Sheriff John said. "The judge will be in tomorrow and go over all of this. You know I had to bring you in. It was more for your protection than anything else. A couple of them movie folks looked like they were apt to find the nearest tree from which to string you up." He absently rubbed at the scars on his throat. Sheriff John had personal experience with being hanged, although it hadn't been at the hands of an angry mob.

Bubba nodded. "I know. That girl either stabbed Kristoph herself, which she seemed awfully put out so that don't seem likely, or she was just hysterical from seeing him like that, because she dint see me stab the fella."

Mebe I should have hit *her. Naw.* A thought occurred to Bubba, "Can I make my phone call now?"

"Why? Your ma already called your lawyer," Sheriff John said and pursed his lips.

Tee pushed the phone over to Bubba. Bubba picked up the receiver and dialed the number from memory. "Willodean?" he asked when it rolled over to voice mail. "I wanted to tell you that I do want kids. Two would be nice. Three would be good, too. Hell, I'll take quadruplets. Did I mention I know how to change diapers?"

●

Later Tee brought a sandwich to Bubba. "One of them deputies brought it from Subway for you. There's chips and a brownie, too," Tee said as he handed the items through the bars. He also passed him a bottle of water.

It turned out Bubba had the whole jail to himself on this particular Sunday evening. So all he could do was stare at a wall, eat his dinner, and think about Kristoph's murder. Either the screaming McGeorge was trying to frame Bubba and she just didn't seem like she was consciously planning it, or she was mistaken, as folks could get when something traumatic happened. McGeorge seemed to be wound tighter than an eight day clock.

The film crew had been on the Snoddy Estate for two hours before Bubba had gotten off the ladder for the second time that day. Bubba hadn't seen Kristoph arrive, but Sheriff John would be on top of that. So while Risley Risto, Schuler, Tandy North, and Marquita Thaddeus came to pester Bubba for what he saw as an inconsequential line in a B-movie, Kristoph had gone to Bubba's house and gotten himself murdered. (And hadn't the redhead said something to Bubba, too? Why, yes she had.)

Unless, Bubba considered, *Kristoph had come much earlier in the day*. Bubba hadn't been in the house for hours. If Kristoph had come any time during that period, Bubba might not have noticed.

Kristoph's murder wasn't the kicker. It was the bayonet. The knife had been in a box upstairs on the top shelf of his closet in his bedroom. It wasn't lying around on a coffee table where someone could simply grab it and plunge away to his or her gory content.

No, someone had gone looking for a weapon in Bubba's house. Someone had been inside Bubba's house with the specific reason of finding something to kill Kristoph.

Or wait. Bubba played with the empty tube of Pecan Pie Pringles. *Why kill Kristoph in my house? With my knife?*

Say Kristoph had been clobbered with Precious's water dish, then Bubba couldn't state it was anything but an opportunity that presented itself. Bubba could even put himself in the position of the murder. *I'm pissed at Kristoph because he's an idjit with a megaphone and poofy pants. In fact, I hate his poofy pants and his megaphone makes my innards clench up. Grr. I'll kill him. Bang. Right on the gourd with a stoneware dish.*

But that didn't happen.

Lah de dah. I'm pissed with Kristoph because he's an idjit with a megaphone and poofy pants. Megaphone = pretentiousness personified. Just looking at the short wool jacket makes me want to scratch like a lazy dog in the shade. So while I'm pissed at him I go looking around for just the right weapon with which to off him. What have we got in Bubba's house? (This is the part where Bubba would hum a cheerful tune while searching for an appropriate armament. "Folsom Prison Blues" came to mind.) One butcher's knife in the kitchen. No, that's in the dishwasher. A set of steak knives. Nope, still in the box.

Bubba hadn't cooked since he'd moved in. *Not really cooked. Microwaving Stouffers' Chicken a la King wasn't real cooking.*

So I meander into the living room and I find a second hand couch with matching pillows. Kristoph ain't goin' to stay still to be smothered with a pillow. There's the little TV, but it is a little TV and prolly would just bruise his noggin instead of killing him. Cain't use that. So I go on upstairs and find an extra-long bed with an antique wedding ring quilt. I could throw the quilt over Kristoph's head and pound him with one of my shoes.

Naw. Prolly would just irritate the man.

Bubba's metaphysical self systematically scanned around the bedroom. *There's a bed. A nightstand. A digital clock.* All had been house warming gifts from friends and relatives. He'd planned to sleep on an air mattress until his mother had said something sarcastic about it to Miz Adelia. The next day the bed with the mattress had appeared on his front porch. True it hadn't been put together and the mattress had been dusty. ("Bin in my mama's spare bedroom for ten years," Miz Adelia said. "Daddy liked to sleep on it on account that Mama snores." But Miz Adelia's father, who had been a tall man, had died a decade before and her mother was in the final stages of cancer and in hospice.)

Continuing to mentally picture the room, Bubba saw the closet and opened it. There was a deer rifle propped against the side. It hadn't been used in years and a "gift" from his mother so he could have a gun in the house. Bubba had removed the bolt, which was very obvious, and he had put both the magazine and the absent bolt in a drawer downstairs. (*Where does Ma come up with all the weapons?* For a raging liberal, his mother had a particular and dogged attachment to the Second Amendment.)

Some clothes hung in there. A suit. Button down shirts on hangers. Three pairs of pants that were clipped to hangers so they wouldn't be wrinkled. There were three pairs of shoes. Two sets of boots.

If a fella looked up, he saw the lone box on the top shelf. Shore. There's a weapon in there so I kin rush down and kill Kristoph. Plain as day. Box = weapon. And what in Sam Hill was Sheriff John talking about a necktie fer?

Bubba glowered at the empty tube of Pecan Pie Pringles. He tipped it over and got a sparse amount of crumbs. He poured them into his mouth. He wouldn't have said that he would like Pecan Pie Pringles, but they weren't bad.

Bubba called out to Tee, "Say Tee, kin I have a piece of paper and a pen?"

"Hold on, Bubba," Tee said.

Tee came back and unlocked the door. "Come on up and watch the game."

"Ain't you goin' to get in trouble?"

"Why, you goin' to cause trouble?"

"I will not. What game?"

"BYU versus San Diego."

"College teams, okay then."

Bubba borrowed a pen and a sheet of paper and started his list. They sat behind the front desk and Tee brought out a tablet. He punched in some information, swiped his finger over the screen, and brought up what he wanted. Then he used the tablet's cover to set it in a position so they could both see it.

"Birthday present," Tee said. "Streaming video is good."

"What do you use for cable?"

"Wi-fi, Bubba," Tee said, "man, you're a dinosaur."

Bubba shrugged. It wasn't so bad being a dinosaur.

He chewed the end of the pen.   Then he wrote, "People who want to kill Kristoph" and underlined it for emphasis. He added Marquita. (That's because it's always the spouse, right?)   Then the redhead was included, (because he didn't know her name and the nameless should always be suspect,) and she had been right on the spot.   McGeorge had to be a suspect.   (She's from Hollywood so she could be a very good actress, and why not blame Bubba because he was right there?) But really Bubba couldn't add the redhead because he didn't know whether she had a reason to murder Kristoph or not. In fact, he couldn't say anything about any of the crew because all of them or none of them could have had a reason to kill Kristoph.   He crossed the redhead off, frowned, and then added, "Any of the crew who had a grudge against Kristoph." It was going to be a long list.

He made another list. He titled it, "People who want to frame Bubba." Then he underlined it.

The bayonet was key. Someone had deliberately gone looking in Bubba's house for a weapon. It hadn't been something they had tripped over.   The usual suspects could be discounted.   Lurlene Grady, AKA Donna Hyatt, and Noey Wheatfall were still in prison and awaiting trials. They had tried to frame Bubba for the murder of his ex-fiancée.   Then there was the Christmas Killer, who had tried to frame, kind of, Bubba and/or Miz Demetrice. She was also in prison. So was her brother, who had pretty much fallen to pieces.   The villains of the latest affair during the 1st Annual Pegramville Murder Mystery Festival were safely ensconced in prison. The judge still languished in Mexico because his Mexican attorneys were fighting extradition. But his wife was gleefully imprisoned and that made Bubba happy because Constance Posey was kind of scary.

So that left the people who hadn't committed felonies that Bubba knew about. Lloyd Goshorn still held it against Bubba that he almost ran him down, but Bubba didn't think Lloyd was up to stabbing a man in the back. Noey Wheatfall's wife, Nancy, still glared at Bubba when they came into contact, as though it had been his fault that her husband was gallivanting around with a psychopathic waitress, waiting for an opportunity to assuage their greed. Nancy still worked at the manure factory and their formerly prospering café had descended into the doldrums. Again, Bubba couldn't see the former Missus Wheatfall (Former due to a divorce) going after Kristoph for revenge against Bubba. Maybe Bubba himself, but that was neither here nor there. Considering the vast differences in appearance, Kristoph couldn't have been mistaken for Bubba at all.

"Baltimore chop," Tee said, waving at the tablet. "See that?"

"Got any more of them Pecan Pie Pringles?" Bubba asked, staring at the game. Maybe an obscure college play would give him the secrets of the universe.

"Nope. There's Chicken and Waffles Lays. Mebe some Old Dutch Crispy Bacon flavored. My wife's cousin from Minnesota brought a whole box of them down. Pert dang tasty. You cain't buy them around here."

"Bacon flavored?"

Tee reached under the counter and gave Bubba a bag. "Don't tell Poppiann."

"Cross my heart," Bubba said. He put his paper and pen on the counter and concentrated on the food. After all, a big man like Bubba had to keep his energy up and going to jail was a particularly trying event.

"So you think Sheriff John will clear the whole murder mess up?" Tee asked, reaching for the bag. Bubba handed it over. Tee opened an insulated cooler bag with the other hand and pulled out a can of Diet Pepsi. He gave it to Bubba and pulled out another one for himself. "I'm on a diet," he chortled. "Seriously, about Sheriff John?"

"I dunno," Bubba said.

"What about Willodean?"

"I really dunno."

"The cemetery thing dint work out?" Tee was one of the few people who knew about Bubba's master plan. Bubba had asked Tee for advice. Tee had asked his wife, Poppiann, when they had taken a trip to South Padre Island. Tee had it all set up and involved the staff of the fancy hotel they had stayed at. Bubba had seen the photographs.

"Zombies," Bubba explained.

Tee sighed. "Zombies. That'll do it every daggummed time."

"Well, I couldn't very well do it after *they* showed up." Bubba put his hand out for the bag and Tee passed it. Bubba took a handful of chips.

Tee shook his head.

"You know anyone who would want to frame me?" Bubba asked.

"There was that fella in the twelfth grade whose girlfriend wanted to go out with you instead of him," Tee said.

"Vance Roe?"

"No, not the one who had a sister who liked you, the other one."

"Phil something, right?"

"Yep. McCracken. His girlfriend was the one with the long red hair and freckles."

"Whatever happened to them?"

"They got married. Moved to Dallas. I think they have five kids. Two sets of twins and a single."

"I cain't see Phil driving down here all in the name of framing me," Bubba said. "Wasn't Phil a protestant?"

"Mebe if he'd been Catholic. Anyway, I reckon not, but he's the only one I kin think of." Tee shoved a handful of chips in his mouth and chewed vociferously. "Lemme think about it. Look, the pitcher's charging the mound."

"And that perty well cleared the bench."

"How about that?"

"You suppose I could telephone Willodean again?"

"Uh-uh," Tee said. "Let her figure things out. You cain't be calling her five times in one day." He chuckled. "And talking about how many children you want. Ain't done, man."

"She said something and I think she thought I was scared, but I wasn't really scared." Bubba thought about it. "Mainly I was surprised. I choked on my chicken."

Tee choked on the chips. "You mean you choked the chicken?"

"No, *on* the chicken, smartass."

They watched the game some more.

Bubba's mind kind of wandered away. He figured out that he should write another list. The third list should be titled "**People who *don't* want to frame/incarcerate Bubba**!!!" Then he should underline it. *Mebe put it in bold, too. Put some exclamation marks on it for good measure. Italicize the "don't." That's got to be the shorter list.*

Bubba had come to a conclusion. Not only did he not know who had murdered Kristoph, he didn't have diddly-poo. He was diddly-pooless.

Chapter Ten

Bubba and the Curious Courtroom Conundrum

Monday, March 11th

Bubba had never slept better than when he spent the night in the Pegram County Jail. This particular stay was no exception until the wee hours of the morning. He had been the only occupant until about three a.m., when two drunk zombies who had been fighting at Grubbo's Tavern were escorted in by Deputy Steve Simms. Simms had to help cart them down the hallway and put them in separate cells. The inebriated zombies argued drunkenly with each other and with Simms. Then it was cut off as the unmistakable sound of barfing carried throughout the jail.

"That one was eating pickles," Simms complained. "He threw up in my Bronco. The other one's prolly about to erupt like Old Faithful. They got makeup all over everything. Yuck. Zombie cooties."

"Buckets," Tee said as he secured the doors. More sounds of retching accompanied his decisive word. Bubba would be happy if the smell didn't carry, as well.

Simms paused by Bubba's cell. "Guess you ain't made of Teflon after all, Bubba."

"Don't you got to go give some tourists some speeding tickets, Steve?" Bubba asked without getting out of the bunk. "You like to target the ones with the expensive cars and the out of state plates, right? You see them when you hide behind the billboard on County Highway 6?"

"What did you say to Gray, anyway?" Simms peered between the bars, into the dimly lit cell. Tee was nice

114

enough to turn the lights low so that the prisoners could sleep during the night. "She asked Sheriff John for a day off, and she ain't done that since she's been here." Simms thought about it. "She did take some time off, but it ain't like she asked to be kidnapped."

Mebe I shouldn't have said something about quadruplets, Bubba thought. *It couldn't have been the thing about the diapers. Don't all women want a man who ain't afraid of a little poopy diaper?*

"Your mama stayed picketing in front of the jail until midnight," Steve commented. "I thought I was goin' to have to take her in, but she was real polite and all. Arlette brought her a glass of lemonade on account that her throat was scratchy from all the protesting."

"Only midnight?" Bubba asked. "I would have thought she would have stuck to two or three of the a.m. She's tough." *Must be all that other illegal stuff she's up to; it's worn her plumb out.*

Steve shrugged. "She had three signs that she switched out. I liked the one that said, 'I'm so ANGRY, I made a SIGN!' Then underneath that was 'Bubba is innocent!' in small letters."

"She had that one made already," Bubba admitted. "Prolly just added the 'Bubba is innocent!' part."

"Miz Demetrice is a card," Steve said with a reluctant hint of admiration.

"Anyone confess to Kristoph's murder?" Bubba asked politely.

Steve chortled. "We got you."

"I dint do it."

"You should just have a t-shirt made. Instead of the ones that say, 'Get your Bubba on!,' it should be 'I didn't do it!'" Steve laughed again and settled his hands on his Sam Browne belt.

115

"Penny bin making her chicken continental again?" Bubba asked when the belly rolled over the side of the belt.

Steve glanced at his stomach and patted it fondly. "Woman's a good cook. Cain't help it."

"Is the judge coming in today?"

"Yep. *Arimithia* Perez will be front and present for your bond hearing," Steve said and laughed again. "She don't take no crap. A woman named Arimithia shouldn't have to take crap."

"I know. I had her before."

Steve strolled off with a satisfied grunt. "You shore you don't want to get anything off your chest, Bubba? I kin get a camcorder in for a confession."

"Your eyes cross when you laugh," Bubba said and rolled over. He could still get a few hours of sleep and he thought he would need them. He thought of something. "Steve! Call Gideon Culpepper and tell him I won't be in there today!"

Bubba's only answer was the door shutting on the far end of the jail. Bubba didn't really need to worry about it. Gideon had probably heard all about Bubba already. Everyone in the town had probably heard it. It was probably why Willodean had fled, not the thing about quadruplets.

Bubba buried his head under his arms and groaned.

●

The drunken zombies bonded out before Bubba. One was released on his own recognizance but only after he removed all of his makeup. The other one had to pay $1000 because this was his third visit to a jail in three months. (Two in California and one in Pegram County, Texas.) Of course, they both had to barf in the buckets that Tee had thoughtfully allowed them to carry with them

116

to the court house. A number of people in the gallery visibly winced at the sound of liquid hitting the bottom of the aluminum containers. A few of them nearly gagged and ran for the doors.

Her Honor, Judge Arimithia Perez, appeared as she had the last time he had seen her in Dallas. She was a Hispanic woman in her forties with a knowledgeable countenance that possessed a suggestion of pessimism. Bubba likened the expression to what some people saw when they looked into cops' eyes. Some police officers had, through years of experience and years of being lied to by the average Joe and Jane P. Citizen, developed that look. It was a bowlful of cynicism coupled with a heaping tablespoon of doubt, and sprinkled with overt suspicion. Willodean even had a touch of it.

And right now, she's prolly brimming with it.

Bubba realized that her Honor had said his name when the bailiff poked him in the side. He stood up and the handcuffs rattled loudly. "Sorry, your Honor."

"Bubba Snoddy again," the judge said. She glanced to one side and asked, "Can someone please, for the love of Clarence Darrow, get some Febreze in here?" Her acute gaze settled upon Bubba once more. "As I said, here again."

"Yes, ma'am," Bubba said because there didn't seem to be anything else to say to that. He hadn't actually seen the judge in this particular court house, although he'd been here before on a number of occasions. Not only was he familiar with it, but he knew just about everyone there. Two of the bailiffs went to his church and the stenographer was distantly related to Adelia Cedarbloom.

"This would be a bond hearing but the prosecuting attorney seems to be a little confused about his case," the judge said, looking at the paperwork before her. She reached up and adjusted her octagonal shaped glasses.

Just then Bubba felt someone move behind him and he turned, hoping it was Willodean, but it was Lawyer Petrie and his mother. Miz Demetrice patted him on the shoulder while Lawyer Petrie muttered, "Again?"

"Alfred Petrie for the defendant," Lawyer Petrie said loudly.

The judge cast him a look that might have melted stone if she'd had an active energy source. "You're late."

"Apologies, your Honor," Lawyer Petrie said smoothly. He had years of experience with recalcitrant judges. "The film crew has three streets blocked off and parking was difficult. There were zombies everywhere."

"Ah," the judge said and there was a note of understanding. "I suppose that means they've taken up the slack without their director."

Sheriff John called from the back of the courtroom, "The assistant director has taken the reins, Judge Perez."

"Okay, give me a minute," she said. "I just switched to decaf and my head feels like a balloon."

The judge perused her papers. She nodded twice and took some notes with a pen. Finally, she called up the attorney from the prosecutor's office and then Lawyer Petrie joined him at the bottom of the bench. The attorney shook his head. The judge glowered. Lawyer Petrie had an expression of utter incorruptibility. Bubba didn't know how the man did it while he was wearing a three piece suit that was reminiscent of what a funeral director would wear.

"Did they hurt you in jail, Bubba dearest?" Miz Demetrice whispered.

"Ma, you know Tee treats me just fine," Bubba said, trying to hear what the prosecuting attorney was whispering.

"It's a wretched place. Why, the last time I was there, there was a young woman who couldn't stop talking about her practices as a lady of the evening." Miz Demetrice considered. "It *was* informative. I gave her enough money to make it to Dallas. I recommended that she reconsider her involvement in that sordid business as she has a very large mouth. Talks, talks, talks." She considered again. "Perhaps a large mouth is a beneficial trait in her line of work."

"Ma!"

The judge glared at both of them.

Bubba shrugged apologetically.

The prosecuting attorney said something, "—witness." Bubba tried to wiggle his ears but he still couldn't hear any of it.

The judge called Sheriff John up and the four of them became very animated. "—cain't help what she said," Sheriff John said, louder than he had intended. "Based on evidence I had at the moment—"

"I got an email from the young woman a month ago," Miz Demetrice went on, as if the judge hadn't glared at them and Sheriff John wasn't saying something very pertinent. "She's taking courses at the community college. I believe she's interested in social work. Very apropos."

Ma's got email? Bubba decided that no matter what he wasn't going to hear what the judge, the sheriff, and the attorneys were saying anyway, so he whispered, "Have you heard from Willodean?"

"Yes."

Now Ma goes monosyllabic.

"You goin' to tell me more, Ma?"

"I do not know what you told that poor girl, but she's all riled up," Miz Demetrice said. She stared over her shoulder at the tableaux of the judge and the three men listening to her low, intent voice.

"Does Willodean know about all of this?" Bubba waved around the courtroom.

His mother shrugged. That was clearly a closed door, but there were always other subjects to explore.

"Okay then, what's with Alfonzo and Pilar?"

Miz Demetrice was the epitome of innocence. Butter would not have melted in her petite southern mouth. "I don't know what you're talking about, Bubba. That dratted jail has rattled your poor brains, along with all the times you've been knocked unconscious. Why you could have a giant tumor from all that bashing in, bless your heart."

A light bulb popped over Bubba's head. He looked up to see if one of the fluorescent lights had actually burst but it hadn't. "Ma, do Alfonzo and Pilar have anything to do with Kristoph's death?"

"Of course not!" Miz Demetrice declared.

The judge looked up again. "Madam, I will cite you for contempt of court if you continue your interruptions. This is a court of law. You will respect that."

Miz Demetrice's mouth opened and then shut. There were few things that she actually respected, but it wasn't her hot dog roasting over an open fire, so she manifestly resisted. Finally and reluctantly, she said, "Sorry, your Honor."

His mother glared at him. "Do you think I would bring a murderer or murderers into our homes?" she whispered. "Furthermore, do you think I would condone you taking the rap for another person's criminal activities?"

Bubba had to think about that for a while. "I reckon not."

The judge cleared her throat, banged the gavel on the sound block, and said, "Case dismissed."

The bailiff modestly unlocked Bubba's cuffs. Bubba stood there.

Lawyer Petrie strutted back to the table. "That girl who said she saw you do it, recanted. She admitted she had seen no such thing and it was all because she was so upset that the director was lying on the floor with a big knife in his back." He leaned closer and whispered, "Apparently, the pair had a thing." He drew out the last word, "a thaaaaang," as if drawing it out made a clearer reference to McGeorge and Kristoph having an affair.

Bubba didn't say anything. He looked around the audience in the gallery and saw some locals, some folks that had to be media reporters, and a few that had the telltale shirts on with *The Deadly Dead* RISES!" with the standard blood dripping from "RISES!" The two people looked at Bubba thoughtfully, as if he might have gotten away with something. Curiously one of them was Risley Risto, who sat with his arms across his chest and studied Bubba as if the other man was a bug under his microscope. By his side was the redhead. She wasn't wearing a film shirt, but she did have a jacket with a zombie staggering across the right breast. More interestingly she had one hand possessively resting on Risley's forearm and was caressing his limb with what seemed like more than an executive's level of interest.

So if Risley ain't directing the film at the moment, then who is?

With that annoying thought riling Bubba's head, Risley got up and headed for his table. The redhead followed along behind. Bubba glanced at Lawyer Petrie who was

121

discussing what Bubba had to do next. Miz Demetrice patted her cheeks with a pink trimmed handkerchief and attempted to appear completely innocuous. She was about as innocuous as the offspring of an irradiated black widow spider that had mated with a Velociraptor.

"Say Bubba," Risley said, the unhappy redhead still behind him, "I didn't think you did it, so how about you come back to the movie? Now that I'm in charge, I'd like to expand your role."

Bubba thought that was just stupid. *Who in their right mind would want a potential murderer on his film set?* He peered at Risley. He had an Oscar, so he couldn't be too insane, or perhaps that meant he was more insane than he appeared. Bubba's head was starting to hurt as it usually did in these types of situations.

But something else occurred to Bubba. Who had a better motive to kill Kristoph than one of his crew? Hey, for all Bubba knew, Risley was the *Scream* inspired, knife wielding perpetrator and was ready to do more damage. But that didn't make sense either. If Risley had stabbed Kristoph and tried to frame Bubba, wouldn't he be screaming, "BUBBA DID IT!" in some form or fashion? He wouldn't be asking him to come back to the movie.

Bubba glanced over at Sheriff John who was staring at them with an intentness that Bubba found disconcerting.

"Why would you do that?" Bubba asked Risley.

Risley appeared surprised. "Most people wouldn't even ask why," he said after a moment. "They'd just yell 'Hell, yeah!' and sign the contract. I know people who would screw over their grandmother to get a walk-on role on a Hollywood film. These are people who are ruthless, vindictive, and more cutthroat than any politician I've ever met."

122

"You should go to one of the meetings of our town council," Bubba said mildly.

Risley chuckled. "Well?"

"Shore. I imagine my phone machine at home's got a message from my boss at the garage about how I should take some time off and deal with this." Bubba looked around. "All of this. So I prolly don't have much better to do." He glanced meaningfully at Sheriff John. "Who knows what might happen?"

"Great. My exec here will give you the details," Risley said. "I took a break to walk over and see what happened with Kristoph's death. The studio is having fits, but any publicity is good for a film, especially a horror film. I hate to demean the director, but Kristoph would have *loved* being the center of attention."

The redhead nodded firmly. "Would have *loved* it," she repeated.

"You dint answer my question," Bubba said.

Risley stared at Bubba. "You're not just a dumb little hick, are you?" And very oddly, he looked supremely discontented.

"I kin be right stupid at times," Bubba said with a smile that didn't reach his eyes.

"Publicity like I said," Risley answered. "I wasn't going to offer you anything if they'd moved you along to the next step of prosecution, but I wasn't sure what was going to happen today. McGeorge already told us she was mistaken about seeing you stab Kristoph. She said you had your hand on the phone and she was upset about seeing his body. She lost it. The other two film crew said you didn't have a drop of blood on you."

Bubba looked down at his shirt. He was wearing the same outfit he'd had on the day before. It wasn't clean but it didn't have any blood on it, either. He supposed

Sheriff John was slipping. The sheriff probably should have taken the clothes and had the crime lab in Dallas do an examination on them, but Bubba wasn't complaining. Sheriff John had inspected Bubba's hands, too. And he had looked at Bubba's shirt.

Bubba couldn't believe that in any world a film director would suddenly want him to be in their movie, so having secondary motives seemed more realistic.

"That really true?" Bubba asked.

"What? That having you in the cast gets us more press?" Risley asked. "Yes. I'm honest. The more press we get, the better the movie does when it gets released, and let's face it, you have been in the news before. Isn't that kid who shocked Matt Lauer with a homemade Taser related to you?" Bubba glowered in response. "Nevermind. The studio will throw some more bucks at us, too. Hey, Kristoph may not be here to appreciate it, but his death will make his final movie a big hit." He lowered his voice to a whisper. "You didn't see all the media out in front? There were five vans with satellite dishes."

"I came in through the back," Bubba gritted.

"It's like Christmastime, the Emmys, the Tonys, and the Oscars all wrapped in one event," Risley said. "Wherever he's at, Kristoph is probably leaping up and down for joy." He shook his head sadly. "Pity because otherwise this would have been a decent movie that would have gotten minimal attention."

"I would call it ironic," Bubba said.

"Maybe so, but bittersweet and appropriate is the way we'll spin it," Risley said.

"Who would want to kill Kristoph?" Bubba asked because he couldn't help himself. Maybe it was because he'd been in a similar position so many times before.

Sheriff John was capable enough but Bubba was right on the spot and the former assistant director was open and talking now.

"You can't get anywhere in this industry without stomping on fingers and toes," Risley said. "The list for such a person would be endless."

"Would you be on it?"

"Sure, Kristoph's stomped on my toes upon occasion but then he's family," Risley said, "so I had to forgive him."

"Family?"

"Marquita is my sister," Risley said. "Okay then, Bubba. See you on the set tomorrow. I'll have my girl here send over some script pages. Practice them in a mirror. Get your anti-zombie mentality going on. We'll be making a *movie!*"

Chapter Eleven

Bubba and the Puzzling Probe

Monday, March 11th

Thirteen messages filled Bubba's answering machine. He didn't know why he needed an answering machine which had been a housewarming gift from his Aunt Caressa. She had informed him, "Ya'll need to give up your club and move out of the cave, Bubba," when she had been at the celebratory party Miz Demetrice had thrown for Bubba once the house had officially been completed. Consequently, he had an answering machine but he didn't have a toaster and since he couldn't find anyone who wanted to trade him an answering machine for a toaster, he kept it. He'd even turned it on, although most of the time there were minimal messages.

One message was from Gideon Culpepper who suggested that Bubba take the week off until his hash was cooked or primed or pumped or something like that. Another message was from Brownie, who demanded to know if Bubba was illicitly solving mysteries without his presence. He threatened to blow off school and bring his two dogs, Bogie and Oscar, to help, but the baby, Cookie, needed him too badly at the moment. Furthermore, Brownie did offer to bite the bullet if Bubba really, truly, vehemently needed his support. All Bubba needed to do was call for assistance. A third message was from Daniel Lewis Gollihugh, who was the largest man in Pegram County at a shade over seven feet tall. He had aided Bubba in a previous mystery and felt compelled to keep up with the other man.

"Say, Bubba, Trixibelle said I should call you on account that you done got arrested again for another murder," Dan said prosaically. "I'm over to Tyler and ain't back for a week, so kin you hold up on this murder business until I'm done with this little ol' conference on the methods of Buddhism?" He paused in the message as if Bubba was going to answer him. Dan had found Buddhism in his last trip to the big house and it was working out well for him. Although he was supposed to be a vegan and practice nonviolence as an integral facet of his newfound spirituality, he didn't always succeed. However, he was successful enough that he had managed to get back together with his last wife and to keep out of trouble for months. "Mebe that fella, David Beathard, would help you out?" he continued in the message, as if Bubba was actively listening when he had been speaking. "Last time I saw him he weren't wearing the pirate gear no more. He looked more like a school teacher or mebe a prison counselor. Anyway, just remember, 'Three things cannot be hidden: the sun, the moon, and the truth.'"

Messages four through ten were from reporters and representatives of the media. Oddly Matt Lauer did not call. Well, not that oddly.

Bubba wondered if he could flush his answering machine down the toilet without causing the toilet to back up.

Message eleven was a hang up. Message twelve was an offer to refinance his house or his boat or possibly his motorcycle from a mortgage company that he had never heard about.

Message thirteen was from Willodean.

"I just heard about what happened, Bubba," she said, and he sighed. Willodean didn't sound upset with him in particular. She didn't sound angry. She sounded a little

127

resigned. "I'm sorry I'm not there. I'll be back in a day or so. John says they didn't find your prints on the knife but that they did find Simms' thumb print on it, so that bit of evidence has just gone bah-bye. And I have no idea what they're going to do about the necktie."

Willodean is giving me inside information. Bubba leaned closer to the answering machine. *She must be feeling bad. Is that good or bad? Wait, what friggin' necktie?*

"I'll call you later," she finished and there was a click. That was followed by a monotone voice announcing that it was the last message.

Precious nudged his leg. Bubba still stared at the machine. He could play it over. There was probably a hidden message in those words. Willodean was telling him something but he had to figure out what it meant.

Precious apparently felt bad about being left alone with Miz Demetrice and Miz Adelia and bit his ankle but not hard enough to break the skin. Bubba cursed and she scuttled off toward the little kitchen but stopped only a few feet away. She wanted recompense for her hours of being spoken to as if she was a baby. *They sprayed me with perfume again,* she thought, *and they said I was an ootsie bootsie whootsie who needed a pink ribbon around each ear. I pawed the ribbons off and buried them by the oleanders and then I barfed on the back stoop. I hate you.*

"Did you hear that, girl?" Bubba asked, rubbing both his ankle and her head at the same time.

I heard nothing. You are dead to me.

"You're a girl, Precious," he said to the dog. "Explain how girls think to me. I thought I understood but they're a complete mystery and I don't understand. What's a fella supposed to do?"

Eat poop and die.

"She called, right? I mean, she did call." He scratched behind one of Precious's long ears and her left rear foot began to thump the floor rhythmically.

I chewed up two of your athletic shoes. I hid them under the bed. You stink.

Bubba began to rub the other side of her head and she tried to get both of her rear legs to scratch at the same time but it couldn't be done.

I rubbed my butt all over the carpet in the bedroom.

"Who's my precious mescious special girl? Want a goodie? I got them gourmet treats that you like." Bubba scratched under her chin and her eyes rolled back in her head.

I do not want a treat.

Bubba scratched harder and alternated spots. "Who does?"

Oh, right there. Harder. Precious finally gave up and launched herself into the kitchen, baying loudly. *I WANT A TREAT! NOW! NOW! NOW!*

Bubba obliged. He got himself an RC cola even though it wasn't past ten a.m. Then he fixed eggs and grits for himself. He poured ketchup over the lot. (Not the cola.) He fed some of the scrambled eggs to Precious, who had, by that time, consumed her donut shaped bounty. He sat at a simple pub table with matching stools. Willodean had helped him pick it out. The kitchen was a little too small for anything else and the house didn't have a formal dining room.

It was time to let his mind settle down and think about what to do.

More lists needed to be made. But what Bubba really needed was information and he had a few ideas about that.

After Bubba finished his brunch he went upstairs and saw that his meager belongings had been searched. The box that had contained the bayonet was on the floor in the master bedroom and the contents messily rearranged. There didn't seem to be much missing.

He didn't feel like staying there, so he went outside and found that someone had thoughtfully returned his 1954 Chevy truck, colloquially called Ol' Green. He still had the keys from when they had been returned to him from being in jail, so it was likely that his mother or Miz Adelia had performed the service. As they had done on multiple occasions before.

So now Bubba had a brand spanking new legal bill, questionable standing in a B-grade movie, a dubious relationship with a hot deputy, and he owed his mama big time. *Can things get worse? Why yes, they can get worse. I done checked the house again and there wasn't a new dead body. I could go back in and one will appear as if by magical means.*

Bubba looked up at the skies.

I need to ask myself a question. Several questions, Bubba thought. *Did I do something to bring this on me? Is it that sign I asked for, God? Is this the sign? Did I offend Thee in another life and now I'm paying for it?*

While Bubba was waxing a metaphysical contemplation with a supreme being, Precious attempted to eat a squirrel. The squirrel hauled butt for the nearest oak tree and went up quickly, only pausing to angrily chirp at the Basset hound.

After all, I was just making a few bucks by saying, "It shore ain't a pink elephant!" What in tarnation does that mean anyway? I wasn't doin' nothing criminal or immoral. Bubba had to stop to think about that. *Movies ain't immoral per se. Most of the time, anyway.* He shook his head. It wasn't illegal or immoral. *Definitely not.* He hadn't murdered Kristoph. Someone else had done that. In Bubba's house. In Bubba's brand new house. In the house Bubba was planning to...

Bubba started to get a little mad. He supposed he should have been getting mad the day before, but instead he'd had another feeling. He had been somewhat embarrassed to get fired in front of the beauteous sheriff's deputy. He had wanted to crawl in a hole. He knew that Willodean wouldn't see it as something to be embarrassed about, because that was the kind of person she was, but still Bubba's pride had been dented. It surely wasn't the first time and it was more than likely not the last time it would happen, but that didn't mean that Bubba had to like it.

But that wasn't the part that made him most angry. Bubba hadn't asked for any of this, yet it had landed in his lap, er, living room, using his daddy's bayonet, and ruining the rug he'd purchased the previous week at Walmart.

Mostly the whole situation *had* to be cleared up before Bubba could do anything else about Willodean Gray.

That was the part that really chapped his tuckus. And if his tuckus was any more chapped, he was going to need the economy sized Boudreaux's Butt Paste Can of Whoop Rash, just like Alfonzo and Pilar had for their daughters' little tender tushies. (The can was so big they were going to be using it on their grandbabies and possibly their great-grandbabies, which made Bubba wonder if he should send some to Fudge and Virtna Snoddy so they could use it on Cookie.)

Speaking of which, Alfonzo was working on the side of the mansion. He had a roller and was painting the side an ivory white that would age well with the oversized house.

Bubba waved genially. He was a little sorry he couldn't help.

But Bubba had another job. It was true Sheriff John would probably figure out who did it. Sheriff John didn't suffer fools gladly. If there was one thing Bubba had learned about John Headrick it was that he liked to get the job done and get it done correctly.

Of course, that hadn't stopped Sheriff John from arresting Bubba on the suspicion that he had done the director in. Bubba frowned. John hadn't had a choice. Although Bubba had saved his life once upon a time, he had been found in the immediate vicinity with a body that had a knife that belonged to him in its back and a woman nearby who was saying that he had done it. Mother Theresa would have had to be taken into jail if she had been in a similar position.

Bubba understood that. He didn't like it but he understood it.

That also didn't mean that Bubba had to sit on his gluteus maximus and twiddle his thumbs singing lullabies and waiting for Sheriff John to figure out who was really the culprit.

Precious leaned on the base of the tree with the squirrel in it and woofed derogatorily.

"Ride, girl?" Bubba opened the door to the truck.

Precious bayed once at the still-chattering squirrel. *"I'll get you, my pretty,"* she thought with a lingering look at the aggrieved rodent, *"you and your little dog, too!"* Then she rushed for the truck before her beloved master could change his mind.

Bubba helped the canine inside the cab and decided on the first step of his master plan. The sooner this was all taken care, the sooner he could get back to the business of Willodean.

●

Fortuitously, the Pegramville Public Library was open and unoccupied by zombies, serial murderers, or politicians. (That Bubba knew about.) It was a nice little building built in 1986 with funds provided by the Lions Club, the Optimists, and Miz Demetrice's group of avid gamblers. The library still received federal monies for one librarian and two aides. Bubba was happy to note that most of the books were fairly new. He often stopped in to check one or two out. He had been reading about a girl with a dragon tattoo lately and she was a rip-roaring character, if the truth be told.

Bubba left Precious in the truck with the windows open. Precious rested her long nose on her paws and glared at him as he walked up to the glass doors. Miz Nadine Clark, the head librarian, (the only librarian, if one wanted to be particular,) was in her forties despite having a mop of completely white hair. A plump woman just shy of five feet tall, Bubba disliked having to stare down at her as much as he had to. It often caused a crick in his neck.

Nadine also did not possess a sense of humor and reminded Bubba of Dee Dee Lacour, who was Doc Goodjoint's nurse. Both women wore a perpetual expression of having just sucked all the juice out of a crate of lemons.

Nadine sat at the front desk, looking at a computer. "Say, Miz Clack," Bubba said. "I wonder if I kin look at some newspapers and such."

Nadine looked up and adjusted her Benjamin Franklin glasses. She'd worn a similar style of frames for many years and Bubba thought she would look strange if she changed them. "Bubba," she said, "I understand you're in trouble again."

133

"It was dismissed a few hours ago," Bubba said defensively. He looked around. It was only the two of them in the library and Nadine didn't look especially uncomfortable with it, but he backed up two steps so she wouldn't feel pressured.

"Dismissed," she repeated. "They could still bring charges against you if they decided to, at a later point."

"Yep," Bubba said. Lawyer Petrie had discussed that in the walk from the jail to the car, but Bubba had pretty much tuned the attorney out. It had been "Charges blah blah blah. Evidence blahity blahity blahity. Murder blahy blahy blahy." Bubba had really not wanted to listen and he didn't want to talk about it with Nadine, not when he was going to have to go all Columbo. "I dint kill no one," he said, and it was very nearly automatic.

A hint of something that might be called a smile crossed Nadine's lips, although Bubba was not certain he'd actually seen it.

"Of course not," Nadine said. "Old newspapers or new ones?"

"I'm not sure," Bubba admitted.

"What are you looking for?"

"Suspects."

Nadine seemed to take that in with implacable inscrutability. "We have five computers, Bubba," she said. "You should Google Kristoph Thaddeus and see what you come up with."

"I should Google Kristoph Thaddeus," Bubba repeated. "That sounds a mite obscene and besides, he's dead."

"Google is a search engine," Nadine explained patiently. "Come on. Let me show you how to use it."

It took Bubba about ten minutes, but it wasn't hard. "Look, I can Google myself. I got 150,000 results. How kin there be so much about me on the Internet?"

Nadine was eminently patient. "There was all the news about you during the whole first, second, and third sets of murder. Then there was the Brownie/Matt Lauer thing. I really would like to know how he made a stun gun from scrap parts. Thank goodness the kidnapping didn't make the news."

"What kidnapping?" Bubba asked benignly. Brownie said he couldn't remember anything about the event, although Bubba suspected that he had somehow tortured the kidnappers until they had fled the state screaming in terror. The two men from the junkyard hadn't been seen in months. They were likely in fear for their lives if they dared to come back.

"And let us not forget about rescuing the beautiful sheriff's deputy from a demented kidnapper and brother of the Christmas Killer," Nadine added helpfully. "You should be glad all the commotion finally died down." She bit her lip. "No pun intended."

"You know the media's back in town because of Kristoph's death, don't ya?" Bubba asked.

"One would have to be stupid and deaf and blind not to know," Nadine said smartly.

"See," Bubba said, pointing to an article from *The Dallas Morning News* he just opened in a new window on the monitor. The title was "Infamous Pegramville Man Arrested for Murder Again".

Nadine sighed. "Just put in Kristoph's name and see what you can find. I gather you're looking for someone other than yourself to point a finger at."

"You gather correctly." He typed with two index fingers and occasionally used his thumb on the space bar.

"Call me if you need further assistance and that Larsson book is due next week," Nadine said.

"It's a long book," Bubba said. "That Lisbeth is a pistol. I don't like the other fella as much. Mikael's a little stuck on hisself."

"I'll extend the deadline for you," Nadine said and glided away.

Bubba immediately lost himself in the wonder that was a search engine. It was easy to get distracted. It turned out there were many search engines. Google was the most famous but Bing wasn't bad and Bing had a pretty picture on its background that was animated. (Elk from Russia breathing out icy air as they romped through a winter meadow.)

Once he got un-sidetracked, he put in Kristoph Thaddeus's name in the little window and made the little curser move over to the magnifying glass with the mouse. Using the mouse was like using a dainty cup of tea that his mother had in a china cabinet in the secondary dining room. One of those cups wouldn't even be a mouthful, but Miz Demetrice insisted on breaking them out at least once a year. Bubba was deathly afraid he was going to pinch it too hard in between thumb and forefinger and it would become a tiny, crumbled footnote in the history of their family. The mouse was exactly the same except the computer would probably short circuit and blow up. Then the library would catch on fire and everyone knows what happens to books when exposed to a flame.

Bubba shook his head. The results numbered in the millions. *Millions*, he marveled, *and I ain't never heard of him before.*

Concentrating, Bubba knew that he had to add words to his search in order to prune down the information.

"Enemies of Kristoph Thaddeus" produced another result in the millions. Bubba glowered.

Then he tried "People who hate Kristoph Thaddeus." This narrowed it down to just over a hundred thousand results, with the top one being a Facebook page titled "We hate Kristoph Thaddeus." It had seventeen followers and Bubba didn't recognize any of the names. Additionally the author of the page seemed to be exceptionally put out with the way that Kristoph had accepted his Saturn award and not for any other reason.

Bubba Googled "People who want to murder Kristoph Thaddeus." It took Bubba little while to understand, but it turned out there was a zombie game that had a segment where the director was a guest zombie. A good number of points could be scored by players who could "kill" him. (In the game.)

Bubba let a huge breath of air out. *This is goin' to be harder than I thought.*

Chapter Twelve

Bubba and the Wonky Witnesses

Monday, March 11th

Two hours later, Bubba had read so many articles about Kristoph that his eyes were starting to cross. Some of the articles were biographical. (He had been born in Kansas and graduated from Satanta High School.) Some of the articles were critical. (*"Night of the Flesh Zombies* was the worst movie ever made!" This struck Bubba as somewhat hypercritical considering that the author of the article had also seen *Jaws: The Revenge.* This was directly noted in the context of the review.) Some of the articles were incidental. ("Kristoph's six bedroom mansion has eight bathrooms! Eight!")

I have a full bath and a half bath now, Bubba thought. *One and a half! One upstairs and a half one for when I don't feel like going upstairs. Pure luxury!* (An elongated man sized potty, not that namby-pamby round one that only a ten-year-old kid would be comfortable on.)

There were articles about Kristoph's personal life. ("Horror Movie Director Marries for the Third Time", which was Marquita. Kristoph's first wife had died of cancer and his second wife had run off to Mexico with a *Lucha libre* wrestler and divorced the director from tropical climes.) He had three grown children who were all in other businesses besides the film industry. (One managed a mattress store.) He owned a production company and he was good friends with Quentin Tarantino. (Supposedly.)

There was article after article about the artistry of movie direction where Kristoph had been interviewed. A slew of articles appeared after his Saturn award. Most of the articles were upbeat and an enthusiastic Kristoph was quoted endlessly.

Bubba switched to the articles written after Kristoph's death was reported. Most of them focused on the arrest of a "local man." Words used included tragic, before his time, unfortunate, and a loss of a Hollywood legend, although Bubba wasn't sure of what the legend really was. There wasn't a mention of the cause of death.

Groaning, Bubba finally gave up. He would bet there wouldn't be as many articles the next day quoting the case's dismissal, which was one more dip in the tar with the brush that was Bubba's life.

Stopping by Nadine's desk, Bubba said, "I reckon that's all I kin do for now."

Nadine seemed to consider Bubba carefully, correctly gauging his frustration. "Let me sum up for you."

"Okay."

"Kristoph fired you on the set. Hours later, he's found in your house, stabbed in the back, is that correct?"

"With my knife," Bubba said. "Well, my daddy's knife."

"Oh, my."

"Yep. Oh, my."

"But they still dismissed the charges," Nadine said. Her eyes appeared huge through the glasses' lenses.

"Their witness changed her mind. Said she was upset. And there weren't any fingerprints on the knife." *Except Steve Simms's and I don't think he would have stabbed Kristoph in the back. He would have given him a ton of traffic tickets and hoped the director would have a heart attack.* "And there wasn't any blood on me."

"So naturally it must be one of the crew or the people attached to Kristoph."

"I was hoping to make a list," Bubba admitted.

"His wife, his brother, his nephew, his best friend, and his dog?"

"Mebe his wife. I don't know about the others." *Kin a dog stab someone? Hmm. Precious kin be powerful inventive-like. Best to put the knives in a drawer from now on.*

"I was being facetious, dear."

Bubba blinked. He knew what facetious meant, but he hadn't realized that Nadine Clack was capable of facetiousness. He, himself, was rarely capable of facetiousity.

"While reading up on the art of detection, I have come to the conclusion that your situation would be best solved by going undercover," Nadine said. "You'll have to integrate yourself into the film and get all the dirty laundry aired. Once you befriend the ones who know where all the metaphorical bodies are buried, you're a shoe-in." She paused. "I didn't mean anything about bodies, really."

"You're reading up on the art of detection," Bubba said.

"It seems like the thing to do of late," Nadine replied with a sly smile. "It's obvious that the sheriff's department and the local police force are woefully inadequate in the practice."

"Most murders are committed by people they know and ain't real complicated," Bubba immediately defended Willodean and Sheriff John, realizing belatedly he was defending Big Joe, as well. Big Joe was the local chief of police of Pegramville and a man who disliked Bubba on principle. He hadn't helped things when he had roundhoused Big Joe in the pursuit of catching the

Christmas Killer before the perpetrator could murder again.

"Yes, yes. Revenge over a past misdeed committed twenty years in the past. Very uncomplicated. Then there was the murder of a wife to get her money by not the husband, exactly, but the secretary. That would be straightforward especially since she also murdered the notary public who witnessed the will and the man who had been part of the original conspiracy and black mailing of her. Unsophistication personified." Nadine's voice dripped with sarcasm.

"Miz Clack," Bubba said, "I did not know that you had a sense of humor."

"I have a hell of a sense of humor," she said promptly. "Why did the chicken cross the road?"

Bubba didn't answer right away because he wasn't certain if Nadine *wanted* him to answer. "Why did the chicken cross the road?" he asked after a long moment.

"Because the chicken had to murder the director of a big film," Nadine answered without hesitation.

"I'm in the film already, Miz Clack," Bubba said, unused to the amount of thinking he was doing.

"Good. Go and detect. Call me if you need some librarial assistance."

Bubba stared at Nadine. She appeared serious. "I'll get back to you," he said slowly. "Do you know where the movie folks are today?"

"The Boomer farm," Nadine said and returned to checking in books.

"Obliged," Bubba said.

●

If a good old boy based his theory on the premise that a killer had to be part of the film crew, *The Deadly Dead*, then a good old boy knew that the murderer still had to be in town. That person would pretend that he or she was unknowledgeable of the crime and that they were continuing to work on the movie. Leaving abruptly would have upset the apple cart.

Unless the person was Marquita Thaddeus, who probably could get away with looking upset. After all, her husband had just been murdered and the one suspicious person had been set free because there was not enough evidence to hold him in jail. Marquita had a right to be upset and leave town.

But Marquita Thaddeus was the first person to notice Bubba walking up to the yellow tape that kept curious onlookers from getting in the way of shots on the Boomer Farm.

Bubba recognized the tall woman in her fifties immediately and stepped backward. Although Risley Risto had rehired Bubba, he didn't know how the wife of the murdered man would react to his presence. He thought it was more than likely that she would A). Attempt to hit him, B). Hit him, C). Scream at him, or D). All of the above.

Instead Marquita blinked, looked away, and then looked back again. "Oh," she said. "It's you. Risley said you were back, but I didn't expect to see you today." She appeared tired and her makeup wasn't applied as flawlessly as the first day he'd seen her. She wasn't wearing the high-heeled boots and her silk shirt was slightly wrinkled. She glanced down at Precious, who was staying behind Bubba, and her eyebrows rose up incrementally.

"I'm sorry for your loss," Bubba said. He supposed the sentiment could have been misconstrued, but it was the right thing to say. Why was Marquita even at the shoot? Shouldn't she be in mourning, arranging her husband's funeral, and doing what widows were supposed to be doing at a time like this? *Just like your mother did?* Bubba's inner sarcastic voice screamed. *That was different*, he told himself. *My father was a complete dick. I don't know why Ma didn't have a ticker tape parade.*

Marquita sipped from a tall Styrofoam cup she clutched in both hands. It smelled like coffee. "I know," she said, catching his glance at her drink. "I preached all the time about Kristoph drinking too much caffeine, and here I am, sucking it down. But today I need it." She deliberately took another drink. If she had been smoking she would have purposefully lit another cigarette.

"I am sorry," Bubba said again. *Undercover, my heinie*, he thought. *I don't even know what to say. I need the Purple Singapore Sling or even Daniel Lewis Gollihugh to plow the road for me. Willodean could use her mace.*

"The sheriff tells me it's unlikely that you did it to...poor Kristoph," Marquita trailed away and sighed, "so that's partly why Risley got you back. Also for the publicity." She laughed bitterly. "Death of the director. That's news and all."

"I didn't kill your husband," Bubba said carefully. "Wonder if you know who might have wanted to." *That was as smooth as a pig on stilts, Ex-Lax.*

"You're asking me if I know who might have wanted to stick a knife in Kristoph's back?" Marquita's face twisted in consternation. "Good God, *that's* a question."

And she's now prolly goin' to have my tuckus thrown off faster than a bell clapper in a goose's butt.

"I assume you mean the people on the set?" Marquita asked politely.

"Had to be here in order to have done it."

"The sheriff has me on the list, too." Marquita frowned.

"That's perty normal. The spouse or significant other is always looked at," Bubba said and thought he sounded nearly professional. "That's bin my experience." *To my eternal regret that I kin say those very words.*

"When Kristoph worked on *I, Detective* that was what the hero said. Murders are nearly always committed by someone the victim knows. Hollywood has dramatized the serial killer to an extent that people think there's one lurking around every corner." Marquita drank more from the cup of coffee and then looked inside to see if any more was hiding from her at the bottom of the Styrofoam container. "I hate to tell you this, Bubba, wasn't it, Bubba?"

Bubba nodded.

"The sheriff has already interviewed me at length. I'm doing a polygraph test later in the week. Apparently my alibi of being in the loo is somewhat questionable." Marquita crumpled the cup in her fist and tossed it at a garbage can stenciled with *The Deadly Dead* on its side. "I was in the bathroom for about twenty minutes and then I saw you on the way out. You wouldn't talk to me. Can't blame you for that since Kristoph was *ever* so nice to you about your dog." She glanced at Precious. Precious sat on her rump, scratching lazily with one back paw. "You know, Kristoph has never liked dogs. He is, was, a cat person. We've got three Siamese cats at home. They're going to be inconsolable. In any case, my stomach has been so upset since we got to Texas that I've been in the bathroom half the hours of the day. Normally I have a cast iron stomach. I went right back there after you walked off." She laughed. "My alibi. Your mother's bathroom. She was nice enough to let me use the one in the house instead of those god awful porta-potties. It's a great house."

"I like it," Bubba said, compelled to fill in Marquita's pause.

But Marquita didn't continue speaking. She stopped and watched the film crew working near the Christ Tree. Zombies were being gathered by the redhead and Risley Risto directed the cameramen with their shots.

"Kin I ask you something personal?" Bubba went ahead and asked because he didn't want her to say no before he could ask. "Why are you still here?"

"You mean, why am I not wearing a hair shirt and pulling out my locks, whilst I wail in distress?" Marquita almost looked amused. The black circles under her eyes took away from the impact of how amusement should appear.

"I would think it would be somewhat painful to stay here," Bubba said.

"This was Kristoph's last movie." Marquita waved all around them. "He'll never do another one because someone killed him. I've got two reasons. Number one is that I want to make sure Risley does it right. If I have to stand behind his shoulder and nag him until the final shot, then I will do so. It's the least I can do for Kristoph. Kristoph had a vision, you know."

"You don't think your own brother will do your deceased husband's project justice?"

Marquita appeared to ponder the question. "I think it'll probably be a better movie for Risley's participation. They had issues working together. Risley used to drive Kristoph nuts and vice versa. But the final products of their association are good movies." She accurately guessed at what Bubba's confused expression meant. "What, you wouldn't think a B-movie would be a good movie?"

"I like B-movies," Bubba said. "*Tremors.* That was a good movie. I liked Fred Ward in that one, and I was scared to walk around holes in the ground for a full week after seeing it."

"I could tell you a very good story about Kevin Bacon and Fred Ward, but gossip is really de trop for me. A hint will have to be enough. It's a very juicy tale. Enough said."

"Okay," Bubba said slowly. "What was the other reason you stayed?"

"I know I'm supposed to be the weeping widow, crying, dashing my tears, fainting, looking wan, not able to eat, but that's never been me. Kristoph was killed, no, he was murdered, by someone who stabbed him in the back. Stabbed him...in...the...back. I'm staying because I want to look the person in the face when they're handcuffed and going to jail. I want to see the dismay and regret in their face. I want to see the tears of frustration and fear coursing down their cheeks. I want to have a little back of what that person has knowingly inflicted." She paused and took a deep breath. "If I leave I might miss that."

Bubba decided that Marquita Thaddeus was a person that he wouldn't want to make mad. A thought occurred to him. He remembered Kristoph and Risley arguing about a scene. "What about your brother? Seems like he shore benefited from Kristoph's death."

"You think Risley would kill Kristoph to gain control of a movie," Marquita restated. "That would be killing the goose who laid the golden eggs. There was no guarantee the studio would let Risley step up to the position, but they didn't have much of a choice at this juncture. Plus I was pulling all the strings to get it there."

"Why don't you direct it?" Bubba couldn't help but ask. "Seems like you know as much about it as the rest?"

"I'm a behind the scenes girl," Marquita said. "I get a hefty percentage of the movie proceeds if it's successful. I'm not a director. I don't have the patience, sweetie." She sighed gustily and reached into the breast pocket of her silk shirt to remove a package of cigarettes and gold lighter. With smooth practiced movements, she extracted one cigarette and put it in her lips, lighting it with the other hand. "God, I miss smoking and especially now. Don't tell my doctor or he'll kill me."

Bubba shrugged. "I don't know your doctor but cigarettes are bad for you."

"So are knives in the back," she snapped.

Bubba figured he wasn't going to get anything else out of the woman and in fact, he was lucky that Marquita was so talkative. "Thank you," he said.

"Are you...detecting?" Marquita asked curiously. "Trying to save your own hide? A man who's on the edge? Sounds like a movie to me."

"Seems like someone would like to point a finger at me," Bubba said. "The least I kin do is point one back."

"Touché." Marquita puffed then blew smoke into the air above her head. "Would you tell me if you find out anything?" she asked. "I'll tell you what. If anyone says anything about you asking questions, then direct them back to me. You've got my permission to talk to any of the crew. Go right ahead. I don't know if they'll talk to you, but you go right ahead and detect away. It should be interesting."

"Why would you do that?" Bubba asked.

"Because it will make the person nervous," Marquita said, "and I like the idea of that. Let him or her be nervous. Maybe they'll do something stupid and confess, so I can systematically destroy them in Hollywood." She looked positively delirious at the thought of performing such an action.

Bubba nodded uncertainly and walked away. If Marquita was a killer, then she was a *good* actress. Bubba had been fooled before, but the director's wife seemed like the sort to deliver her own brand of private justice if she was so inclined and she seemed so inclined.

Just as he was about to walk around a van, he saw the redhead approach Marquita. Marquita said something to her, but Bubba was too far away to hear. Then the redhead wrapped a comforting arm around Marquita. Marquita stood it for a moment and then pulled away. The redhead seemed distraught herself. It was curious but Bubba couldn't think of any particular reason he should be concerned with it.

Bubba followed up with a best boy grip.

The best boy grip was Bob Southwell and he wasn't a boy and he wasn't a grip. To be precise he was in his thirties. Bob didn't have a lot of time when Bubba stopped him. "I have to get some of this equipment over to the next set," he explained.

"You're the best boy," Bubba said. "What's a best boy?"

Bob grimaced. "There are usually two best boys. On bigger films, there could be a half dozen or more. In ours, one helps with the crew. One helps the key grips. I'm the best boy grip. I deal with lighting, electronics, et cetera. But the union says I don't actually touch the lights. The electricians do that. I make sure everything is where it needs to be so that the director can do the next take. Understand?"

"You deal with the lighting but you cain't actually touch it," Bubba said. He didn't understand.

"Union rules," Bob explained.

"Were you on set yesterday at the Snoddy Estate?" Bubba asked.

"Of course I was," Bob answered. "And that's not an estate, it's a rambling house with a few extra bedrooms and termites up the hoo-ha."

Bubba glowered. "Did you see Kristoph come to the set?"

"He came with Marquita," Bob said, "and you're not a cop, you're a bit role. So why all the questions? Wait, you're that guy. The one they arrested." He stepped back from Bubba so quickly that he nearly tripped. "Jeez, they let *you* back on the set?"

"The charges were dismissed," Bubba said irately. "And someone's got to ask questions."

Bob shook a finger at Bubba. "The cops already asked me. The real cops." He turned away, gathered some equipment that resembled large suitcases and started toting them off.

"Well, now I know what a best boy grip is," Bubba said to Precious. Precious lay on a section of grass and rolled around until she was thoroughly saturated with the smell. She didn't know what a best boy grip was, and she didn't care unless a best boy grip had bacon on him.

Chapter Thirteen

Bubba and the Dillydallying DEA

Monday, March 11th

Several frustrating hours later, Bubba drove back to the Snoddy Estate. From his conversations with the various and sundry members of the crew from *The Deadly Dead*, he had ascertained several things.

A list was necessary to properly appreciate what he'd learned and a list was what Bubba said to himself silently as he turned into the long lane that led to the Snoddy Mansion.

A). Bubba Snoddy was considered, to several members of the film crew, a poopoo head.

B). Kristoph was a merciless jerk who didn't like dogs, tuba players, or white shoes after Labor Day. He also was a caffeine fiend and a man who would unceremoniously steal cigs. Sometimes he would steal the whole pack.

C). Pegramville didn't have a Starbucks and that was just god-awful.

D). Sheriff John and Steve Simms had already questioned most of the crew about all things Kristoph. Some of them had even been taken to the sheriff's department for further questioning.

E). The mayor of Pegramville, the honorable John Leroy, Jr., was a letch who had systematically hit on every female attached to the film. This libidinous behavior had included snooking on the sixty-five year old sound producer and grandmother of six and a cross-dressing cameraman.

F). The standard form of equation for a parabola is $(x - h)^2 = 4p(y - k)$. (One crew member was studying for a college algebra/geometry class and the formula was prevalent on his mind which then became prevalent on Bubba's mind.)

G). Alex Luis was probably gay but there wasn't a clear consensus. He had winked at Bubba, but Bubba couldn't tell if there was something to it or not.

H). Tandy North could do a triple smoke ring when properly motivated. (One of the grips bet her ten dollars she couldn't do it. Bubba witnessed the whole thing. And the grip had griped when he'd had to fork over the bill.)

I). Bubba had nothing.

Some of the crew wouldn't even look at Bubba, much less speak to him, although most of them had gotten the word that the charges had been dismissed against him and that Marquita was supporting his "investigation."

Certainly no one was pointing fingers at anyone else. There *had* to be a reason for Kristoph's death. The man was stabbed in the back with a rather large knife and that was indication enough that someone was irked with him. But no one was speaking about reasons. They were concerned about their next paycheck. They were concerned about whether the studio would close the movie down. Half of the crew didn't have gigs lined up because they had been counting on the two months of work from *The Deadly Dead*. (The amount of work varied depending on what the crew member did. One woman would be working on the film for another three months if it didn't go belly up like a fish in a dynamited pond. Her words, not Bubba's.)

Snippets of information did spill over. Kristoph had been eccentric. He had a little clout. The film was fully funded and it wasn't over budget. They were on a schedule and surprise of surprises, it was only three days behind schedule, which was practically like being on schedule. A crew member said, "That's because of Risley. He's a stickler for schedules. Kristoph would have run off filming butterflies, er, zombie butterflies. Hey, you're the guy who got arrested for it, aren't you? And hey, hey, that's the zombie Basset hound. She's gone viral."

And how could Bubba argue with any of that? Why, he could not, and consequently he gave up just as the sun was setting. Mostly he gave up because he was tired, but mostly he gave up because he was starving and Willodean was supposed to call him at home.

Truck parked, he turned off the ignition with a sigh. He climbed out of the vehicle and Precious tumbled out after him. He saw his mother's Cadillac in its normal spot. Alfonzo and Pilar's minivan was next to it, taking up what was Bubba's typical parking locale, but he didn't really mind parking in the grass. The grass was getting particularly long and needed to be taken down a peg.

As Bubba trudged toward his house, he heard the sound of tires on gravel. He looked over his shoulder. Three black SUVs charged down the drive. Furthermore, and more telling, was the large white letters on the sides of the SUVs. D-E-A.

DEA, Bubba thought. *DEA. The Drug Enforcement Administration? Really?* He immediately thought about Miz Adelia Cedarbloom and her mother, Charlene. Charlene was in the later stages of cancer and used marijuana as a pain killer. Miz Adelia's cousin Ralph grew some of the plants to help out his aunt in her hour of need. He also grew some more of the plants as a financial boon to his pocketbook. He had briefly been put out of business when the massive search for the beauteous sheriff's deputy included the place where Ralph's pot patch had been growing. He'd destroyed the evidence and had found another spot. Last Bubba'd heard, this newest crop was good. Miz Adelia kept a special canister of "tea" in the house for the occasions when one of the two women had needed a little mood alteration. The canister had conveniently vanished the last time the FBI had visited the Snoddy Mansion. That had been during Brownie's kidnapping and the canister hadn't reappeared, leaving Bubba to believe that Miz Adelia had relocated the illegal item to a place not so easily discoverable by the average law enforcement official.

The canister, by itself, couldn't possibly be the object of three DEA SUVs roaring down the drive. At least that was what Bubba thought. *One mebe. Not three.*

But his mother and Miz Adelia had been talking about "shipments" and "—they're suspicious." Bubba never would have guessed that his mother nor Miz Adelia would have anything to do with illegal drugs outside a few ounces of medicinal marijuana, but they had been acting very oddly lately and very protective of the Garcias.

The SUVs squealed to a stop in unison, leaving Bubba to wonder if they had regularly practiced the maneuver. Men and women in black jackets bearing the same initials poured out, apparently seeking targets. Bubba sighed. At least they hadn't drawn their weapons.

"You!" One of them settled his avaricious gaze upon Bubba and yelled, "DEA! Don't move!"

I'm not *moving.* Bubba froze. He didn't want to get shot by a DEA agent while in an attempt not to move. Suddenly his nose began to itch. *What in hellfire and brimstone are Ma and Miz Adelia up to?*

The agent swiftly approached Bubba, halting a few yards away and looking at him with a patented law enforcement look that was equal parts disdain and I-got-you-ness. "Special Agent Warley Smith, DEA," he announced, not even flashing a fancy badge. He cast an eye upon Precious, who was waiting and growling behind Bubba's legs. She obviously knew a cop when she saw one. Most of them were hardly a step above the people who came treasure hunting on the Snoddy estate with shovels and metal detectors. (Willodean didn't count because she took the time to feed Precious roast beef.) "You are?"

"Bubba Snoddy," he said.

"The son," Smith said with a note of arrogant understanding. "We've got warrants to search the premises. Where's your mother and the two immigrants?"

Bubba hushed Precious under his breath. "I imagine my mother is in the house. As for the immigrants, I'm not real shore who you're talking about."

"Garcia. Alfonzo and Pilar Garcia," Smith snapped.

"Mebe they ran out the back door," Bubba suggested.

Smith snapped at several of the agents who ran around the back of the mansion in response.

"I was joking," Bubba said.

"What do you know about the Garcias' trips to Mexico on the fourth, sixteenth, and twenty-eighth of last month?" Smith shot out.

"They like Mexico?" Bubba said, irritation beginning to trickle through his being. "And I don't reckon Alfonzo or Pilar are Mexican citizens. I believe they're as American as you or I."

"We'll see about that," Smith said.

Just then Miz Demetrice barreled out of the front door. "What in the name of all that's holy is happening here?" She paused upon seeing the three black SUVs and took in the initials on the sides of the vehicles. "DEA?" she said loudly. "Why would the DEA be here?"

154

"Hey, Ma," Bubba called, "is there something you forgot to tell me?"

"Shut up, Bubba!" she said. "At least I didn't get arrested yesterday."

"The charges were dismissed." Bubba sniffed.

"What charges?" Smith snapped. Obviously he liked to snap. He was quite the expert at it.

"Suspicion of murder, I believe," Bubba said. "I don't think Sheriff John actually got around to telling me."

"The movie director," another agent called.

"I am totally innocent," Bubba said. It was getting easier to say something like that.

"You need to go back to your house and stay there until we're done with the search," Smith said to Bubba after a moment.

Bubba's eyebrows lifted. He might be well aware that his mother was doing *something*, but it didn't mean he wouldn't have her back. "Ma? Man says he has a warrant. Asking questions about the Garcias. Hope he don't wake up the babies."

"I'll just need to see the warrant," his mother responded loftily. She had a lot of experience doing that. "I'll need my reading glasses. I'll have to validate its authenticity before anyone gets to touch anything. Or do I need to call my lawyer and the local police to get involved?"

Smith bristled like a long haired cat upon seeing a werewolf on Halloween. "Make sure those other people don't have any way of getting away," he directed his people.

"They're drinking tea in the kitchen," Miz Demetrice said. "Oh, yes and eating some cookies, too. Oh, the criminality of it all." The last oozed with sarcasm.

155

Another two agents ushered the Garcias outside beside Miz Demetrice. Pilar was crying and saying, "Why are they doing this to us? We've done nothing wrong. This is racial profiling! This is illegal! Don't you dare wake up my babies!"

"I'm calling LULAC," Alfonzo said, and pulled out his cell phone.

"They went to Mexico three times and you think they done something wrong?" Bubba asked Special Agent Smith.

"Start with the Dodge Caravan," Smith called. "Then we'll work on the big house."

"I don't think so," Miz Demetrice said snidely. She had her reading glasses on and was perusing the warrant one of the agents had handed to her. "This says nothing about accessing the land-based property at this address. It indicates the physical persons of Alfonzo and Pilar Garcia and their vehicular property, the Dodge Caravan."

"Fine," Smith snapped again. "Pull that van apart. I want to see rivets."

Bubba began to walk toward his mother and the Garcias. Smith put a hand up to stop him. "I told you to go inside your house."

Bubba smiled coldly at the other man. He had had a long day, which was made all the longer by the abrupt presence of DEA officials on a snipe hunt. He immediately recognized when the agent comprehended the imminent peril he was in. Smith's hand twitched toward the gun holstered under his DEA jacket. Bubba stood about a half foot taller than the other man and weighed fifty pounds more. Bubba blocked out the crescent moon. The other man was isolated from the other special agents and the scowl on Bubba's face was both fierce and chilling.

156

"*That*—" Bubba said and pointed to Miz Demetrice "—is my mother. I will be going to my mother and standing by her and her friends, who she has invited to stay with her in her house, which is clearly not covered under the mandates of your warrant." Bubba stepped one pace closer to the agent and purposely crowded him. "So you don't get to tell me where I have to go and what I need to be doing. The last I heard, it was still a free country and a free country frowns on folks who trample all over the U.S. Constitution."

Bubba strode past Smith and joined his mother. Precious followed right at Bubba's heels. Miz Demetrice continued to read the warrant but she whispered, "Bravo, Bubba."

"Ma, they goin' to find anything?" he whispered out of the side of his mouth.

"Of course not," Miz Demetrice replied indignantly. "What kind of person do you think I am?"

•

Bubba thought a lot of things about his mother. Some of them were even good things. The one thing that he did not think was that she would do anything that would garner the specific interest of the DEA. And it *was* Demetrice Snoddy that the DEA was interested in, as well as Alfonzo and Pilar Garcia.

Three trips to Mexico didn't necessarily a criminal make.

Bubba considered all the options. The question wasn't whether his mother was up to something but exactly what she up to. She suddenly was making very private conversations with Miz Adelia and to a lesser extent, Willodean Gray. She suddenly had guests who went off on midnight drives with their two young children. It wasn't as if they could be driving all the way to Mexico

157

from Pegram County. It was four hundred miles to the nearest point to cross over into Mexico. Even if a fellow was doing the speed limit, it would take six hours to drive one way.

Unambiguously, the DEA had taken note of the Garcias crossing over to Mexico and even traced them back to Pegram County to the Snoddy Mansion. At some point in time they had convinced some judge (Bubba didn't think it was Arimithia Perez but her Honor did have a good poker face) to grant a warrant based on some evidence he didn't know about to search the Garcia's car.

Something bumped his leg and Bubba looked down. Either Carlotta or Blanca curled a little arm around his calf. The DEA had, in fact, woken up the children and Pilar had gone up to comfort them. She had returned with a child in each arm, muttering, "*Hombres estúpidos* woke them up. *Hombres estúpidos* can listen to them cry." But both babies weren't especially upset and one of them had begun to toddle around the veranda, going from adult to adult, curious at why they were doing something different. The other one started to pull on Precious's long ears and Precious was being remarkably patient with the child.

The baby gazed up at Bubba with large brown eyes and raised her arms in supplication. Bubba couldn't resist that and picked her up. She was wearing footsie jammies with Dora the Explorer exploring all over them. Under the jammies, Bubba could feel the heft of a diaper that was about due to be changed. "What's the matter, sweet pea?" he asked.

Bubba caught the simultaneous glance of his mother, Alfonzo and Pilar. They all froze in place for a moment and stared at him holding the child. Bubba blinked and Miz Demetrice was looking at the stars while Alfonzo was looking at a scrape on the back of his hand. Pilar still looked at Bubba holding the child.

"Is this Carlotta or Blanca?" Bubba asked.

"Blanca," Pilar said.

Bubba continued to murmur sweet baby words to the baby and Blanca stared at him entranced. He glanced over at the group of DEA agents who were systematically dismantling the Dodge Caravan. Mentally he catalogued three items that the agents had broken that he was going to suggest that Alfonzo sue the DEA over. As a first generation Caravan, it would be hard to replace those specific parts.

Since Miz Demetrice had thwarted Special Agent Warley Smith, he seemed to be taking his wrath out on the van. Based on the way that his mother was relaxed in the Adirondack chair, Bubba would say the DEA wasn't going to find bubkis in the vehicle.

Blanca tugged on Bubba's lower lip and let it snap back. "You like that, sweetie pie? Bubba needs that to et the chow. Say, you hungry? I bet Auntie Adelia left some cake in the kitchen. Miz Adelia makes good cake. *Muy delicioso.*"

"There's snickerdoodles," Miz Demetrice said. "And milk for the babies. They don't need much. Carlotta can gnaw on a cookie ifin Pilar doesn't mind."

Bubba beckoned at Carlotta. "You want Bubba to carry you, too?"

Carlotta glanced at Pilar and put her head down.

"I'll bring her," Pilar said. "A few bites and a drink won't bother them much."

"You look a mite tired," Bubba said. "Shall I take the younnun?"

Pilar gently eased Carlotta into her arms and with a little shrug she passed the child over to Bubba. Both of the children stared at Bubba as if they hadn't seen such a thing ever. Perhaps they hadn't. Tall rednecks that weighed 240 pounds didn't tromp over hither and yon.

"It's okay. Them nasty pants law enforcement folks won't hurt you," Bubba said quietly. "I won't let them. They just have a problem with a lack of fiber. They need more bran flakes in their diet, don't they? If they didn't keep all that poopoo inside they wouldn't have so much vitriol."

Carlotta gurgled. Then Bubba heard her insides make a very distinct noise. "But you don't have a problem with that, do you, sugar lips?"

"Aie," Pilar said. "*La niña* is pooping every five minutes. I think it's the change in milk."

"There's children's medications in the kitchen," Miz Demetrice said. "There's one that helps with their digestive systems."

Bubba thought about it. "Mebe that's why this one seems a little smaller," he said. Pilar paused in front of him as if something had suddenly tugged her to a complete stop. After a brief moment, she continued down the long hallway into the kitchen.

Bubba continued to murmur at the children as he carried them along. Both stared at him as they placidly sat in his arms. It turned out that cookies were just the thing to make an apprehensive baby besties with a fellow.

•

The DEA finished with the van after midnight and Bubba had a conversation with Alfonzo about the repairs needed for the vehicle. They put most of it back together but Miz Demetrice made a big show out of taking photographs with her cell phone.

Special Agent Warley Smith glared at them as he got back into a DEA SUV and the rest of the agents appeared disgruntled.

Bubba said, "Perhaps they should have et some of them snickerdoodles."

Pilar and Alfonzo carried half-asleep children inside and Bubba stopped his mother with a single stare.

"Ma," he said, "what the blazes?"

"I'm tired, Bubba," she said pertly. Miz Demetrice wasn't that tired. She simply didn't want to have this conversation with her son at that moment. "And you've got a movie to do tomorrow. My son, the zombie actor. How thrilled your grandmother would have been."

Bubba watched the huge door shut and heard the lock being thrown.

When he went back to his house with his dog trailing along behind, he discovered someone had left a script on his front porch in a neat binder with the words "The Deadly Dead" on the front in a blood red font. He also discovered that Willodean had called and that he had missed the call.

Consequently, Bubba went to bed feeling very discouraged.

Chapter Fourteen

Bubba and the Gregarious Goodjoint
And
The Gregarious Gangsta

Tuesday, March 12th

When Bubba woke up the next day it was lightly raining outside. Precious had her head underneath his pillow and her large rump sticking out. She was dreaming and her tail thumped against his stomach lazily. While he lay in bed, Bubba decided he needed to think like the people on CSI. The ones in Las Vegas, Miami, and New York. If no one was going to offer up a convenient suspect (beside himself) then he needed to know as much as he could about the corpse.

So in between work on the film, finding out what Ma was doing, and trying to catch up with Willodean Gray, Bubba was going to have to investigate to the fullest of his abilities. Therefore, he would start the way most investigators would.

Breakfast. Eggs with bacon and a bran muffin, just in case what afflicted the DEA agents started to afflict Bubba. Bubba knew that a fellow was never too young to eat bran muffins to ensure prevention of digestional intractability. In fact, he liked bran muffins, especially the ones Miz Adelia made. If he happened to see Special Agent Warley Smith, he would recommend them to him. *Good for his constitution.*

Bubba showered, made his breakfast, and ate while looking at the script. "'I think we got big trouble,'" he read laboriously. "Who writes this stuff?" He gave Precious a bite of bacon. "Do you write this stuff, Precious?"

Precious woofed while she dragged the hapless piece of bacon under the small table in order to subjugate and devour it properly.

Bubba glanced at the clock on the wall, a black Kit-Cat Clock with the tail swinging and eyes that moved back and forth. It had been another housewarming gift, although he couldn't remember from whom. It was just after eight a.m. and he knew he had enough time to continue his investigation before he had to get to the set for makeup.

The set was at the high school that day and Bubba's stop was on the way. He left an irritable Precious with Miz Adelia in the mansion and the dog had to amuse herself by graciously allowing the Garcia children to play with her Dumbo sized ears.

The Pegramville Family Medical Clinic and Chiropractic Care Center was open at the crack of dawn because the doctor in charge happened to be an early bird sort of person. George Goodjoint was an elderly man who'd attended both Harvard and Johns Hopkins for his various degrees. Bubba knew of three degrees but had an idea that Doc had a few more than that. He was also a tall thin man with a shock of white hair that he swept back over his forehead. Furthermore, he was a personal friend of the Snoddy family, often invited to regular dinners with Miz Demetrice. Bubba would have thought that there was a romantic interest between them, but over the course of years it became apparent that the pair were fast friends and nothing more. They had dinner once a month, at which other guests were occasionally invited, and sometimes very interesting things occurred, like the thirteen cannon salute of the previous month. (One of the old oak trees had suffered an everlasting indignity in that

163

sorry incident. Who knew they could actually get one of the antique cannons to work?) Finally, and most importantly, Doc was the coroner of Pegram County. (He might not know where all the dead bodies were buried, but he knew about how they had died.)

Bubba arrived at the clinic at half-past eight and shouldered his way past three people coming out. One had a bloody nose to which he held an icepack. All three glared at the light rain and paused under the clinic's awning. They all wore film crew standard shirts. Black background. Red lettering. "The Deadly Dead RISES!" The last word dripped with silkscreened blood ad nauseum.

"Broken?" the one with the bloody nose said. "Do you know how much the damn insurance covers? I'll be able to afford a quarter of the x-ray. Maybe they can take a little itty-bitty x-ray of just the nose."

The second one patted him on the shoulder. "We'll just bill Schuler. He broke it. Let him pay for the x-rays."

The third one said, "What the hell got into Schuler, anyway?"

"I dunno," bloody nose said. "All I said was 'Where's the scarf?'"

"God," the second one said sarcastically, "no one said that Hollyweird was so glamorous."

"Well Schuler doesn't look like himself if he isn't wearing the ascot, or whatever."

Bubba held the door for the three men and one of them said, "Hey, aren't you Zombie #14/Farmboy?"

"I reckon," Bubba said.

"He's the one with the zombie dog, too," another one added as they walked away.

Once he was inside he told the receptionist that he needed to speak with Doc for five minutes. No more. No less. The receptionist was new. He didn't know her name

164

and she didn't have a name plate, but she looked a lot like Doc's intractable nurse Dee Dee Lacour, a woman with the least amount of sense of humor that Bubba had ever known.

Doc popped out thirty seconds later. "Bubba, dear boy," he said. "You're in luck. No business right now." He waved around the empty room. "I had to send the last young man to the hospital for an x-ray. Very unfortunate. He's going to need an ear, nose, and throat man to put that nose back where it belongs." He gestured for Bubba to follow him back.

Bubba went and looked around for Dee Dee. "Where's the sourpuss?"

Doc chuckled. "The acting bug took her but properly. She's on the set, being made up into a zombie. She texted me a photo. I'd show you but I don't want to spoil your morning."

He ushered Bubba into his office. "I assume you're not injured, seeing as you're not unconscious upon this splendiferous occasion."

"It's true I don't get much occasion to see you when I'm awake and all," Bubba acknowledged.

"Let me guess the reason for your visit," Doc said and sat in his high backed leather chair. He motioned at the other chairs and Bubba sat.

"Do you know what Ma is up to?" Bubba asked. *Might as well kill two birds with one stone. I might get lucky.*

"The eminent Miz Demetrice is capable of many things, the dear lady. Her brilliance and glory are a force to be reckoned with." Doc swept a lock of white hair away from his forehead and grinned. "As you well know."

Bubba studied Doc. It was good that Bubba didn't play poker because Doc could and would bluff. The physician knew something but he wasn't going to blab about it. "The DEA came calling yesterday," Bubba said, "out at the mansion."

"The DEA," Doc repeated. "How fascinating. Did they search your mother? I always wanted to know how in depth such a search would go. Well, not with your mother, of course, but such an agent would have to be highly motivated, would they not?"

"They searched the Garcias' minivan," Bubba said. "You know the Garcias? Alfonzo and Pilar and the two babies."

"Of course. I looked at the children yesterday. Healthy young ones, although Blanca could use soy milk for a bit until we determine if she's allergic to dairy or not."

Bubba pursed his lips. *Dead end.* "Okay, next subject."

"You want to know about Kristoph Thaddeus," Doc answered. Doc was a doctor for no little reason. He was hardly stupid. "As does Sheriff John, Deputy Gray, the DEA special agent, your mother, thirteen representatives of the media, and Mayor John Leroy, Jr." Doc lowered his voice. "I think the mayor was just trying to make sure the town couldn't be sued for the death. I was happy to inform him that the director did not die in the town proper of Pegramville but in Pegram County, thus the jurisdictional influence of the Pegram County Sheriff's Department."

"Yes, I know. He died in my house, with my knife in his back. My house is located in Pegram County, not Pegramville, or I'd still be in Big Joe's jail playing pinochle with Butterfingers Moran and Pretty Boy Floyd."

"A confounding conundrum," Doc admitted.

Bubba stared at Doc. "How is that confounding or a conundrum? He was stabbed in the back. It sorta implies death all by itself."

Doc steepled his fingers together, folding them in and out and looking at his ceiling. "It didn't bleed."

Thinking about stuff was Bubba's biggest issue of late. If he had to think hard about a subject then it was bound to give him a massive headache. He was thinking about his mother, about Willodean, about the Garcias, about the DEA, about the film, and about Kristoph Thaddeus. So he thought about that only. *Infamous director was stabbed in his back. It didn't bleed. One didn't lead to the other.* "Kristoph didn't die because someone stabbed him in the back," Bubba said slowly, comprehension making his synapses, neurons, and dendrites ever so happy.

"No."

"How did he die?"

"That would be the confounding conundrum part, stalwart lad," Doc said dramatically. "It really is a puzzlement."

"And John said something about a necktie," Bubba said, half to himself. "I didn't turn the man over. He looked dead to me. Perhaps I should have turned him over to see if he was dead. He *was* dead. Wasn't he dead, Doc?"

"Kristoph was dead. Still is dead, I would think. It would be rather ironic, wouldn't it, if he happened to turn into a genuine zombie at this point?" Doc chuckled at his own black humor.

Bubba leaned forward in the chair. "Necktie. Willodean said something about a necktie, too."

Doc looked at Bubba. "I say, categorically and without hesitation, that there was no necktie involved."

"Then how do you think he died, Doc?"

"It's my sincerest belief that his heart stopped beating," Doc said. "The problem is determining *how* the heart was caused to stop."

"You don't know how he died?" Bubba sat back in the chair, confused. A knife in the back was one thing. It was clear. It was irrefutable. It was like a bulletin board announcing its presence and intention. "I killed Kristoph! All six and three-quarters inches of my blade! Yes me! What are you going to do about it, huh? Pussies!"

"You know that I'm not supposed to discuss particulars with the general public, Bubba," Doc said with a grin.

"I know that rules are applied only when you think they should be applicable," Bubba said, "which is a trait that you share with my mother."

"I love it when your education is clearly illuminated," Doc said immediately.

"I reckon," Bubba said promptly.

The receptionist pounded on Doc's door, startling both of them. "Your five minutes is up and you have a patient, Doctor Goodjoint!" she bellowed.

"Lordy," Bubba muttered. "Cain't you find a nice helper?"

Doc sighed. "Unfortunately not. She's a friend of Dee Dee's, as one might surmise."

●

By the time Bubba swung by the Pegram County Sheriff's Department to see if Willodean was about, the rain had blown off to the east. However, Willodean was not about. Furthermore, Mary Lou Treadmill, whose job description meandered from 9-1-1 operator to receptionist, would not give him any information about the lady in question. "I will pass your message onto her, Bubba," she said.

"What?"

"Arlette was telling me about your recent break-up," Mary Lou stared at him coldly.

"I ain't bin broke up," Bubba said.

"That's not what Arlette says."

Bubba lowered his head and looked at the floor. Linoleum squares of black and white, they hadn't been changed since the building was built and Bubba couldn't remember when that was, even if he had wanted to remember when that was.

"You said you were going to pop the question," Mary Lou accused. She smoothed over her scarlet red hair done up in its usual bouffant. Her blue eyes studied him with a clarity that he found alarming.

"I dint say that exactly," Bubba said.

"I think you're breaking that poor girl's heart," Mary Lou pronounced.

I am? What'd I do? I told her I wanted quadruplets. I told her I kin change diapers. If that ain't a declaration of my undying love, then I don't know what is.

Bubba left the Pegram County Sheriff's Department feeling mildly dejected.

●

Pegramville High School was pretty much exactly like Bubba remembered it. Except now it had zombies wandering across the vast lawn. (High school students first thing in the morning could be mistaken for zombies but mostly they didn't have blood and brains all over them.) Several were gathered around the giant rock that got repainted every year with a new school theme. (This year's theme was "Education ROCKS!" Bubba was certain the pun was intended.) Other zombies gathered at a chuck wagon, drinking coffee and eating whatever they were serving. (Brains probably weren't on the menu.)

169

Bubba parked on the far side of the lot and waded through onlookers. Clearly the high school had called a day off to accommodate the film crew. Many of the curious spectators were obviously high school students hoping to be extras.

"BUBBA!" someone yelled as he moved through the crowd. Bubba stopped to look and saw a man in his thirties approaching quickly. He wore a Saint's jersey and purple leather pants with glossy black knee high boots. His white grin lit up his entire face and set off his mahogany skin.

Bubba knew the man from somewhere. It finally dawned on him. "Bam Bam," he said as the other man approached, bumped fists with Bubba, and then performed an elaborate set of hand gestures that would have confused an expert on nonverbal communication. Bubba's eyes followed the gestures with both bafflement and interest, trying to detect the meaning but failing miserably.

Bam Bam Jones had been one of the first people that Bubba had met in Dallas while searching for Willodean. He was several parts street guy, several parts entrepreneur, and all friendliness.

"Bubba, I was so glad to hear that you found that missing gal," Bam Bam said, "and I sent some flowers when she knocked you on your ass. I got to say I thought there would be a big A. hole in your head but I don't see nothing."

"I remember. White carnations," Bubba said. Was there a man rule about acknowledging flowers from another man? If there was, he couldn't remember it. "Thank you. I liked 'em."

"The least I could do," Bam Bam chortled. "Bizness was tremendous after I got connected to you. Peeps coming from all over to talk with me. Wanting to know what that was like. Peeps from jail. Peeps from South Dallas. Peeps everywhere." The hands kept moving.

"Glad I could help?" Bubba said.

Bam Bam chortled again.

"What are you doing in Pegramville?" Bubba asked. "It don't seem like the sort of place you'd like to go, or am I making an assumption?"

"You be correct, ma man," Bam Bam said. "Small towns are so damn small. Your peeps be looking at my boots and saying, 'What the hell?' They don't know when a man needs to dress for success." He stopped to adjust the jersey as if he was straightening the lapels of a fancy suit. "And I got a tip about six months ago from a fella I know who's in the movie business, wanting to know about good areas to film in. Places with at-mo-sphere. You know? I thought of you. Small town. Needs some cash. Has some famous fella who rescued his woman. How kin I go wrong with that?" More hand gesturing ensued well after Bam Bam's words trailed off. "So I hooked him up. Got some deals cookin' with peeps supplying the movie. Got some deep discounts. I got me a quarter percentage point on the film."

"So you came to see how your investment is going?"

"That fella, Kristoph, up and died, man," Bam Bam said, "in your house, homes. With your knife in his back. You damn tootin' I came down to see how the investment is going. Of course, I know a stand-up fella like you wouldn't stab a man in the back."

"Mebe you should share that," Bubba said. Several of the people around them were blatantly eavesdropping.

"Ma man, Bubba, wouldn't kill no one that way," Bam Bam said loudly. "If he were of a mind, he would likely punch them in the face and knock their asses down. *Never* in the back."

"Thanks," Bubba said.

"I hear you're in the movie," Bam Bam said. More explosive hand gestures followed apparently indicating his approval of the news. "A redneck zombie." He grinned widely and nodded. "That be the way it be."

"That be the way it be," Bubba repeated. "I got to go, Bam Bam. You should come out to the house. My ma would love to meet you." And Bubba would love to see his mother meeting Bam Bam Jones.

Bam Bam produced a card. "Ma numbuh," he said. "Call me."

Bubba turned away, toward the cordoned-off set, but paused when an odd thought popped into his head. "Bam Bam," he called, "who was it that you told about Pegramville?"

"Risley Risto," Bam Bam said instantly. "I told him it be a hotbed of intrigue and murderous scenarios. The shizz is happening around here. Bodies left and right. Missing gold, blood, little kids with Tasers, and rock and roll. I mean, a fella's got to take advantage, am I right?" He didn't wait for an answer. "I'm right. Don't hurt none that the place is infamous. That's why they make movies on Alcatraz Island, and in Washington, DC."

"I reckon," Bubba said. "Catch you later, Bam Bam." As Bubba walked away he heard a young woman say to Bam Bam, "So you're in the movie business?"

"I am but a lowly associate, my dear," Bam Bam said suavely. "Do the firemen know about you because you're smokin'?"

Bubba got admitted and walked to the makeup tent while he thought about why he'd asked Bam Bam that very question. He couldn't imagine why someone would want to film in Pegram County. It was isolated. There weren't enough hotels and motels for the film crew and people were packed in every spare room available. The scenery was nice but it wasn't as spectacular as a mountain range or a yawning gorge on a dusky evening. It did have some infamy though most of that had died down. As for financial availability, it might be advantageous. The Honorable Mayor John Leroy, Jr. was probably letting the film use whatever they wanted for free.

I am *confounded.* Bubba frowned. *And it* is *a conundrum.*

Chapter Fifteen

Bubba and the Acrimonious Assault

Tuesday, March 12th

Simone Sheats was Bubba's makeup artist again. "Bubba," she said, "so glad to see you. Sit down. I didn't think you could have killed Kristoph. I can tell, you know. It's a trick that all artists have. A skill that we have. We can divine everything when we're doing a session. We're like makeup gods and goddesses. You're supposed to be a zombie again. So you need to find your gear and change again. Remember it's Zombie #14/Farmboy. Go ahead, stand up. Don't forget to go pee pee."

Bubba bumbled his way through wardrobe. Once Bubba was back in her chair, he listened to Simone chatter with only half an ear. "—thinks an insane critic did it. Some of those critics are like the phantom of the opera. They're all warped inside because such and such director or so and so producer said their review sucked the great big lemon. It can be such a horrible business with dog eat dog going on."

Then why do you do it? Bubba wanted to ask but it was too late. The shotgun blasted face prosthesis was already attached and he couldn't move his mouth. He'd forgotten to take another antihistamine so who knew what was going to happen. He briefly thought of one of the FBI agents who had been investigating Brownie's disappearance and who happened to be violently allergic to poison ivy. The man had blown up like a water balloon. Doc Goodjoint had hinted that he'd had to treat him with more antihistamines than he'd ever given to one single person before.

Simone was already filling in the blanks without being prompted. "It's not *that* horrible of a business. You establish your network and you keep abreast of latest innovations in the field. There's a con in July just for makeup, wardrobe, and special effects. It'll be killer. I shouldn't say killer. It'll be fantastic. We all do our best to outdo each other. Just imagine every conceivable costume and makeup possible wandering around Las Vegas in July." She frowned. "We're going to melt." She brightened again. "But we'll have a blast melting." She grinned. "Some of the effects people in Vegas make six figures regularly with bennies. No diving for the next movie to come out or for the television show with all the aliens on it."

Bubba yanked his head out of the clouds. He couldn't talk to Simone and pump her for information but he could think hard at her. *Who else might have done it? Tell me how to get Willodean Gray to talk to me again. Is the DEA really going to arrest my mother for complicity in drug smuggling?*

Simone was exactly as she was the previous times Bubba had spent with her. Her everyday prattle was numbing and she was happy that the person with whom she was chattering couldn't answer her back and thusly distract her. "I'm doing a giant daisy. My entire body naked except green paint and appropriate leaves. Stark mother naked. Buffness. Wearing nothing but a smile and some body paint. A special headdress with the flowers on top of my head. Bejeweled, too. I mean, Swarovski crystals all over all of the petals. I wish you could see it. Well, they'll take pics in July so keep an eye on the web. Hey, you could friend me on Facebook. I'm on Twitter, too. I have two thousand followers. Last year I was Lady Godiva."

Okay. Ifin it was Willodean who was naked just for green paint, mebe. Bubba wanted to shake his head to get the image out of there, but his jaw was immobilized by Simone's fingers. He stared in the mirror in front of him, trying to catch Simone's eyes, but she was lost in the moment of transformation appreciation.

"Oh goodness, you look very zombie-ish," Simone said approvingly.

Someone else came up behind them. It was Schuler and his purple hair was styled into a fancified, plum colored rooster's comb. "Great work, Simone, as usual," he said to Simone. "Hey, Zombie #14," he said to Bubba. Bubba grunted. It wasn't like he could give an oral treatise on the simplicities of the Bazooka Launcher Platform Concept Theorem. (What were the simplicities of the Bazooka Launcher Platform Concept Theorem? Bubba did not know.)

"Do you have your dog with you today?" Schuler asked. His tone was short. He towered over Bubba sitting in the chair and made Bubba think of the three men at Doc Goodjoint's clinic and the one with the broken nose.

Simone generously allowed Bubba to shake his head. He hadn't thought bringing his dog was a good idea at all. Someone might take Precious' presence as Bubba flaunting his freedom. Or she might have tried to eat someone. Either one would have been bad.

"Bring her by tomorrow," Schuler said. "She was so good in the first take, we'll use her in a few more. She can be Farmboy's bosom companion." He smiled wanly and wandered away, stopping to critique another artist's work in progress. "God, that needs more blood. Did you look at your Polaroids? Do you want to get a Razzie for worst makeup?" There was a pause and Bubba was sorry that he couldn't turn his head to look. "Are you crying? Makeup artists DO NOT cry! Mascara running!"

"Scarfie is just the biggest bitch today," Simone said quietly. "I don't know what crawled up his butt and died, but it must have something with sharp claws and teeth. He totally needs a good humor enema."

Scarfie doesn't have his scarf today, Bubba observed when Simone moved to the other side and he was able to move his eyes to where Schuler still chastised a hapless makeup artist. The man's neck was oddly empty, which is why the crew member had asked about it. *What makes a man so temperamental that he hits a fella when he asks about something like that?*

"He's generally so-so," Simone went on, "but ever since Kristoph got murdered, he's been a pure pain in the ass. Well, who wouldn't be? Not me, but I'm easy. Everyone is nervous about their jobs. No one wants to hear that the studio is freaking and is thinking about axing the movie dead in its tracks." Simone paused. "That wasn't a pun. Oh, that sounded terrible."

Bubba understood. It was something about people dying that did it. You wanted to make a joke so you wouldn't have to cry instead. Some people didn't understand that, but Bubba did. He also wanted to ask Simone where she was when Kristoph was getting stabbed in the back or whatever it was that had killed him, but then another thought occurred to him. He should have asked Doc when Kristoph died. Doc could usually put a time frame on those sorts of things. It might be hours but it might put another completely different spin on events. It could clear Bubba irrefutably or it could damn him even more. But Bubba had forgotten to ask and now he couldn't even talk.

Bubba concluded that he was a terrible detective. He needed the Purple Singapore Sling or Daniel Lewis Gollihugh or Brownie. He needed someone.

"BUBBA!" someone yelled and Simone jumped. She swore under her breath.

Bubba could only look into the mirror. Bam Bam Jones appeared behind him, his hands gesturing wildly. "Yo, homes," he said. "I be thinking and all that. I expect a fella needs to know what the dealio is. And seeing as how you were the main suspect and all—"

The charges WERE dismissed! Bubba yelled in his head. If there was ever a time that he needed a sudden psychic ability brought on by a nuclear accident and chemical experimentation in an era of free-love, it was now. Alas it was not to be.

"—well, you be the man who needs to find out who the real murderer is," Bam Bam concluded. He spared a long glance at Simone. "Hey, baby, I wish you were DSL so I could get high speed access."

Simone shoved Bam Bam aside. "If I don't get his face finished in ten minutes I'm going to be history, so step away from the zombie."

Bam Bam smoothly stepped back and then presented a card. "Bam Bam Jones, sweetness. Entrepreneur, businessman, investor." He grinned widely at Simone.

Simone took the card and dumped it on her work bench. "Simone Sheats, makeup, wardrobe, and bitch. You can talk to him but don't expect him to answer. His face is *mine*." She resumed her work with a vengeance.

Unruffled by Simone's rejection, Bam Bam looked at Bubba and said, "Dah-amn, Bubba. You look like you be ready to tear into somethin' like it be fresh brains on toast."

Simone grunted approvingly. "He should be."

"Well, I just wanted to say that I think we should get together and start interrogating all the film crew," Bam Bam said. "I'm shore the po-lice ain't doin' a proper job and all. Of course, I don't mean your girl, the deputy." He glanced at Simone again. "Sorry, baby, but that deputy girl melts me like fudge on a sundae."

Bubba growled.

"Okay, big man," Bam Bam soothed. "I just be thinking that we don't want this film to fold, am I right, brotha?" He didn't wait for Bubba to answer. "So we be asking folks, who be wanting to kill Kristoph? Like you, sugar lips," he said to Simone, "who do you think would do poor Kristoph in?"

Simone frowned. "Everyone is thinking about that very subject, you know." She brushed something across Bubba's forehead and then checked the Polaroid shots on the work bench. "Bubba is the one who just got fired. So he's suspect number one, except the charges get dismissed on account that they couldn't find any fingerprints on the knife." *They found Simms's fingerprint.*

"Maybe Bubba used gloves. He's a smart white boy," Bam Bam suggested.

Oh crap balls! Stop trying to help me, Bam Bam! Bubba thought hard. He also grunted eloquently.

"In his own house with his own knife?" Simone asked sarcastically. "That seems unlikely. Besides what was he doing in Bubba's house?"

Bubba would have answered if he'd been able. *Risley Risto said something about Kristoph wandering into weird places in the name of filming unusual shots or somethin' like that. It had gotten him in trouble before. Mebe that was why Kristoph had been in my house.*

"To frame Bubba, of course," Bam Bam declared. "If I was a bad guy, and I can be, you know. If I was a bad guy, I

179

would call Kristoph up and say, 'Yo blood, meet me at the redneck's house because we need to deal.'"

"I don't think our killer talks like that," Simone said.

Bam Bam's eyes rolled. "Okay." His voice mimicked an average Middle American accent with no inflection. "'Please, sir, meet me at Bubba's residence promptly at four p.m. so that I can stab you in the back.'"

"Kristoph wouldn't have come to that," Simone sneered.

"It's just for example," Bam Bam said. "I'm just saying a fella would have to be a little clever in order to get the man over where he wanted him to be and then it was a done deal. Where you be at when the man be getting stabbed, Bubba?"

Simone and Bam Bam both looked at Bubba. Bubba grunted again.

"Oh, he cain't talk," Bam Bam said understandingly. "Mebe we should get him something to write with. We need an alibi for when the director got shanked. You know, I know a gal who would vouch for you. She's like a professional alibi person. She provided one for Knobby Knees Macaroy back in '10 when he robbed that bank."

But Bubba was thinking about what Bam Bam had actually meant. If one needed a fall guy for a murder, then who better than a man who went in and out of jail faster than a hound will swallow a boiled egg. Everything about Bubba practically screamed "SCAPEGOAT!"

And where does a fella find a scapegoat? Why, Pegram County's got all the best ones. They fall right out of the trees there.

•

"Here's your mark," the redhead said. One day Bubba was going to have to take some time to ask what her name actually was. "In this scene, you're about to eat Alex," she indicated Alex Luis, who winked at Bubba again. Bubba was afraid to blink lest it be misinterpreted as something it was not. He didn't have anything against a man or a woman's sexual proclivities, but unfortunately he was a product of his culture and upbringing. "You go from here to here. Then you have to hurry. No saying brains. A little moaning. Remember you died from a shotgun to the face that missed your spinal cord and didn't disconnect your central nervous system. Shuffle, shuffle, bite, bite."

Okay, Bubba thought. They were in the high school's gymnasium. The lights were flickering on and off above them and it appeared as though the room had been under attack by people throwing mud. It was possible that Bubba didn't really understand the genius that was the art of special effects.

On one side of the gym, Risley Risto perched on a director's chair watching the redhead and the others get organized. Finally the redhead backed out of the scene and called, "Okay, Risley."

"Shake and bake," Risley called. "Cameramen!" The cameramen, er, persons, because one of them was a woman, started filming. Then he motioned at the baldheaded kid with the multiple piercings. He rushed in, used the clapboard, then rushed out. Risley gestured at the actors. "Action!" he said.

Alex held a shotgun and pumped it loudly. The bullet casing ejected and flew through the air and hit Tandy North in the eye. She caught herself before saying what was obviously going to be a vicious and four-lettered word. "Sorry," Alex said.

Risley said a bad word.

"Sorry," Alex said again. He pumped the shotgun again.

"Don't stop," Risley commanded.

181

Alex took a deep breath. He aimed the shotgun at Bubba and the three other zombie actors who loomed and leered at the two "live" people.

"Dakota," Alex said to Tandy North. Bubba took that to mean that her character's name was Dakota. He couldn't remember if he had heard it before. He didn't think much of it but then he was named Bubba so he supposed he couldn't complain much. "We're in a corner here." His tone was urgent, determined, and ready for his big denouement.

"Riker," Tandy, er, Dakota said, which Bubba also took to mean that Alex's character was named Riker. (Perhaps after a jail or a first officer from the Star Trek universe, not that Bubba would ever admit to watching the entire series of *Star Trek: The Next Generation* in a marathon session over a long holiday weekend.) "We knew that it was a long shot."

"You know, I have a hankering to go back to Jamaica and lose my necktie," Alex, er, Riker said suavely, clearly lost in the moment of being the hero who was about to die a wretched cinematic death.

He ain't wearing a necktie, Bubba thought and moaned. Risley shot Bubba a quick look. *Too loud?*

"You're not wearing a necktie," Tandy, er, Dakota shot back wryly.

Bubba stumbled forward. The other zombies followed suit. He tried to remember if he was supposed to drag his leg and went ahead and dragged it some anyway. No one screamed "CUT, you big dumb goober!" so he figured it was okay.

Alex and Tandy tried to back farther into their isolated corner. The flickering fluorescent lights above were similar to strobe lights in a dance club. The on and off actions showed their desperate faces, waiting for something to happen, for someone to save them.

"I just wanted to say that I think I love you," Alex said to Tandy.

It was a little hard to see his mark, Bubba stumbled another step forward. He could see Risley leaning forward to see him better. One of his hands was twitching a gesture at him. *Don't stop. Don't stop.*

"Aren't you going to tell me something?" Alex demanded.

"When we're not in a shadowy gym with a bunch of dead freaks!" Tandy said forcefully. "I want candles and a table with a real cloth tablecloth." She brought up her shotgun and pumped it once. It was clear to everyone that she was trying to aim the ejecting shotgun shell at Alex but she missed abysmally. "I want you on one knee and by god, I think you can find a two carat rock in a ring my size." She jerked Alex's head down to hers and kissed him hard once. "But now, we've got other things to do."

They brought their shotguns up in unison and aimed at the approaching zombies.

Bubba saw Risley clamp his hands together in anticipation.

There was a loud clicking noise and a boom. Bubba saw flashes of light coming from the ends of the shotguns and there was an immediate burning on his arm. Almost instantaneously there was a huge explosion of breaking glass and Bubba swung his head around to see one of the lights behind him burst into pieces. He looked forward again and saw both Alex and Tandy staring horrified at the shotguns in their hands.

"Oh snap," Tandy said. "You know, I think this gun had real bullets in it."

Risley had been frozen and then he said, "Cut, cut, cut!"

The special effects supervisor rushed in to see what Tandy was saying.

"I've fired shotguns before at the range," Tandy said, "and this felt like the real deal. I think I hit the portable light. Damn, I'm good. I was aiming at the redneck zombie like I was supposed to."

"Of course it's not real," the supervisor said, "it's just a special load that we—"

Alex sniffed. "Smells like the real thing to me."

"Uh, Risley," the supervisor said, carefully taking both shotguns away from the two lead actors and examining them closely, "we got a problem."

Bubba looked around at saw people staring. A lot of people staring. And there was McGeorge, watching him with a funny little twisted smile on her face, just like the cat that ate the zombie canary.

One of the zombies glanced at Bubba and her eyes went very large, even with the pale white contacts. "I think you've been shot, guy," she said. Bubba didn't know her except as Zombie #64, and she wasn't someone he recognized.

Bubba wanted to say, *Shore, I've bin shot. That's what the good guy and gal are supposed to do. They're supposed to shoot the bad, hungry, brain-eting zombie. Right?* Bubba looked down at his stinging shoulder. There was blood on his face that was fake. There were some spots on his shirt that Simone had reapplied. But there hadn't been a large spreading patch of bright crimson blood on his upper left arm. There also hadn't been a stinging that was rapidly turning into a fierce scorching of his flesh.

184

He brought his hand up to cover it and then brought it away to see the redness dripping from his palm. *Crap,* he thought. *I mean, Carp.*

Chapter Sixteen

Bubba and the Heinous Hospital

Tuesday, March 12th

So this *is what the hospital looks like when I'm coming in while I'm actually conscious,* Bubba thought. The ER people weren't particularly impressed with the shotgun wound in his upper arm. (Hunting season in east Texas brought a whole other level to Cheney-like "accidents.") They thought the face prosthesis was real for a brief time until one nurse experimentally poked him in the face. *I shore hope the movie people are goin' to pay for this visit. It wasn't my fault the gun was loaded. It wasn't—*

Wait.

Bubba mentally rewound what Tandy North said, "I was aiming at the redneck zombie like I was supposed to." The character was aiming at Zombie #14/Farmboy. The character was supposed to specifically shoot Zombie #14/Farmboy as was stated thusly in the script. In another take he would be filmed falling down as blood exploded out of his chest. Bubba assumed that meant they would put the same kind of thing on him that they had put on David Beathard. *I had no idea the movie bizness is so dang dangerous.*

The hospital staff threw him on a gurney and rolled him into a back area. It was a large room with rooms separated by curtains hanging from the ceiling. A child was coughing and an elderly man was arguing about his diagnosis. "I don't have no gallstones, dagnammit! It's my lumbago!" he screamed at a clerk.

And Bubba remembered the special effects supervisor saying something like, "It's just a special load that we—" and his words had stopped because he had been staring at the weapons. His words had trailed off because he recognized those had been real bullets. There had been real bullets in the scene where Bubba's character was supposed to have been shot.

Someone tried to murder me. That's just ducky.

The staff got busy on Bubba's arm while the redhead tried to tell some other staff that what had happened was just a tragic misadventure.

"Do you feel lightheaded, Bubba?" a nurse asked. Bubba didn't recognize the nurse but they were used to having him in the hospital so that was a no brainer. (Groaner.) (All the nurses knew him, but he didn't always recognize them because usually he was unconscious in the hospital.)

Bubba shook his head.

"How do we get this crap off his face?" another one asked.

The shirt was neatly sliced up the sleeve with scissors and exposed the wound. The nurse blinked. "That's a nice little shot pattern. Notice the expanding pattern of beads around the main wound. He caught only half of it. We're going to have to pick out each pellet and then do an x-ray to make sure we got all of them."

Bubba understood about shotgun wounds. Tee Gearheart had been shot by his cousin, catching most of the pellets across his buttocks. He hadn't sat down for a full month and his cousin had his shotgun returned to him with a bow tied barrel. (Tee was mostly genial but he hadn't liked being shot in the ass at all, which had inspired a bout of creativity involving a vise clamp, a blow torch, and a hydraulic pipe bender.)

187

"Let's get an IV in him," one nurse said. "Call the doctor and have him take a looksee to make sure he doesn't want anything else done. Bubba," she said to him, clasping thick white pads of gauze across the wound, "are you hurt anywhere else? Side?"

Bubba shook his head.

Simone Sheats appeared on the other side. She stared at Bubba and then at the gauze on his upper arm. "It looks just like the fake blood, except it's not. Oh, Bubba, I'm sorry. I think people are just really ticked off about the thing with Kristoph and you're the one they're blaming."

Someone tried to murder me because I might have killed Kristoph? But the charges were dismissed! Wait, how does Simone know that?

"Let me just take the prosthesis before the staff whacks it off with a scalpel," she added, plopping a plastic box on top of his stomach and deftly opening it. It looked like a tackle box but had makeup accoutrements inside. "The clothing is history." She looked around and saw the pants in a neat pile on a table. "I can take those and I'll remove the jaw piece so we can use it again. I'm pretty sure we have a bunch of those shirts that we can use."

Simone got to work and then a person in scrubs came in to start an IV. Bubba would have scowled when he saw that it was Dee Dee Lacour, the dourest nurse on the face of the planet, but Simone had his jaw fixed in one hand.

"Oh, joy and wondrous felicitations," Dee Dee said sardonically when she saw Bubba. Her face was set in a perpetual glower. "It's Bubba Snoddy, the man who wants to ruin it for the rest of us."

Belatedly Bubba remembered that Doc had said that Dee Dee caught the acting bug. He could see how she might blame him for the potential loss of her fifteen minutes of fame. *Did Dee Dee have access to the weapon props? Hmm?*

"Just keep around his head," Dee Dee instructed Simone snidely, "so I can get this needle in him." She roughly rubbed some kind of orangish disinfectant on the back of his hand. Bubba thought she might be rubbing her way to China when she finally finished and deftly stabbed him with a needle appropriate for an African elephant. Without hesitation she finished connecting the IV and hung the bag on the pole attached to the bed. "Have a tetanus shot lately, Bubba?" she asked with just the right note of condescension.

Bubba shrugged. He couldn't remember anything about a tetanus shot.

"Great," Dee Dee said cheerfully, or as cheerfully as a woman of her sort could be, "that shot will sting like a son of a beach ball. Just wait until we're picking shot out of your shoulder. That'll really hurt."

Simone finished with the prosthesis and packed it away in a plastic bag. "There," she said. "Now you should be able to talk."

"Weebadoo," Bubba said.

"And there's a little more of that swelling," Simone said.

Dee Dee stared at Bubba's jaw. "I've got just the thing for that," she said wickedly. "Biggest gauge needle we have. It's like an ice pick. Be right back."

"I think I'll get out of here before that nurse decides to use a needle on me," Simone said, closing the lid of her kit. "Sorry about the shotgun holes in you, Bubba. Risley's all happy though, because it means more publicity for the film. He said to tell you that they'd shoot around you until you could film again, but I don't think that will be a big problem."

"Fahkah hee," Bubba said crankily. He was a little tired. He supposed the adrenalin rush was rapidly receding and he was starting to crash. He needed a glass of milk and a nap. What he really needed was to ask Doc Goodjoint if he'd determined a time of death for Kristoph, so he could eliminate suspects. Then he needed to ask Sheriff John or Willodean if the necktie they had talked about was really Schuler's scarf that he was missing and how that related to Kristoph's death. If Bubba could work in something about what was bothering Willodean, that would just be swell.

Bubba fell asleep before he could make any specific plans and he didn't even wake up when Dee Dee Lacour injected the tetanus shot directly into his gluteus Maximus.

●

"Are you a parking ticket, hotness? Because you have fine written all over you," someone said in a way that implied lechery, luridness, and hopefulness all wrapped up in a question and a brief statement. It almost made Bubba jealous because clever pick-up lines had never been his forte. His idea of being saucy involved a wink and a "Hey, you like catfish?" Truthfully though, he was only saucy with Willodean of late.

When Bubba opened his eyes a halo of light that brightened the entire room was centered over the dark haired, green eyed being that was...

"Wee-oh-dee," he said and then, "Cwah. I mean, cahh." His mouth was as dry as the Gobi Desert on a sunny day in a drought.

Bam Bam turned from where he was attempting to hit on Willodean Gray. Willodean transferred her solemn glance to Bubba and her expression didn't change.

190

Bubba sighed. She was beautiful and she could shoot a gun. What woman could be more perfect? She made him feel like he was a puppy dog who could pull a freight train. Except for now, he felt like a puppy dog unable even to pull his own leash.

"You be the deputy?" Bam Bam asked politely, the lechery, luridness, and hopefulness toned down. Possibly it was the holstered gun that made him slightly reticent.

"I be," Willodean agreed. "And you be?"

"I be Bam Bam Jones," he said, snapping out a card from seemingly nothingness. Willodean took it and looked at it once.

"You helped Bubba while he was in Dallas," Willodean said.

"Bubba talked about lil' ol' me?" Bam Bam grinned and even Bubba had to admit it was an infectious grin. "I knew he liked me a little." Willodean didn't say anything and Bam Bam shifted uncomfortably. "I guess I should go get some Mountain Dew," he said and sidled out the door.

Willodean looked back at Bubba.

Bubba gestured with his hand, beckoning her closer. She hesitated and then stepped up to the side of the bed. He took her hand with his right hand, the one with the IV, on account that his left arm was all strapped to his side now and he couldn't really move it. "Saw-ree," he said. He swallowed and tried to speak more coherently. "Tha makeup makes my skin swell up something fierce."

"That's what the doctor said," Willodean said. With her free hand she picked up a glass sitting on the little table and shook the straw around so that he could sip from it. "Also that they gave you some antihistamines and antibiotics and they got all the buckshot out. You slept through the procedure and the x-ray and them moving you up here." When Bubba was done with the water, he let

191

his head fall back and watched as she put the glass back on the table.

"Ain't bin sleeping good lately," Bubba said. He looked around. He had been moved to a regular hospital room. He was all bandaged up and had a new IV. The ceiling mounted television was on CNN. But all of that faded to the background as he watched the woman whose hand he held.

"Listen I'm sorry about what I said," Willodean said slowly. She pursed her lovely ruby lips and Bubba was entranced. "It didn't come out the way it should have and I had to leave for a day to get my head clear."

"About the...children," Bubba said tentatively. "I wasn't mad. I don't always make myself plain but mebe it's time for us to be talking about things like that." *That's good. Real good. Sounded adult. Sounded like I was opening a door and ready to let her in. Yep.*

There was obvious tension in Willodean's shoulders. *That's not good. What's bothering her?*

"You know I don't like seeing you in here," Willodean said. The unspoken part was "At least it wasn't my fault this time."

"Totally not *my* fault this time," Bubba said before he considered that it *might* be his fault. Certainly Simone had implied that he had been the target of someone who was mad that he might have killed Kristoph and thusly might have hurt the picture's staying power. But Bubba wondered if the killer might be thinking about stopping Bubba from getting too close to the solution. After all, Bam Bam was blaring it all over the countryside. *I would think a fella in his...special line of bizness would be more circumspect.*

"Sheriff John is talking to the special effects guy," Willodean said. "They're trying to figure out if it was an

192

unfortunate accident or deliberate. The special effects supervisor says they don't keep real ammo around...*ever*."

Which makes it lean to the side of deliberation, Bubba thought because he didn't want to emphasize it more to Willodean. She already knew.

"Everyone on the set has access to that area," Willodean added. "Well, practically everyone. All they would need would be a fresh set of shotgun shells."

"What gauge?"

"20," she said.

"Ma's got one of them," Bubba said woodenly. "So does half the county and their brothers, too. What about the necktie?"

"I don't wear a necktie," Willodean said immediately. The corners of her perfect mouth lifted just a touch.

Bubba took the moment to drag her hand close to his mouth where he pressed a kiss to it. He could see Willodean melting on the spot. He wished he wasn't lying on his back in a hospital bed and that he had a certain something he was going to give to her. But reality was the shift of heavy cotton sheets and the pull of a needle and tape in the back of his hand. This wasn't the place. This wasn't the time. Little cupids blowing trumpets from the corners wouldn't have made a hospital room the place or the time.

"Hey, baby, are you from McDonalds, because you are McGorgeous," Bam Bam said/asked an unseen someone outside the room.

Willodean blinked. "Does he memorize those?"

"Would it help ifin I memorized some?" Bubba asked optimistically.

They both heard the response to Bam Bam's hopeful query. "Good Lord, I'm old enough to be your mother," Miz Demetrice said.

"This should be interestin'," Bubba said. "Tell me about the necktie because I think it's really Schuler's scarf."

Willodean opened her mouth and then shut it. "Can't you keep out of it?"

"I got arrested for it," Bubba said, "how kin that not be my bizness?"

"The charges were dismissed," Willodean said.

"I dint turn over the body, so was there a scarf wrapped around Kristoph's neck?" Bubba persisted. If his mother made it past Bam Bam, it would be the end of his impromptu interrogation. Besides Willodean clearly felt guilty enough to give him a little information on the sly. "Then did someone stab him in the back to make certain he was well and truly dead?"

"All those arrests are making you crazy," Willodean stated. "Or have you been watching *Murder, She Wrote* reruns again?"

"Angela Lansbury's character solves everything all in sixty minutes," Bubba protested. "Forty-five ifin you don't count the commercials."

"You know the sheriff doesn't want you interfering," Willodean chastised.

Bubba stared at her. *Really? Seriously? How kin I not?*

"Oh, Lord Above save us," his mother said and saved Willodean from further questioning. It was obvious that Willodean was well aware of that fact. She strode over to the opposite side of the bed and stared down at Bubba. "You got shot." She looked at the ceiling as if in deep thought. "Has Bubba been shot before? Shot at, but never shot that I recall."

"It wasn't supposed to be loaded," Bubba said, "otherwise I reckon I would have ducked."

194

Miz Demetrice looked at Bubba, sighed, and looked at Willodean, and sighed again. His mother correctly assessed the air of discontent in the room and made an abrupt decision. Bam Bam appeared behind her holding a bottle of Mountain Dew. Miz Demetrice turned back to Bam Bam. "You," she said to him.

"Me?"

"You shall escort me to the cafeteria and tell me all the wondrous ways I remind you of something you'd like to...tap. Tell me, do I still qualify to be called a MILF?"

Bam Bam choked on his Mountain Dew. Miz Demetrice grinned. "Then I'll tell you all the ways I killed my late husband," she added.

"Did you have Lucky Charms for breakfast, " Bam Bam said as he led Miz Demetrice toward the door, "because you be looking magically delicious? Yo daddy must be a drug dealer, because you're dope. Know what's on the menu? Me N you."

A moment later, when they were finally alone, Bubba looked at Willodean. "Sheriff John said necktie. You said necktie. Doc said no necktie. I suspect scarf. And the only man around here, or woman for that matter, wearing a scarf that could be mistaken for a necktie is Schuler, the head of makeup and a man with a purple high top. And suddenly he ain't wearing that scarf no more."

"We're not going to talk about children?" she asked.

"Yes, we will talk about children," Bubba said. "Not today." It might have been a mistake but the larger problem was the fact that it was entirely likely that a murderer was actively trying to murder him. *Get past that and then get back to the issue of children.*

"It was a scarf," Willodean said, "and don't you dare tell Sheriff John who told you. You're going to get Doc and me into trouble."

"So was the scarf around Kristoph's neck?"

"Yes. Scarf around his neck, tight enough that someone might think he got strangled with it."

Bubba thought about those words. "Kristoph wasn't strangled to death?"

"No."

Bubba kissed Willodean's hand again. She tried to pull away, but it seemed halfhearted at best. "Sometimes you're as closemouthed as I am," he observed. "So someone *tried* to strangle Kristoph?"

"We don't think so."

"You have a time of death?"

"From four to seven p.m.," she said.

"Well, that doesn't narrow it down," Bubba said with sarcasm.

"I'm not in charge of time of death estimates," Willodean replied with equal sarcasm.

"So he was in my house for some time while I was outside scraping paint with Alfonzo," Bubba stated.

"That's what Alfonzo said."

Because Sheriff John and Willodean already checked my alibi. Bubba frowned. "Did you hear about the DEA?"

Willodean nodded. Suddenly there was a great deal of tension back in her shoulders.

"Did you know the DEA was coming?"

"They didn't deign to inform the locals," Willodean said and the words struck Bubba as careful and considered.

Bubba thought about it. "I don't believe my mother is smuggling drugs or anything else the DEA would be interested in."

"That's not something your mother would do," Willodean agreed.

Bubba rubbed her fingers with his own much larger ones. *Secrets everywhere and not a drop to drink. What does history tell us about secrets? It tells us that the man with the most secrets wins.*

"I don't suppose Kristoph's death has anything to do with whatever Ma and Alfonzo and you are up to." It wasn't exactly a question, but Bubba knew that Willodean would understand the gist.

"I don't think it does."

"Okay, that's good. Is what Ma's up to illegal?"

Willodean didn't answer that right away. Finally she nodded. "Very."

"Going to jail illegal?"

There was another nod without words.

"You could go to jail, too?"

A third nod.

"And ya'll don't want to tell me," Bubba said.

Willodean didn't nod. She stared at their joined hands.

"Okay, I kin probably help with it, ifin you change your mind." Bubba took a deep breath. "I reckon they'll let me out of here in a few hours."

"That's what the doctor said," Willodean said, and he could tell she was relieved that he wasn't pushing the issue.

That's what she thinks.

Chapter Seventeen

Bubba and the Problematical Pursuit

Wednesday, March 13th

The next day Bubba had been released from the hospital and was sorely contemplative. He sat on a chair on his tiny porch, drinking an RC Cola, thinking about going inside to get a Moon Pie, or maybe a Twinkie, to eat. (Not the reproduced kind of Twinkies but a *genuine* Twinkie hoarded from the days immediately preceding the discontinuance of the product. Miz Adelia couldn't stand the remade version. Bubba couldn't tell the difference, but she said it was glaring and that his taste buds must be as dead as the Dodo bird.) His left arm was in a sling and he watched as Alfonzo rolled paint on the side of the mansion.

Perhaps Bubba should be actively investigating or searching for clues about exactly what his mother was doing, but he couldn't bring himself to care much. He wasn't supposed to be any particular place at the time, Willodean was working, and the sun was shining. Sitting on the porch was the thing to do for the moment.

Alfonzo's two children played on a blanket under one of the oak trees. Pilar giggled and played patty cake games with one. Bubba studied the three on the blanket. He'd heard them go out again the night before. Rather, he'd heard the van start up and leave. He'd also heard them come back in right away and park again. He wondered if that was because a plain van was still parked at the end of the lane which had a satellite dish on top of it. It didn't say DEA on it, nor did it scream "WE ARE

WATCHING YOU!" but it might as well have. Every time Bubba drove past the two people sitting inside the van changed, but they all wore the same brand of sunglasses and dark jackets.

Great. Suspected of murder and now the DEA is practically parked on the front stoop. Bubba eyed the skies. *Next, a space station surely would crash on my new house.*

Bubba had heard the van start up in the early morning again. This time the engine hadn't moved down the long lane, but instead went down the two ruts that led past the swamp and through part of the rear forty acres of prime worthless land. Clearly Alfonzo had been instructed to use the back way. He'd taken his time, likely slowly to avoid the holes dug by common treasure hunters. Most people didn't know about the back way. Bubba had used it a time or two in high school. He seemed to remember his mother complaining about his father using it regularly, but then his father had been a hose monkey of the finest caliber.

Pilar lay on the blanket and pillowed her head on a folded sweater. The morning had started off in the fifties and was probably going to climb into the seventies. It was a mite warm for March and undeniably beautiful once the wind had stopped blowing. The babies loved it. One of them drank from a sippy cup with Spongebob Squarepants on the front. The other one swung a small branch around.

Precious had been chasing squirrels but stopped to collapse in the grass while she kept a wary eye on the floor apes that could come at her without warning.

One of the babies started to crawl for something Bubba couldn't identify. Her little hands and knees worked like a little powerhouse. Bubba waited but Pilar's eyes were shut. *I reckon it gets a little tiring to go out gallivanting all night. Shore tuckers a soul out.*

Bubba looked at Alfonzo. He was busy rolling paint. Bubba should be helping him but it was hard to hold onto a roller and a ladder at the same time with only one hand.

Bubba looked for his mother. She had checked his wound that morning but remained remarkably absent otherwise. *As if she's afraid of the questions I'll ask, hmm.*

After rising out of his chair, Bubba walked over to rescue the errant baby from a patch of sticky goat head. "Hey pumpkin," he said. He wasn't sure if the baby was Blanca or Carlotta. She looked up at him and said something like, "Boovadoo."

Bubba carefully gathered the baby in his good arm and settled her against his right side. She looked up at him with big...hazel eyes. *That's funny. I don't remember them having hazel eyes. Big brown eyes. Brown like Hershey's chocolate eyes.*

"Best to keep away from them plants," he said to the child, pointing awkwardly with his left hand. "*Afilado,*" he said, trying to remember the correct word in Spanish. "Uh, *penetrante.* Owie." He pretended to touch a plant and then yanked it back with an exaggerated yelp.

The baby giggled. Bubba carried her back to the blanket and sat down. The other child immediately gave up the Spongebob sippy cup and came to sit in his lap. It didn't matter; he had a lap big enough for two children. They proceeded to amuse themselves by pulling on his sling and yanking at his belt buckle. He took his keys out and divided them into two sets. The girls jingled and jangled to their little hearts' content. One cooed like a bird and happily blew spit bubbles.

After a while, Alfonzo looked over and visibly started. Bubba nearly cringed. He didn't want the man falling off the ladder. He waved because he didn't really want to wake Pilar up. Poor woman had a long night behind her. *Who knows where the Garcias are goin' tonight?*

Miz Demetrice came out of the mansion and brought a box of age appropriate toys for the children. There wasn't a single butcher knife to be found. She dragged a chair over and sat watching Bubba play with the girls. Little was said and Bubba was okay with that for the time being.

A half hour after that Miz Adelia brought lemonade and treats outside, carrying them on a silver tray. Alfonzo came down from the ladder and drank a glass and ate a sugar cookie. He lay beside his wife and watched the babies while rubbing one of Pilar's arms.

"I figure the DEA will be watching the other road tonight," Bubba said. He might as well be remarking that the weather looked good enough to go fishing on the lake. Bubba needed to go fishing. The fish probably missed him. After all, he fed them a lot of worms. Plus they also loved Velveeta Cheese balls.

Miz Demetrice crossed her ankles and soothed down her dress. Miz Adelia paused in giving a cookie to the older baby. Alfonzo's hand hesitated midstream.

"I kin show you the other road," Bubba said. "It'll be a tight squeeze in the van. Branches will scrape some, but it'll get you over by Sturgis Creek and then you can get down the road. Do you suppose them DEA people put some kind of tracker on your Dodge? I suppose I should look for something on there. Is that legal?"

"Bubba," his mother said politely, "wherever do you get your ideas?"

"Ma, please," he said solemnly. "You got Willodean all wrapped up in your shenanigans. It ain't done to be caught by a couple of folks who are so tight a corn cob couldn't be—"

"Bubba!" Miz Demetrice interrupted him.

"Just sayin'."

"*Gracias*," Alfonzo said.

They became aware of the sound of a car driving down the lane. Bubba didn't recognize the engine, so he tensed a little. Then a purple thing inched around the corner and parked itself next to his truck. They all watched entranced. Bubba had never seen one exactly like it before.

"Is that a...Gremlin?" Miz Demetrice asked with a note of awe.

"Yep." It *was* a Gremlin. A metallic sparkling purple AMC Gremlin with silver and purple trimmed rims for the wheels. Bubba didn't know what year it was because he didn't know much about that particular type of car, and this one had been somewhat modified. It had been lowered a tad in the front and had gold plated curb feelers on the sides. A pair of fuzzy dice hung from the rear view mirror.

Bam Bam Jones climbed from the Gremlin. He was wearing a Knicks shirt combined with shiny gray pants and black leather boots that were only ankle high for a change of pace. "Yo, Bubba," he said and his hands snapped and gesticulated wildly. "So this be the mansion."

"Bam Bam," Bubba said, "this is my mother, who you met yesterday. That's Miz Adelia, Alfonzo, Pilar, and their two daughters. Cain't remember which one is which." Bubba added the last part darkly with a quick glare at his mother, who went just a little pink in her cheeks. *Dint know Ma could still blush. Go figure.*

"A pleasure," Bam Bam said suavely. "I just be coming out here to see if Bubba needed anything, but of course, he does not with so many lovely ladies about to tend to his every need."

Pilar woke up at that moment and Alfonzo said something to her in Spanish. She blinked and rubbed her eyes.

Bam Bam knelt by one of the toddlers and said, "I get a toothache just by looking at you, my petite darling."

Blanca, Bubba thought it was Blanca, giggled. Even at her young age, she knew when she was being flirted with.

"And you," he said to Carlotta, "you be so beautiful that I forgot my pick-up line."

Carlotta grabbed her sippy cup and presented it to Bam Bam, who took it graciously.

"Ladies and gentlemen," Bam Bam said. "I must speak with Bubba about dem ugly matters of late." He handed the sippy cup to Pilar.

Bubba collected his discarded keys (The keys had lost to Bam Bam's contagious presence and the blinding motions of his nearly unstoppable hands.) and climbed to his feet. The two girls muttered tiredly but gave in graciously.

"Nap time," Pilar announced and pulled both girls into her arms with obvious skill that spoke of a long time with small children. Alfonzo returned to painting and Miz Demetrice and Miz Adelia wandered inside the mansion.

"Nice," Bam Bam said, looking around. "I'd say you be rich, but you ain't, not really."

"Not really. I got what I need." *Mostly,* he added silently. "Food on my table. Clothes on my back. A family."

Bam Bam nodded gravely. "Well. I spent the morning on the set. I tell you, these Hollywood types be busier than gals on Harry Hines Boulevard."

"Busy?"

"Biz-ah," Bam Bam confirmed. "I be asking questions all on the low down, and it ain't who knows what but who's doing who? Whom? Whatever."

"Which has what to do with Kristoph's death?"

"Well, Kristoph was doing McGeorge," Bam Bam said. "That's what everyone be saying. But then Marquita be doing someone. And they's married and all, so not all married folks are okay with their spouse doing someone else, so that's all that."

"So who was Marquita—" Bubba trailed off because he didn't really want to ask who was having sex with whom. It wasn't a manly question. In fact, it was a tacky question, even if Bam Bam was correct.

"Some say it be Alex Luis," Bam Bam said and motioned at the little caretaker's house, "that be the one that got rebuilt?"

"Yep," Bubba said. "You want some coffee? Or mebe an RC Cola?"

"RC Cola?" Bam Bam repeated thoughtfully as his hands snapped out intricate movements. "I ain't bin hit with that since I was a little kid, stealing cigarettes from the corner store. You bet." As they passed Precious, Bam Bam said to her, "Baby dog, did you eat Campbell's soup today because you are mmm-mmm-good?"

Wow, he's even got a pick-up line for my dog.

•

Bam Bam drank his RC Cola and burped vociferously. "Pardon me," he said. He pulled a little notepad out of his pocket. They sat at Bubba's small table in his kitchen because Bubba wanted to make sure that his mother couldn't approach and eavesdrop, or anyone else for that matter. *Who knows what the DEA can do with them listening devices?* Bubba nearly shuddered. *I'm starting to*

204

think like Newt Durley or Lloyd Goshorn. And I ain't even had a lick of 'shine to show for it.

Bam Bam touched an index finger to his tongue and began paging through his notepad. "I tole you about Marquita and Kristoph. Marquita is doin' something with someone but ain't no one for certain. Then Risley is doin' someone but he ain't married and Marquita is his sister so he ain't doin' it with her." Bam Bam paused. "No, no, no. No one said anything about that."

Bubba pushed a Moon Pie toward Bam Bam.

"Then there's this sound technician who's doin' it with a best boy and a key grip, at the same time," Bam Bam said. "They call it being polyamorous. They be doin' it all at the same time. That makes me wonder who's doin' what and to who? I mean, it's two men and a gal. If this one is doin' that, then what is the other one doin'? Bam Bam has an open mind and all, but I be thinking two is enough. Could be two boys. Could be two girls. But just two. Three sounds like something be wrong." He shook his head.

"What does that have to do with Kristoph's death?" Bubba asked. He couldn't imagine what three were supposed to do either, but he wasn't going to discuss it with another man. In fact, he couldn't think of who he would discuss it with.

Bam Bam frowned. "Nothing, I guess, but I be a people person, as you know and folks like to share. Sometimes they be sharing too much, but who am I to tell them to stop."

"Anything else?" Bubba asked, hoping Bam Bam would say no.

Bam Bam did not say no. He said, "That Tandy North is a wild girl. I don't think she's interested in boys or girls.

She just wants to play games and act and toke out. Cain't figure that girl."

"Did Kristoph give Tandy a hard time about the smoking?"

"Nope. She disappears and comes back happy. Uses a lot of eye drops, but theys used to that." Bam Bam touched his index finger to his tongue again and flipped more pages. "This fella likes to surf the net for porn. He was sitting in a chair using his Xoom right out in the open. Don't care who be walking behind him. I did give him a card so if he comes to the Big D, he can hook up with this phat girl I know, Sugar Passionsweet. I hear tell she can do things with her tongue that—"

"Bam Bam!" Bubba said.

"Okay, country boy," Bam Bam said. "I cain't help being all business like. Let's see." He flipped a few more pages. "There's that redheaded girl who's all executive like. She be sneaky. She saw me watching and she was gone faster than yesterday's wind. I think she be up to something, but I'll be danged if I know what."

"What about Schuler?" Bubba asked.

"Schuler," Bam Bam said. He flipped a few more pages. "He's a grumpy mutha. He went around tearing folks up. Said someone done stole something from him. The po-lice had him for an hour yesterday, asking him about the shotgun shells. You know, the ones that weren't supposed to be real. But your sheriff's deputy brought him back to the set and he seemed like he was in a good mood."

Bubba finished the rest of his RC Cola. Willodean had taken Schuler in for questioning, which was what Willodean would do. But was she questioning the head makeup artist about Bubba's shooting or about Kristoph's death or both? "That's pretty much nothing. I need to talk to Willodean again."

"I could go back to the set," Bam Bam said. "Try to pick up this, that, and the other. You never know when some dumb person is apt to confess that he shouldn't have tried to kill that person they tried to kill. I cain't talk about my work to my cousin on account that he's a patrolman in Alabama. We have these big family get-togethers and I have to pretend I own a fast food place or something. That be embarrassing. My auntie, she be all like, do I have to do what I do? I got great hours and I'm not living on the street. And most of what I do be legal. Mostly."

"Willodean said Kristoph's time of death was between four and seven p.m.," Bubba said. "Mebe ifin we find out where everyone was at during those times."

"I'll work on it, but my brotha, that ain't easy, asking questions like that. 'Baby, do your legs hurt from running through my dreams all night, and by the by, where you be between four and seven the other day?'" Bam Bam chuckled.

"This is what's gotta happen," Bubba said.

"Don't be fretting, my crazy-cracker-companion," Bam Bam soothed. "We'll find the perp and you be as free as a bird, and this movie will make 150 million, of which I will get a quarter percentage point. I done figured that out. Ifin the movie grosses 150 million, then I get 2.5 million out of 100 million profit. You know because the film be costing about 50 million and I be danged if I know what they spending it on."

Bubba glanced out the window and saw the Pegramville Department of Police vehicle pull up beside the Gremlin. Bam Bam saw it at the same time and said, "And that be my cue to leave your fine domicile." He stood up, snapped his hands, and offered a fist for Bubba to bump. He glanced at Precious, who was lying on her back in a sunny spot on the floor, "My gorgeous darling, it pains me grievously to part from your buxom being."

One of her back paws twitched. Like the Garcias' daughters, Precious knew a flirt when she heard one.

Bam Bam hurried out the door and slunk past Big Joe as he climbed out of his cruiser. Big Joe cast Bam Bam the big hairy eyeball, but didn't say anything as the other man rushed to the Gremlin. The large police officer simply watched as Bam Bam ground his gears once and then nearly backed over the pile of paint cans that Alfonzo had put nearby.

Of course when Bam Bam had driven away, Big Joe turned his attention to Bubba's house and to Bubba himself.

Lovely.

Chapter Eighteen

Bubba and the Iconic Investigation
And
Bubba and the Wondrous Willodean

Wednesday, March 13th

Big Joe sat in the same stool that Bam Bam had so recently vacated. (It wasn't all that strange because there were only two seats in his kitchen.) Bubba didn't offer Big Joe an RC Cola or a Moon Pie. Instead he sat on the opposite stool and adjusted the sling on his shoulder while the two of them got the staring over and done with.

"Joe," Bubba said finally. It was a comprehensive word. "What do you want?", "Why are you here?", "Are you going to arrest me?", and "I think your feet smell like limburger cheese." were all contained in the single word.

"Bubba," Joe responded in kind. Encompassed in his lone word were "I'm here to question you.", "You're still a redneck.", and "I don't know ifin I'm goin' to arrest you, but don't get too comfy."

"So, you got shot," Big Joe continued, breaking the monosyllabic conversation.

Bubba nodded, trying to compensate by saying nothing at all.

"I reckon you know it was likely on purpose," Big Joe went on.

Bubba nodded again. The conversation was getting lopsided, but he was determined to give it his best shot. (No pun intended.)

"I expect someone was right upset at you for killing the director," Big Joe said.

"I dint kill Kristoph," Bubba said immediately. He forgot all about the single word effort. "The charges were dismissed."

Big Joe nodded sagely. He was a big man as the moniker "Big Joe" implied. He wasn't as tall as Bubba, lacking only two inches in that department, but he was ten pounds heavier and his gut showed it. The people in Pegramville liked their law enforcement on the southern heavy side and Big Joe was a prime example of how southern and heavy a man could be. It was rumored that he loudly played Jim Nabors records to force his prisoners to confess. There had also been rumors of the police chief playing Justin Bieber singing "Baby" and, when he was particularly feeling obnoxious, any cut of the Spice Girls' larger-than-life collection.

"So where's the gruesome twosome with the steel tipped boots?" Bubba asked, referring to two of Big Joe's more enthusiastic officers, who had once kicked Bubba in the head with said footwear. It had never been definitely proven which one had accomplished the deed, but Bubba had always leaned toward Haynes. "My head don't feel right unlessin' one of them fellas is kickin' it."

Big Joe smiled. It was an unnerving smile. He had never liked Bubba, and specifically he had liked Bubba a whole lot less once Bubba had punched him in the face while distracting him. It had been a sleazy move, but Bubba still believed that it was something that had needed to be done. Lives had needed to be saved and Big Joe would have held Bubba back.

"Patrolling," Big Joe answered. "Lots of work on account of all them movie people. I'm surprised the film company stayed after the director got plugged."

Bubba knew that Big Joe was a little miffed because the case of Kristoph Thaddeus wasn't his. Kristoph had died in Pegram County, not in Pegramville proper and that made it a sheriff's department's case. However, Bubba's shooting *had* occurred in Pegramville High School, which was smack in the middle of Big Joe's jurisdiction. Big Joe had probably done a perky little dance when he heard, so that he could stick his interfering head right in the middle of Sheriff John's investigation.

"Uh huh," Bubba said. It was as noncommittal as he could get. Big Joe knew why the movie people had stayed just as much as Bubba knew. There were almost as many news people wandering around the streets as there had been after the Christmas Killer had instigated her bloody path of revenge. (That meant there were a lot.)

Precious click-clacked into the kitchen, looked at Big Joe, and a canine sneer crossed her face. She growled once and retreated for safer climes. She knew a flirt on first sight, but she also knew a walking, talking jack wagon, too.

Big Joe steepled his fingers. "Who you bin ticking off, boy?"

Bubba thought about it. "Lloyd Goshorn is still unhappy about me. I dint hit him with Roscoe's car, you know, but he seems to think it was personal. Jeffrey Carnicon wanted me to sign a petition about declaring the separation of church and state impenetrable, but I dint care for his wording, so I said no. He seemed a mite put out." Big Joe's mouth opened but Bubba went on. "That professor from Dallas keeps wanting to tear columns down from the mansion and he seems to think I should give him permission since Ma threatened to give him a 'rectal shotgunostomy.' But I don't want a rectal shotgunostomy anymore than that fella does so I said no and he left in a huff."

Big Joe chuckled once before he remembered he was supposed to be a dickhead.

Bubba went on, "Lurlene Grady, er Donna Hyatt, sent me a nasty letter from the women's prison. You remember her? She helped kill Melissa Dearman, my ex-fiancée and Neal Ledbetter, and had a map about where the Civil War gold was located. She would like it ifin I recanted and she threatened to 'get me.'"

"Found an old rusted car instead of the gold, dint they?" Big Joe asked reflectively. "Civil War gold would have been nice."

"Ain't no gold." Bubba nodded firmly because he was tired of saying that, and went on, "Then there's you."

"Me?"

"You ain't forgiven me for roundhousing you."

"Boy, ifin I hadn't forgiven you, you wouldn't be sitting here. You'd be in Huntsville. Don't matter a lick ifin you were goin' to save Jesus Christ from the cross, you still hit a law enforcement official. And in the great lone star state of Texas that is still a felony." Big Joe smiled again, proud of his statement.

"And I am grateful that you let that one go," Bubba said, attempting to add a note of contriteness.

Big Joe digested that for a long minute. "You tick anyone else off?"

"Not that I know about."

"What about the director's wife?"

"Marquita?"

"Someone said you and her were right friendly the other day," Big Joe said.

"I asked her about Kristoph," Bubba said. "She said I could look into it."

Big Joe snorted and unsteepled his fingers. "Does she know about your track record?"

Bubba shrugged. *Is there someone who doesn't know?*

"So you looked into it," Big Joe said. "You find anything? Mebe that's why someone's trying to shoot you while not actually shooting you? Would have been funny as hell ifin that cute little movie star had plugged you proper."

Bubba thought about it. The image of McGeorge with her funny little smile popped into his head. "Nothing springs to mind," he said and it was half a lie.

"You ain't playing tiddlywinks with...Marquita Thaddeus?"

Bubba was outraged. "I got a girlfriend," he protested. "Damn fine girlfriend."

"That's not what I hear," Big Joe said and looked at his fingernails as if contemplating a manicure. "Heard tell ya'll broke up."

Bubba wasn't sure how to take this. Sure, Mary Lou Treadwell had said something similar, but most of Pegram County made the fine art of gossiping seem like a trait learned right after they began to walk at a year old. Rumors got twisted around faster than green grass through a diarrheic goose. Willodean had been acting oddly. She had been avoiding him. She didn't answer her phone when she was off. She had seen him in the hospital and had offered to drive him home, but Bubba knew she was working.

Bubba knew very well that doubt was an ugly thing and the last thing he wanted to do was let Big Joe know that he'd hit the mark with his pesky little arrow.

"Besides Marquita Thaddeus is old enough to be my mother," Bubba stated steadfastly. "Good looking woman, but I like Willodean Gray just fine." *More than that, but I ain't saying it to Big Joe.*

213

Big Joe nodded knowingly. Between the shrewd affirmation and the Jim Nabors music, he probably had a very high rate of confessions. Even Bubba had a barely suppressed inclination to confess to something when Big Joe cast his unerring legal glance upon him. "I stole a piece of Bazooka Joe Bubble Gum from the corner grocery store!" Bubba thought he might yell if he didn't bite down on his lower lip. It didn't even matter that he had been nine years old and he had brought it back before he'd even opened it. The grocer had thought it was funny as heck. Bubba hadn't thought that cleaning the grocer's windows until his arms almost fell off was funny, but his mother wanted him to learn a lesson about consequences.

"So ain't no one you kin think of?" Big Joe asked.

Bubba shook his head. *McGeorge = funny little smile. McGeorge = access to special effects.* But then half the film crew had access to the special effects and weren't they a little more secure with the firearms? That was because it would hardly be the first time someone had been killed with something they'd thought was safe. A crew member had been talking about Bruce Lee's only son's death for that very same reason.

"The director fired the special effects guy and they brought on a licensed weapons specialist for the duration of the film," Big Joe said.

I expect that's a little late, Bubba thought a little mutinously.

"Mebe you should wear a bullet proof vest when you're filming, boy," Big Joe suggested. "Although you ain't my favorite person, a hole in you just ain't fun."

He stood up and towered over Bubba for a moment that the police chief clearly savored.

"I'll show myself out," Big Joe said. "Don't leave town for the time being."

214

"And where in hellfire do you think I'm goin'?" Bubba couldn't help himself from asking. "It ain't like I have a passport and a ticket to Rio."

Big Joe didn't reply but turned and walked out of the kitchen. Bubba heard the front door open and shut a moment later and watched as the police chief meandered out to his car. He paused to give Alfonzo an intense glance. Alfonzo was back at work on the mansion. The paint was starting to look good on the big house and Alfonzo was working hard. However, Pilar and the babies had remained inside. It was entirely likely that the two youngest Garcias were napping.

As Bubba was looking at the house, he saw the curtain twitch in an upper window. It was the red room on the third floor. The entire room was decorated in crimson and stayed that way for decades. A Snoddy ancestor (It had been a great, great grandfather, Bubba believed.) had kept his mistress in the room while his wife was dying in a second floor bedroom. The colors were fading and the gilt needed to be refinished, but it was a perfectly serviceable guest room that afforded the room's occupant, Pilar in this case, an unobstructed view of Bubba's house.

Bubba retrieved another RC Cola and popped the lid with his good hand.

Precious wandered in for a look and decided it was safe since Big Joe had departed the house. If she had known he was outside she probably would have gone to mark his tires, which was a habit of hers since she tended to make certain people she did not like were urinated upon.

Bubba had been told that female dogs do not mark items but clearly it had been from an individual who had never owned a canine of the feminine persuasion. He sat back at the table and looked out as Big Joe climbed into his patrol car.

As the official vehicle backed out, Bubba noticed the crimson curtain twitch again. Of course, these were people who were in collusion with his mother, Miz Adelia, and Willodean Gray. They took midnight trips down rutted lanes out the back way of the Snoddy Estate and avoided the DEA van parked in the front. Naturally, Pilar would be curious and cautious about who was coming and going on the Snoddy properties.

Bubba grunted. Alfonzo and Pilar were probably regretting the moment they climbed into bed with Miz Demetrice Snoddy.

Shaking his head, Bubba looked around. The world wasn't going to stop spinning on account of any issues he was having. He reached into his pocket and touched the check from the movie people. He'd found it when he'd cleaned out his shirt pockets. He'd forgotten to cash it and he needed to do it before something else happened.

Bubba grabbed his wallet and his truck keys. Precious heard the jingle and her head came up inquisitively. Bubba nodded. "Ride, girl?"

Oh, yes. Ride. Dogs love trucks.

●

The bank was open. People stared at Bubba and he pretended not to notice. He deposited the check into his checking account and took the receipt with the hand that wasn't restricted by a sling. When he returned to Ol' Green, Precious was resting her prodigious nose on her paws as she looked at chipmunks frolicking nearby.

Bubba saw a nondescript van parked across the street from the bank. It was about as obvious as a sore thumb among the plain sedans and plainer trucks in the vicinity. The driver was hidden behind a newspaper. Bubba could

216

tell it was the Pegram Herald, although he wasn't sure how much the driver was getting out of it since it was upside down.

Huh, he thought. *The DEA is following me now. One more thing on my big list. God,* he prayed to himself. *You, the God. I don't doubt that, and I know bad things happen to good people. All the time. Your testing of us. I totally get that. But God, I've already bin shot this week and arrested and in jail and I'm thinking my girl is getting ready to break up with me, so can you oh, cut me a little slack? Thanks in advance. Amen.*

With that thought, Bubba decided that he would find the girl in his head and demand that she eat some lunch with him so that he could cajole some answers from her. It took him about thirty minutes to find her out on the highway. She had pulled over Stella Lackey's Lincoln Continental. The Conny was in front, the Bronco, with its red and blue lights flashing, in the rear.

Bubba pulled in behind the Bronco, got out of his truck, and leaned against the door. Willodean stood beside Stella's car door using a gadget that looked like a cross between a remote control and a cell phone from the nineties. She looked back at Bubba only once, but that was enough to make him stay where he was. She didn't need his assistance with Stella and she didn't need any body language that implied that she needed his assistance.

"I know, Miz Lackey," Willodean was saying as she punched buttons on her device. "It's hard to do the speed limit when there's places to go, but having to go back home to get your dentures does not qualify as an emergency."

"That's because you don't got dentures," Stella retorted.

217

"Perhaps when I do have dentures, I'll understand," Willodean said soothingly. "In the meantime, would you really want to cause an accident because you couldn't chew your ribs at the restaurant?"

"Thems good ribs," Stella said, her voice a little more compliant.

"I'm sure the owner of The Hogfather's will put them in a to-go box," Willodean said. She was using her best calm voice. Bubba likened it to her school teacher voice. She was patient and she was willing to be polite, but she wasn't in the mood for nonsense.

"Don't taste right after it's gotten cold," Stella complained.

"You were doing 79 in a 55 zone, Miz Lackey," Willodean said. "That's almost 25 miles an hour above the speed limit. One more mile above that and it would have been a felony. What if you had caused an accident and gotten someone killed? Could you really live with that? Just because your ribs were getting cold. That's not worth it."

"I reckon you're right," Stella admitted. Then she grinned slyly. "Say, ain't you getting married to Bubba? I hear tell you have so many bridesmaids and groomsmen that you lost count."

Bubba hesitated in scratching his nose.

Willodean didn't say anything for a long moment. "That's just Lloyd Goshorn telling big stories, Miz Lackey. His stories get bigger and bigger the more drinks you pour into him."

"My son *was* buying," Stella admitted.

"Lloyd really needs to go into detox," Willodean said, "and he should probably stop telling stories, too." There was a whirling-clicking noise and Willodean handed something to Stella. "There. You're on the docket. If you want to take a defensive driver's course in lieu of paying the ticket, you can do so. This is your first ticket in over ten years, so that would be one way of getting out of paying for it, but it will cost to take the course and it's a full eight-hour day."

"Will there be men there?"

"It's my experience that there will be," Willodean said.

"Well, a widow like myself could always use a new way to meet men," Stella said and her tone was hopeful.

"Good luck, Miz Lackey," Willodean said, "and slow down, please."

The electronic window on the Lincoln Continental went up as Willodean walked back to her Bronco.

Bubba chewed on his lower lip. Now that he had Willodean to himself, he wasn't sure what he was supposed to say. He had asked God to cut him some slack and now that the slack was cut, he was at a loss.

Willodean glanced at him as she paused by the Bronco. She put the gadget inside the vehicle, turned off the dome lights, and simply looked at him.

"Lunch?" Bubba asked. "The Hogfather's sounds good right now."

The edges of her perfect mouth twitched just a little.

The Conny spit dirt as its wheels spun. Stella got the big car back on the highway with only a slight slide of the rear end as she gunned the big V8 motor. Willodean winced.

Chapter Nineteen

Bubba and the Winsome Willodean
And
Bubba and the Delightful DEA

Wednesday, March 13th

The Hogfather's was fairly crowded or everyone in the immediate vicinity had heard Bubba was taking Willodean to the locale and immediately rushed over to witness what might or might not happen. Bubba grimaced as every face turned in unison to watch them as he held the door open for Willodean. It was as if a spotlight suddenly settled upon them.

Bubba glared at their audience. Ted Andrews, Pegramville Fire Chief and general busybody, grinned broadly from a nearby table. He sat with Melvin Wetmore, a local mechanic Bubba had once worked with, and the Teasdales. The missus Teasdale was Miz Demetrice's sworn evil archenemy. (There had been a certain incident where both women had worn the exact same hat to a church function. Hat? Dress? Something like that. Words had ensued, which escalated into insults that respectable southerners and Texans would never repeat in polite company. Blood oaths had been sworn that they would never speak to each other again.) Bubba's mother would cross the street in order to avoid coming close to Susan Teasdale.

At another table the honorable Mayor John Leroy Jr. sat with Tandy North, Alex Luis and Risley Risto. Tandy blinked at Bubba and swatted the mayor's hand away from her thigh. Alex winked at Willodean, although it

220

might have been intended for Bubba. Risley's eyebrows lifted as if he was surprised to see Bubba alive and walking around. Then his eyes came to rest on Bubba's sling.

Nearby, Wallie, the construction contractor who'd built most of Bubba's new house, chewed on a rib while elbowing Wilma Rabsitt who then snarled at him. At the same table sat Alice and Ruby Mercer. The three women were all active participants in the Pegramville Women's Club and fervent gossips. The four of them at the table eyed Bubba and Willodean as if the pair was the main entrée and they had been marooned on a desert island for a long time.

There was even a group of zombies in one corner booth. It was somewhat difficult to tell where the fake blood ended and the barbeque sauce started.

A few people took their cellphones out and started tapping away in a way that was less than surreptitious. One even took a quick photo of Bubba and Willodean.

"Mebe we should go someplace a little less crowded," Bubba suggested.

"I'm hungry," Willodean said, glaring down the sisters Mercer with a single expressive look, "and I only have an hour."

And wasn't it interesting that two people cleared out a table just as the words came out of Willodean's perfect mouth.

Bubba glowered at the pair, Roy and Maude Chance, owners and editors of the Pegram Herald, moved to the counter with their plates. Roy said, "Get this to go, Jethro? We got a call about a story."

"Your cell phone dint ring," Bubba said darkly.

"It's on vibrate, Bubba," Roy said cheerfully. "Get your head out of that T-rex's ass."

Willodean tucked herself into the seat that Maude had vacated and presented her back to the remainder of the room.

Bubba sat down opposite her and looked out the window where Precious gazed longingly at the restaurant from the open window of the 1954 Chevy truck. Apparently, she knew what the giant neon pig in front of the building meant. So did the two men in identical sunglasses and jackets in the gray van parked three cars down from Bubba's truck. They had lost their insouciant expressions and looked somewhat famished. One said something excitedly, and Bubba didn't have to be a lip reader to understand that he was trying to convince the other one that they *needed* the Michael Corleone special featured on the great hog-shaped blackboard out front.

Bubba looked back and found that everyone in the restaurant had rearranged themselves to have Bubba and Willodean in their direct line of sight. Some of them had actually turned their chairs and slipped into already crowded bench seats so that they could eat and watch at the same time. It would have only been better if there had been popcorn, but Texas barbeque would have to suffice.

A waitress appeared and Willodean said, "Tea. Unsweetened tea."

"You don't want sweet tea?" the waitress asked. "But it's the best sweet tea in the—" Willodean turned her glare toward the waitress and the waitress said, "Unsweetened tea, oh-kay."

"The pork and chicken plate," Willodean added. "I want okra and the slaw on the side and make sure it's a big bowl of bread. Just go ahead and bring the butter out. The real stuff and I'm going to need several napkins so don't skimp. Then follow those suckers with peach

222

cobbler. Big scoop of vanilla on that." She tapped the table. "You want something to eat, Bubba?"

Bubba said, "Uh, you goin' to eat all that, Willodean?" Then he wished a bolt of lightning had just struck him instead of being allowed to open his mouth. "I mean, you don't usually...you don't, um." Perhaps someone would take pity on him and slit his throat on the spot. If he acted up enough perhaps the DEA guys out front would shoot him. Perhaps it would be in the head and someplace that would permanently shut his mouth. "I think I might have the special."

"Sides?" the waitress asked.

"Beans and potato salad and pardon me, do you have some pliers so I kin get my feet out of my mouth?"

"What?" the waitress stopped writing on her little pad to ask.

"The sausage special," Bubba said slowly. "Beans, and 'tato salad. Co-cola, ifin you have one cold in a bottle. No dessert for me."

Willodean sighed gustily.

"Or I could order the red velvet cake and share?" Bubba half asked.

"Shore nuff," the waitress said. "I'm Mamie and I'll be your waitress. We always make you an offer you cain't refuse and—"

Willodean looked at Mamie again. Mamie fled for the kitchen. After all, Willodean did have a loaded gun on her person. And a full container of mace. No one could forget the mace.

Bubba was no coward. "The only way this could be better is ifin Ma showed up," he said with a halfhearted chuckle.

Willodean gestured at the window. Bubba saw his mother's Cadillac pull into a space four cars down from the

DEA's van. She got out of the car. Then Alfonzo and Pilar got out of the car, too. They extracted babies from the car seats that had been transferred to Miz Demetrice's driving boat.

"I suppose that Mary Lou Treadwell spread the word when you called in your break," Bubba said.

"Mary Lou does have a big mouth," Willodean said agreeably.

Bubba looked around. He thought it might be cold inside the restaurant but it also might be the cloud of icy air surrounding Willodean. He wanted to say, "What'd I do?" but that was a tried and true method of self-immolation.

"Something wrong?" Bubba asked. It was all he could come up with.

"It's fine," Willodean said and his heart sank.

There was one thing he knew about women. One who answered with "fine" could mean three things. A). It really is fine. (Very unlikely.), B). I'm right. You're wrong. (Significantly more common.), or C). If you continue along this present discourse, the world will end as we know it and you will be a puddle of nonexistence Bubba goo. (This was something that happened more than Bubba liked to admit. He had had an ex-fiancée and had lived with her for a number of months.)

"It ain't fine," he said. It was an expected answer. "I cain't do anything about it ifin I don't know what the problem is. Is it because of what I said about kids?"

Mamie brought the bread, butter, and drinks and Bubba's mouth snapped shut. She scuttled off as soon as Willodean cast her green eyes upon her again. Behind Willodean Bubba could see everyone in the restaurant leaning forward incrementally in order to hear better. He would have glowered at them but he didn't want Willodean to think that he was glowering at her.

The door opened and his mother came in, followed by the Garcias and their children. Bubba pretended not to notice. Willodean smiled wanly and waved.

It was to his mother's credit that Miz Demetrice headed for the opposite side of the restaurant. Bubba looked around the restaurant, pulling at his shirt collar. First it was cold in the place, then it was blazing hot. He thought he might be going through menopause except there was an integral problem with that theory. (He was way too young, and oh, yes, more importantly not a woman.)

The door opened again and the pair of DEA agents crossed the threshold. They sat at the counter on the far side probably so they could order and watch Bubba at the same time. They must have been happy that his mother and the Garcias had come into the same restaurant at the same time. Or perhaps they were thinking that it was a big conspiracy and The Hogfather's was the in place to smuggle...what? Pigs feet? Pork ribs? The secret recipe to The Hogfather's prize winning barbeque sauce and rub?

"No," she said.

Now what does that mean? Bubba asked himself. *It could mean "No." Or it could mean "Yes, but I'm not telling you." Or it could mean "You couldn't be more wrong and I hate you."*

Using a bread knife, Willodean slathered butter on a roll and began to eat. Bubba watched with fascination. Typically Willodean didn't eat half of what he ate. But if she was really angry with him she wouldn't be eating with him at all. *That had to be something good, right?*

"Herb butter," she said around a mouthful.

Bubba took a slug from the bottle. It was icy cold and just what the doctor ordered. He was hungry but he wasn't sure he could eat. His stomach was in knots. Relationships were hard.

Willodean buttered another roll and handed it to him.

She seemed to be waiting for him to do something.

Bubba thought about something he could do. But there was the huge, looming, lurking "but" hanging out in the corner like a mutated, irradiated albino elephant. It was the wrong place. It was even worse than in the cemetery with a swathe of zombies lurking about them. They sat in a barbeque joint called The Hogfather's with thirty people staring at them and he didn't have a clean shirt on. There was no way in hell he would be saying something to her now. Furthermore, he could still be in danger and he didn't want to put her in the way. In fact, he shouldn't even be eating out with her in public.

"It's not bad," Willodean said as she watched his face go through a series of expressions. It took him a moment to realize she was talking about the bread and butter.

"It's good," Bubba said and swallowed a lump of half-chewed roll. It could have been a mouthful of dirt for all he noticed. "Kin we talk about it?"

"Talk about what?" Willodean asked and her eyes slid away.

"Something's bothering you," Bubba said. "I want to help."

The plates arrived. Mamie set them down in various available locations on the table. It was difficult to find room because the ribs and chicken each had their own plate as did the sausage and each of the sides. The table filled up quickly. Bubba looked up because it seemed as though Mamie was pulling the plates out of thin air. Somehow she had managed to carry seven plates, napkins, and a bottle of Tabasco without dropping anything. There was a woman who deserved a tip or possibly a job in a circus show.

Willodean murmured appreciatively and dug into her chicken. Bubba poked his sausage. He sniffed. It smelled good. He looked to one side. Precious had managed to get out of the truck and was leaning against the window nearest to Bubba, front paws on the glass. She also pressed her nose against the glass. Her tongue resembled a transmogrified alien slug intent on consuming the pane by disintegrating it with her transmuted, extraterrestrial mollusk slobber.

Bubba looked up again and saw that a few people had lost interest. There was a bit of whispering and poking, but some folks had gone back to their conversations and their supper as if the big excitement had been called off. The DEA agents still stared at Bubba, although it was a little difficult to tell because they still wore their matching sunglasses. Mamie brought the agents a glass of milk and a glass of iced tea. *Might be sweet tea or not.*

Bubba heard the door open again and saw his mother exiting the restaurant. She whistled for Precious and Precious went like a shot, ever hopeful. Bubba poked his sausage again. *Think, stupid,* he told himself. *Say something wonderful. Say something meaningful. Say anything.*

"You have the most perty lips," he said.

Willodean had a piece of chicken in her hand. She had tucked a napkin into her collar to protect her work shirt from accidental hits and a dollop of sauce immediately fell there. "And I think your eyes are the nicest shade of blue," she said wryly. She pointed with her chicken. "Your mother just put your dog into her Caddy."

Bubba glanced at Miz Demetrice. The woman petted Precious and then took something out of her car. She shut the door while making sure to leave the window open for the dog, and Bubba could almost hear her promising to bring Precious some sausage if she was a good dog and stayed there. He blinked. "Yeah, I should have done that," he admitted, but he had been lost in thought. Too much was happening at once as tended to be the case.

A Smart car pulled up and he saw that it still wore the Jolly Roger wraps. It probably was a pain to get those decals off a car like that and put on something that denoted normality. David Beathard climbed out and waved at Miz Demetrice. David was still dressed like Mr. Rogers and Bubba supposed that was a good thing. Then Bam Bam Jones clambered out of the other side of the car. Bam Bam was not dressed like Mr. Rogers. In fact, he was the polar opposite of what Mr. Rogers would dress like.

Bubba would have groaned if he thought it would have helped. The loony from the Dogley Institute of Mental Well-Being and the street pimp from Dallas together and ready to find out who really did the wretched deed to Kristoph Thaddeus, famous movie director.

"Oh, the fried okra is divine," Willodean said, inhaling some of the cut up and deep-fried vegetables as if she was a Hoover.

Miz Demetrice passed the window near their booth, and it had occurred to him that she had taken something over to his truck, opened the passenger door, and put it inside. *Now why dint she put my dog back in my truck?*

Then his mother paused in front of the restaurant to pull her cellphone out of her purse. She glanced at the window and caught Bubba's eyes. Then she shrugged apologetically. He wasn't sure what she was being apologetic about.

Why hadn't the two DEA agents sitting at the counter seen what she had done? *Why, because they're eating bread and staring at Bam Bam and David.*

"And the slaw. Yum," Willodean said, holding a fork in her hand. "I wish I could eat with both hands."

Bubba frowned. Ma began to punch digits on the phone. She deliberately turned her back on the window as she made her call.

"More bread," Willodean said. "Are you going to eat that sausage?"

Bubba wasn't normally disinterested in food but it wasn't really calling his name at the moment. Willodean simply pulled his plate over to hers and stabbed one of the sausages. "Go ahead," he said a little late.

Bubba transferred his attention back to the window.

The door opened again and David Beathard entered, accompanied by Bam Bam. Bubba glanced at them but hoped they wouldn't join them. David grinned and waved and tugged Bam Bam toward a table that had just opened up. "You've got to try to the Don Vito," David said as he pulled.

"The Don Vito?" Bam Bam repeated.

"It's the ultimate sandwich. Pork, chicken, sausage. Killer," David said.

"Oh, *The Hogfather's*," Bam Bam said understandingly. "I done got it. It's like that movie, right? Except with food. They don't serve horse meat here, do they?"

"No horse meat. They have the Sonny Soup and the Fredo Surprise, too," David said. "You'll like this table better."

"But Bubba be over there," Bam Bam protested, "and I gots to speak with him."

"You can talk to him after lunch," David said. He lowered his voice, but Bubba could hear it anyway, "He's with his *irlfriendgay.*"

Bam Bam stopped to stare. "That mama's so fine it hurts to look at her."

"Come on," David said with one more pull.

"They got lemonade here?" Bam Bam asked.

Bubba looked at his mother again. She had finished her conversation and was putting her cellphone back into her purse. She glanced at him before she turned back to the door. She wasn't going to look at him anymore. It was a big warning flag. She reentered the restaurant without saying anything to her only son.

"Somethin' goin' on with Ma, today?" Bubba asked Willodean once Miz Demetrice was out of earshot.

Willodean swallowed a bite of sausage and said, "Um. There's just a little thing." Her eyes came up and caught Bubba's. "Are you sure you don't walk to talk about what's bothering me instead of what's bothering your mother?"

Sighing, Bubba wanted to bang his head on the table. It sounded better than it would actually feel. "Is what Ma's doin' the thing that's bothering you?"

"No," Willodean said.

Mebe I should be asking open-ended questions instead of yes-no questions.

"I love you," he said instead.

Willodean dropped her fork. Slowly her head came up.

"I want to make things right," he added. "Ain't a mind reader, though. I'd buy you flowers but I just bought you flowers and you thought I'd swiped them from the cemetery."

230

Willodean grimaced. "Sorry," she said. "I shouldn't have said that."

This ain't the right place, Bubba told himself. *Don't do it, dumbass.*

His mouth opened and outside the window, a black SUV suddenly pulled up and screeched to a halt behind his green truck. Its wheels squealed to a halt in the gravel parking area. Half the occupants of the restaurant turned to look. Special Agent Warley Smith got out of the SUV and went to the truck. He peered into the open window of the passenger side. He tilted his head and turned it this way and that.

After a long moment, he called another agent over.

Then the two agents inside the restaurant sighed loudly and got up. One tossed two twenty dollar bills on the counter and looked longingly at the remainder of his meal. They trudged past Bubba and went outside to confer with the rest of their brethren.

Willodean turned her head to watch. "DEA again," she said. "What the goat cheese, Bubba?"

Agent Smith put on plastic disposable gloves, opened the truck's door, and extracted a package the size of a ten pound bag of flour from the interior. It looked like a white substance that had been enclosed in clear wrap and packing tape. Another agent held a large plastic baggie, into which the item was deposited. Agent Smith used a black Sharpie to write something on the large baggie. The other agent took the baggie and went to the SUV.

Agent Smith turned toward the restaurant and grinned at all of the observers. He saw Bubba and Bubba wanted to turn to stare at his mother, but he didn't want to give her away.

Bam Bam said loudly, "There be a back way to this place?"

"Bubba," Willodean said, "what did you do?"

"Who me?" Bubba asked innocently. The Agent Smith came into The Hogfather's and arrested him.

Chapter Twenty

Bubba and the Contumacious Constabulary

Wednesday, March 13th

Agent Smith handcuffed a nonresistant Bubba and led him out to the official DEA SUV. Bubba apologized to Willodean for interrupting their lunch and glared at his mother as he went out. Miz Demetrice looked innocently at the ceiling fan above her. Smith got Bubba into the back seat and slid in beside him. Another agent got into the driver's seat and started the vehicle up.

They left The Hogfather's immediately. It became apparent that they were headed into Pegramville and Bubba wasn't surprised when they pulled up in front of the Pegramville Police Department. Big Joe had been very happy to loan the DEA a room while they did their interrogational thing.

By the time Bubba got to Big Joe's lair, he was seething. He sat in an interrogation room, waiting for Agent Smith to get his ducks in a row while he thought about why it was that he was, in fact, sitting there. Bubba's mother, his very own flesh and blood, had systematically and deliberately set him up. She had put his dog in her Caddy. She had taken the package out of the Caddy. She had put the package into Bubba's truck. Then, she had probably called the police department with an anonymous tip. (That was Bubba's best guess of who she had called on the cellphone. *Wait until they trace your cellphone, Ma. Mebe you should have taken a class in technology instead of that quilting course last semester, huh?*)

While Bubba was sitting there, one of his handcuffs attached to the table which was, in turn, attached to the floor, he just knew his mother was making her getaway. She was probably taking the Garcias. How had his mother known where he was located? Well, he could probably thank Mary Lou Treadwell for that little tidbit.

It hadn't been Willodean because Bubba had seen the look of amazement on her face. She'd been surprised. Miz Demetrice had not been. His mother had been measured and insidious. Sometimes Bubba wished he had inherited that gene but it had passed him by. He especially wished he had it at the moment where he was planning his revenge.

Oh Bubba had an idea of what had really happened. His mother had thrown him to the wolves so she could do something in relative obscurity. While the DEA was focused on Bubba and a packing tape-wrapped package of something white and fluffy, she was likely doing the thing that she didn't want to get caught doing. At Bubba's expense and with great glee and afore malice in her heart.

Bubba could be investigating Kristoph's death or getting to the bottom of the Willodean problem, but instead he was handcuffed to a table, looking at a mirror that he knew was one-way. He thought about picking his nose and flicking a booger at the mirror, but that really wasn't his style.

Ma is goin' to have to do some fancy footwork to get out of this one, he thought.

Agent Smith came into the room holding a clipboard and an expensive pen. He paused beside the table, probably for effect. Bubba leaned his head down so he could reach his fingers that were limited by the handcuffed wrists. He scratched the side of his nose and then his head.

"So Bubba Nathanial Snoddy," Agent Smith said, "I think you would like to make a deal. You know what they say about people who make the deals first?"

Bubba did not know what they said about people who made the deals first. Agent Smith was willing to fill the blank without waiting for Bubba's answer.

"They get the *best* deals and *only* deals," Agent Smith said.

"You know, Warley sounds a mite too close to Wartly," Bubba said. "Is that what they used to call you in elementary school? I thought I got teased about Snoddy, but that ain't nothing on Wartly."

Bubba heard faint laughter. Whoever was watching on the other side of the one-way mirror was chuckling. It sounded a little like Sheriff John.

Smith turned an unbecoming shade of pink that started high on his cheekbones and went down to his chin. Then his chin turned pink. It was kind of like a person with rosacea, splotchy and high pink.

"We know everything," Smith said arrogantly. The agent couldn't quite pull the statement off with the pink cheekbones and chin. It simply didn't look correct. He should have had one of those waxed mustaches that he could spin with his index finger and thumb while he made his aggrandized statement that was obviously a big fat lie.

"Everything?" Bubba repeated. "Then you know about the time we did you-know-what to you-know-who." He shook his head sadly. "That was a terrible day. I was ashamed to admit I had done it. But what else you goin' to do when you have a Big Wheel, duct tape, and a gallon of moonshine, I ask you?"

"Your mother is the ringleader, isn't she?"

"Frequently," Bubba said. "She's an instigator, too."

235

Agent Smith made a notation with his pen. He looked up. The pink was fading fast. "We're aware of your association with the crime lord in Dallas known as Big Mama. Her warehouse was under surveillance when you visited her there some time ago."

Big Mama was a friend of his mother's. Big Mama had sent her son and nephew looking for Bubba while he was rushing around Dallas looking for Willodean Gray. The fact that Big Mama was also a crime lord was incidental to Miz Demetrice. They played poker together upon occasion. Sometimes Big Mama was up in winnings. Sometimes Miz Demetrice was up, but always they were on friendly terms. Big Mama also could make a good pot of gumbo. Better than Miz Adelia's, but Bubba would never tell the housekeeper that. *God forbid.*

Agent Smith produced a photo and shoved it across the table toward Bubba. It came to a crooked halt in front of him, revealing that Agent Smith was very good at sliding photographs across interrogation room tables. The photograph was a grainy black and white shot, obviously taken from outside a window. It showed Bubba, the Purple Singapore Sling, Janie, and Big Mama sitting around a table inside the warehouse. Bubba remembered the occasion very well.

"Who's the man in purple?" Smith asked. "Is he your connection from Asia?"

Singapore was in Asia, right? Bubba nodded. "They call him...the PSS."

"And the little girl? What's her role in all this? A juvenile criminal mastermind?"

"She just wanted to tag along," Bubba said. Janie was Willodean's eight-year-old niece and a devotee of all things police. After all, pretty much everyone in her family was in the police department or some various thereof. At the time Janie thought trailing after Bubba was the way to find her beloved Auntie Wills. That had been true. Kind of. "She's not involved. I dropped her off at her granny's house after that."

"Do you distribute for Big Mama?" Smith asked. "Did the missing boot have anything to do with it?"

Oh, how to answer that? "I've only seen Big Mama once," Bubba said. *I was kidnapped by her son and nephew. There was gumbo. When I got back to my truck there was a boot on my tire, so I took it off. It wasn't really much of a thing and I paid for the boot.* "Did you know Big Mama drives a Toyota Prius? She says the gas mileage is kickin'. It's hard to imagine a woman like that in a Toyota Prius. Doesn't fit her image, you know?"

Smith's eyes narrowed.

"Can I have a phone call now?" Bubba asked.

Smith nodded and reached into his jacket. He pulled out a cellphone and slid it across the table to Bubba. Bubba caught it awkwardly with his hands. He swiped his finger across the screen to unlock it, pleasantly surprised he was able to remember how to accomplish the task. Then he punched numbers in and hit the send button. He bowed his head down close to the phone while numbers clicked and a tone sounded. He glanced up to see that Smith watched from across the table.

Bubba put the whole thing on speaker phone. It was just easier since his head wouldn't quite reach the phone.

The phone on the other end rang twice. "Snoddy Mansion," a woman said.

"Ma," Bubba said.

"Bubba," his mother said.

"I'm still with the DEA," he said darkly. "We're having a conversation. You know, about things."

"Is that so, dearest?"

"You're not picketing today?"

"The weather is a little trifling."

"I see. Can you take Precious to the movie set? Schuler, that's the makeup fella, wanted to shoot a few more scenes with her. In all this excitement, I plumb forgot. I'd hate to let the dog down when she could be a big movie star. Kind of like that Spuds MacKenzie."

"They're over by the Boomer Farm again, is that right?"

"I reckon so. So hello to them film peoples. Bring some treats for Precious in case she has a mind to bite someone. Seeing as how she dint get no barbeque sauce she might be a mite testy."

"Surely," his mother said. There was an obvious note of wariness in her voice.

"Got to go now, Ma. This fella, Smith, wants to ask more questions. You know, about stuff."

Bubba pushed the end button and slid the phone back to Smith.

"You wanted to tell your mother to get your dog to the set," Smith said blankly. "Is that code for hide the drugs?"

"No, the fella who took over for the dead director wants Precious in the movie because he loves dogs. You know Basset hounds have a kind of wide-eyed, dead look to begin with. All that jowly skin, and all."

"Uh-huh," Smith said and put the phone into his jacket pocket. "Now tell me more about the PSS."

"He likes purple. He even wears purple underwear. I bet you didn't know that you cain't buy purple underwear in men's sizes, so he wears women's underwear."

"He's a cross dresser?"

"No, just the underwear. Although he doesn't use that persona anymore."

238

"Persona?" Smith jumped on that with all four feet. "Is that his disguise to keep people from knowing what he's really up to? A drug lord persona?"

"I don't reckon he really wants to keep people from knowing what he's up to," Bubba said. "The PSS don't think like that. He just wanted to be a superhero. He was helping me find Willodean Gray. He done told this one gal he could read her mind and, do you know what, she told him exactly what we wanted to know. I don't believe he could actually read her mind."

"The deputy," Smith said. "Is she involved?"

Bubba frowned. "Willodean was missing at the time. Kidnapped by this fella who was the brother of the Christmas Killer."

Smith frowned back. "Let's start from the top."

About an hour later, when Bubba explained to Agent Smith the difference between being involved with a crime lord in Dallas and being kidnapped by her son and nephew, another agent knocked on the door. Smith had discarded his jacket by that time. His necktie was loosened and his cuffs were unbuttoned. He'd jotted three pages of notes and Bubba was wondering when Smith was going to realize that he wasn't actually getting any "real" information.

The other agent opened the door about a foot and gestured at Smith. Smith got up from his seat and went to confer with the man. The man said something. Smith said something sharply. The man repeated himself. Smith said a four-lettered word and then asked the man to repeat himself.

Bubba heard it that time.

"—self-rising, whole wheat flour," the other agent said again. Then he said something that ended with "—used a disposable burner phone for the tip."

239

Bubba nodded. He rattled the handcuffs. *So Ma had a burner phone for emergencies. Oh, that sneaky woman.*

Agent Smith swung around and stared at Bubba. "Do you have any reason to be carrying a packing tape-wrapped package of self-rising, whole wheat flour under your bench seat of your truck?"

"You never know when you might want to make a loaf of bread?" Bubba said weakly.

•

Sheriff John was waiting for Bubba when the DEA officials, all of whom were furious, cut him loose. Agent Smith had developed an interesting ability to open and shut his mouth without actually saying any words and had turned pink again. This time it went down his neck and disappeared into his chest, from what Bubba could see of the unbuttoned button-down shirt. But the DEA agents didn't say anything else as they did the paperwork to release him. Bubba saw all the special agents watching him as he left, and he heard Big Joe guffawing all the way down the hall.

The sun was shining outside and Bubba looked up. His truck had been towed to the police impound lot. Agent Smith had thoughtfully given Bubba the paperwork that said in complicated legalese that he could collect it when he was of a mind. No fee. At the moment, he didn't have a ride and he was too ticked with his mother to call her. Furthermore, he was confused about Willodean. Finally, he didn't know what had happened to Kristoph except that it had been in his house.

Bubba wanted to blow a long and loud raspberry. That would sum things up appropriately.

"Say, Bubba," Sheriff John said. His voice was husky, like grated stone being run through a rock crusher as a result of being hung by the neck by a homicidal maniac. Fortunately he had been rescued in the nick of time.

Bubba turned to see the big man leaning against the wall of the police department. Still very much gray in color, John Headrick still exuded an aura of power that he used effectively in the execution of his job. There was a reason the county kept reelecting him. Bubba kind of liked the sheriff himself, but only in a manly, masculine, respectful manner, and not when Bubba was being thrown into the jail.

"John," Bubba said. He could have asked if Sheriff John knew what was going on. The DEA might be working with both Big Joe and Sheriff John. It wouldn't be abnormal to garner information from local law enforcement. But Sheriff John wouldn't talk about that.

"I figured they would cut you loose about dinner time," Sheriff John said, stepping away from the wall. "And Gray's busy with a car wreck out on the highway, so I thought I could run you home."

"You figured," Bubba said.

"That fella that does the testing for narcotics might have let something slip about oh, a product containing 0.0 percent illegal drugs." John chuckled darkly. "He done tole Mary Lou Treadwell that he ain't never seen something with that little amount of drugs in it that was actually associated with a narcotics case. There was something said about finding more drugs in a convent than in that bag they took out of your truck."

Bubba had to think about it. "I reckon they couldn't hold me for having a bag of flour in my truck."

"I reckon," Sheriff John agreed. He gestured at the official Bronco parked down the block and Bubba followed him there.

Bubba couldn't help but notice that there wasn't a crowd to see him being released because there was no evidence that he had done anything wrong. His only error had been to be in the wrong place as his mother.

Once they were inside the Bronco and Bubba was getting used to sitting in the front for a change, Sheriff John said, "I suspect your mother is up to something."

Bubba grunted noncommittally. It was best in the situation not to acknowledge anything, lest it be used against him later.

"Half the people at The Hogfather's saw her putting somethin' in your truck," Sheriff John added. "'Cepting the two DEA agents who were following you."

"Ma don't need my permission to get into my truck," Bubba said and thought, *But she's goin' to from now on.* "Besides, the locks don't work on the truck no how. Anyone who tries to steal that truck will have to know how to prime the carburetor and good luck with that."

"You know I think highly of your mother," Sheriff John said.

I didn't know that.

"And you, too. Despite a slew of problems over the last few years, you've held yourself up to a standard that few people could have done. I don't know what I would have done ifin I had been in your shoes."

"A man's got to live the way he wants to be remembered," Bubba said. "Ain't no shame in circumstances beyond his control. But ifin he wants to look Saint Peter in the face on that certain day, a fella can control the way he reacts." *That even works for me...sometimes.*

"I figure your ma used you as a distraction," Sheriff John said. "Perty cold thing to do to your only son, but if I know Miz D, then it was because she believed that something was important enough to do so."

That's about right, Bubba thought sourly.

"And I figure that you dint know in advance. Gray said you were…somewhat dismayed." Sheriff John started up the Bronco. "Fasten your belt," he instructed.

Bubba struggled with it for a moment because the sling was in the way, until Sheriff John gave him a hand. *What good would it do anyone to say I was hoodwinked by my own mother, who probably has some very good damn reason for doin' what she done?*

"What about the investigation into Kristoph's death?" Bubba asked. He had a captive law enforcement audience right there and would have him for approximately ten minutes.

"What about it?" Sheriff John asked in his best I-don't-know-what-you're-talking-about voice.

"You figure it out?"

"Not exactly," Sheriff John backed out, looking behind him. "It ain't just open and shut."

"What do you got?"

"Marquita was the last one to see Kristoph in your house," Sheriff John said. "Kristoph had a thing about always looking for something new to film in. So I think he and she walked right into your house. Then she says they got into a tiff. Her words. A tiff. She left. He was fine and dandy when she left."

"Believe her?"

"Polygraph indicates she was telling the truth. Besides Kristoph had a will. His stuff goes to his kids. Marquita's got her own money. A lot of it, too."

Bubba chewed on his lower lip. Marquita was a prime suspect even though she seemed really interested in finding out who had killed her husband. It was always difficult to mark through a name on a man's list of suspects when the pickings were slim.

"Then your ma saw her at the mansion about the time of death, but of course, the TOD is way too arbitrary. I think we can rule the wife out. I don't believe your mother or Miz Adelia would have kilt the director. At least they wouldn't have put a knife in his back." Sheriff John chuckled. "In his front, mebe. Prolly with a cannon straight on through."

"But the knife dint kill him," Bubba said and wished he had kept his mouth shut.

Sheriff John glanced at him. "Someone's had loose lips. Not Gray, though, am I right?"

Bubba didn't say anything. Then he asked, "What about the scarf?"

Sheriff John mumbled under his breath. It sounded like "Lord, save me from amateurs." "We ain't quite figured things out yet."

"The film wraps next week," Bubba said, "and they'll roll outta here, leaving you as the man who couldn't figure out who done in the famous movie director."

"I know that," Sheriff John said. "I bin called by each and every member of the town council, the mayor, and twenty-three other concerned citizens, including your esteemed mother."

"Only them?"

"The week's only half over."

"Schuler pass his polygraph?"

"Says they're unreliable."

"Huh."

"Ain't a law against refusing to take a polygraph," Sheriff John said, "although mebe there should be."

They reached the long driveway of the Snoddy Estate and Sheriff John turned the Bronco down it. After two more minutes he pulled up in front of Bubba's house. They passed his mother's Cadillac and the Garcias' minivan.

Bubba climbed out and nodded at the sheriff.

Sheriff John backed up and paused to yell out of his window. "Stay out of trouble, Bubba!"

Bubba watched the Bronco return the way it had come. His shoulders slumped. He was tired, hungry, and had a sense of inadequacy that permeated every inch of his being. Then he glanced up and saw the curtain of the red room twitch.

Bubba's head tilted curiously.

Chapter Twenty-one

Bubba and the Shady Suspects

Thursday, March 14th

Bubba woke up to the sound of yelling outside his house. He peered out the window and saw Marquita shouting at Risley.

It was true. The film crew had returned to the scene of the crime. Vans were parked around the front of the mansion and people moved in a coordinated effort to get the set into working order. Most of them seemed to be steadfastly ignoring Marquita and Risley. Clearly the pair had moved away from the main group in order to secure a modicum of privacy, something which the whole yelling thing had negated.

He rubbed his eyes and raised the window so he could shamelessly eavesdrop. Since it was a new, it opened nearly soundlessly, which he admired tremendously. Sometimes it was appropriate to appreciate the little things in life.

"Kristoph wouldn't have wanted you to do it that way!" Marquita yelled.

"Kristoph is dead! D. E. A. D!" Risley strode back and forth, waving his hands about. "I want the world to remember his name, too! You wouldn't believe what I've gone through to ensure that this film is a success!"

Bubba's ears perked up. *What has Risley gone through? Killing Kristoph?* He shook his head. *Confessing in front of my window? That would be insanely easy. The only way it would be better is if there was a camera rolling.*

Bubba looked toward the movie vans parked around the front of the mansion. It appeared that one of the crew was surreptitiously filming Marquita and Risley with a compact digital camcorder. He held the camera at arm's length and followed their movements. He recognized the fellow after a moment. It was none other than Mike Holmgreen, confessed high school arsonist and would-be blogger extraordinaire. He went around listening to his police band so that he could show up and film whatever was going on. And here he was on the spot. *A fella never knew when the next clip would go viral. He was prolly plumb sorry he'd missed out on Zombie Dog.*

There was even a small group of zombies watching avidly. One of them held up a cellphone, also apparently taping the confrontation.

Yeah, go ahead. Confess. That camera's running. Name details. Don't leave nothing out.

"I know you're jumping through hoops!" Marquita roared back.

"Hoops the size of Cheerios!" Risley yelled. "You wouldn't believe how my balls get caught!" He demonstrated with his index finger and thumb the size of a Cheerio, or possibly the size of his balls.

Bubba winced.

"It's just this whole thing!" Marquita yelled. "And that guy almost getting killed, too! You know damn well, dummy bullets don't just magically get replaced by *real* rounds. If that Bubba guy decides to sue us, he's going to own the film and then where we will be?"

I can sue the film? Bubba shook his head. *More lawyers' fees. Mebe ifin they just pay the hospital bill.*

"Mar, honey," Risley said entreatingly, "we're getting lots of yummy publicity. If we can just get through the shooting this week, we can film the rest on the sound

247

stage. We can let those local police officers sort the whole thing out with Kristoph and we can move on. This can be our tribute to Kris. They're going to catch the person. I just know it."

Marquita began to cry and Risley grimaced. After nearly a minute he enfolded his sister in a brotherly embrace.

Bubba sighed. No one was going to confess anything in front of his house. What was wrong with those people? He glanced back at the vans and saw Schuler carrying makeup cases toward the tents. He also saw the redhead staring at the brother and sister in a very odd manner.

Just then Precious stuck her cold, wet, and demanding nose against Bubba's groin and he bonked his head against the bottom of the window.

Risley glanced up and frowned. Bubba waved weakly.

●

Bubba got dressed. He disregarded the sling, let his dog outside with the admonition to not eat any of the film crew and/or zombies lurking in the vicinity. Precious's ears drooped more than they typically did but she trotted outside to do her dogly business.

He stopped to make himself a pot of coffee and thought about what he was supposed to do. There was the old standard. Find the bad guy/girl. Figure out what Ma was up to. Straighten things out with Willodean. It hadn't changed.

Oh, yes. Working as Zombie #14/Farmboy. I got one line. One stupid line. "If it weren't for that dagnammed sprocket." What does that mean, anyway? I might as well say "Hey, there's a friggin' zombie about to bite my tushy."

Bubba checked the Kit-Cat clock and saw that he wasn't late yet. But he might be if he stopped to take a shower. He had been tired the night before. The previous day had been chock full of unpleasant surprises and the inability to get the job done, which had translated into going to be early.

I ain't myself lately, he admitted. *I feel like my feet are slogging through molasses in December and it ain't but March.*

Then he looked out the kitchen window and settled on Snoddy Mansion and specifically the red curtains in the window of the room where the Garcias were staying. He saw the curtain twitch again and knew that Pilar was watching again. She had seen the same thing as Bubba. The brother and sister had been loudly fighting and she was probably trying to get the babies to go back to sleep.

But the kids are up with the sun. Isn't that what Alfonzo said? Yep.

Bubba frowned and took the entire carafe of coffee with him. *Why mess with a mug?*

●

Bubba found himself in the makeup tent a half hour later. Since he had the single line to say he knew he was playing the Farmboy as opposed to Zombie #14. This was good news because Farmboy had a lot less makeup to be applied than Zombie #14. This also meant that he wouldn't have a physiological reaction to the glue the artists used and he would be able to speak coherently for the rest of the day. This was a good thing.

Simone was doing his makeup while she chattered nonsensically. "How's that shotgun wound? I don't think I've ever known someone who got shot before. Except my Uncle Sebastian. But he tripped while he was hunting and shot himself in the foot. He used to bring a baby food jar full of shotgun pellets at Thanksgiving and rattle it at the kids as an object lesson. Did you know that those pellets are like little mouse droppings? It made me afraid of guns

249

because Uncle Sebastian was a little messed up in the head. I don't think it had anything to do with being shot in the foot. Of course, one of those pellets could have traveled through his blood stream and deposited itself in his brain. Hmm. I'll have to run that one by my mom. I bet she would know. She's a registered nurse, you know. Did you pee?"

Bubba took a moment to realize that Simone was actually waiting for him to answer. He nodded. But there was that empty carafe sitting on her makeup table and his bladder said something nasty to him. It went something like, "Go ahead and wait, dumbass. I double dawg dare you. No, I triple dawg dare you."

"I'll go now," Bubba said instead of actually responding to his bladder, which was always the right thing to do.

So Bubba went and took care of coffee inspired business. On his way back he paused by Schuler, who was cooing over Precious. He noticed that the purple-headed man wore a scarf tied jauntily around his neck. It was a different color this time. Blues shot with greens swirling about. Bubba was quite certain he could never get away with wearing a scarf around his neck. He'd be shot as soon as he stepped onto Main Street.

Bubba couldn't think of a way to ask a man if he had killed another man without sounding like an utter jackass, so he said, "You like dogs."

"I do like dogs," Schuler said. "I have five at home. All rescues."

"Precious was kind of like that," Bubba said. He'd gotten her from a breeder of hounds. She wasn't apt to hunt when she was supposed to, but it didn't really matter to Bubba. She was a good dog, even when she was chasing folks with metal detectors through the Sturgis

Woods. (Her legs were stubby and she usually gave up before the people did, so it was all gravy.) "Fella gave her to me because he wasn't goin' to be able to sell her as a hunter."

"Is that right?" Schuler asked. He scratched under Precious's jowls. She tilted her head to properly maximize the human's marvelous fingers.

"She did okay, though," Bubba said. "Found a woman who went missing." *Precious had found Willodean. Precious is a dang fine hound.* Dang fine.

"You found a missing woman?" Schuler asked Precious. Precious drooled down one side of her mouth. One of her back legs thumped in time with the man's scratching. "Aren't you the queen?"

Bubba was at a loss. He was supposed to make some smooth transition from discussing canines to what had happened with Kristoph, but nothing was coming to his mind.

"They found a scarf on Kristoph," Bubba said quietly, because they were still in a tent with a few other people. "Was it yours?"

Schuler froze and Precious whined in an annoyed fashion. The human had ceased scratching the sweet spot, and she was not happy about it.

"What do you care?" Schuler all but snarled.

"Well, they found my daddy's bayonet in the fella's back and they say that dint kill the man," Bubba said. "So someone stuck it in the poor bastard after he died from something else. They also said he wasn't strangled. So mebe that same someone took one of your scarfs and put it around his neck to point the finger at you, too. That's perty much why I care."

251

Schuler looked up at Bubba. "The police didn't say that he hadn't died from strangling." His tone was a whole less snarly.

"Mebe they was hoping you would confess," Bubba said. "Same as me." He scratched at the side of his nose and Simone called across the tent, "BUBBA, DON'T *TOUCH* YOUR MAKEUP!"

"It was *my* scarf," Schuler admitted. "It was the one Liza Minnelli signed. I loved that scarf. I saw her in London when she did 'Liza's Back.' I had a friend who introduced me to the fine actress and singer. Such a lovely lady. So sweet."

"I saw *Cabaret* once," Bubba said.

"I think she gets much better with age," Schuler said with a wistful sigh, "like a fine bottle of wine."

"Where did you keep your scarves?"

"In my kit," Schuler said. He gave Precious a last scratch and stood up. He waved at a massive Craftsman tool chest that was moved around on rollers. Bubba had a similar one, but his was about thirty years old and looked like it had been pushed down the side of a mountain. Schuler's had rainbow stickers on it and one bumper sticker that said "Marriage is SO gay!"

"Do you keep it locked?"

Schuler shook his head. "The artists are always coming and going, borrowing this, that, and the other. It would be stupid to keep it locked. I told the police that anyone on the set could have helped themselves to the scarf. Especially if they wanted to frame me." His expression revealed the innate bitterness. "I didn't miss it until the sheriff asked me about it the next day."

"Why would they want to frame you?"

"Because everyone knows how much I hated Kristoph," Schuler muttered.

"And you hated him because...?"

"He killed my dog."

•

"Kristoph did not kill Schuler's dog," Simone whispered in Bubba's ear when he was back in her chair. "At least, not on purpose." Schuler vanished from the tent as soon as Bubba had stepped away from him, unsure what to say to the other man. Why Simone was whispering, Bubba didn't know since Schuler was gone.

Bubba was about to ask her what she meant when Simone just went ahead and answered him.

"Schuler brought his dog on the set and Kristoph was backing up in his Mercedes. Didn't even see the dog. But Kristoph has never liked dogs so Schuler said it had been done on purpose. Schuler even sued Kristoph for the cost of the dog, the cost of the funeral, and mental anguish. The dog was buried in the Los Angeles Pet Memorial Park. They have Hopalong Cassidy's horse there. Also Rudolph Valentino's dog."

Simone efficiently powdered Bubba's nose. "How could you possibly have messed this up in five minutes?" she asked.

"Why would Schuler still be working on Kristoph's film ifin there was so much bad blood between them?" Bubba asked.

"On account that Schuler's company, the company I work for, has a contract with the studio, not with Kristoph. Kristoph didn't have a choice. So they avoided each other like the plague. Kristoph couldn't fault Schuler's work with makeup and wardrobe."

"What happened with the law suit?"

"Kristoph settled with Schuler out of court. I suppose it was a payoff to shut the man up. Who wants someone running around bitching about the director running over

253

his pet dog?" Simone sighed. "Good dog too. Looked kind of like Benji. That dog would do a dance for a treat and Schuler had her trained to stay in her crate during prime working hours. Never bothered anyone."

"But the dog was out of the crate and Kristoph ran over her," Bubba surmised. "Doesn't sound quite right."

"It was an accident," Simone said. "The guns were going off and the dog freaked out. The cage wasn't latched. That was Schuler's own fault. The dog ran and Kristoph was sorry about it afterward, although he did try to blame it all on Schuler." She sighed again. "I thought I was going to have to move back in with my mother because we weren't going to get any work from the studio ever again. The people in this business are such drama queens."

"So you know Schuler perty well," Bubba said.

Simone dabbed a little on his eyebrow. "Jeez, the hair on your brows won't stay in place. Let me put some hairspray on that. Yes, I know him pretty well."

"You think he might have killed Kristoph?"

Simone sprayed something on Bubba's face and he choked because of the fumes.

"I don't think so. He might have stomped on Kristoph with his size 13 stiletto heels, but strangling. No. It's way too masculine."

Bubba choked once more. *What does that mean?*

●

Either Bubba was getting better at the acting business or he had gotten incredibly lucky. The single line was said in one take. Risley nodded at the actors and said, "Cut! Great job. One take. I love it."

Bubba didn't understand why a dagnammed sprocket was integral to the story line but then he wasn't a writer and he didn't think he could write his way out of a paper bag. That was the same for most of the situations in his life. He was simply glad that one single thing had gone right for a change. But he grimaced as he thought about what he had just done. He had probably jinxed himself.

"Yo, dude," Tandy North said to Bubba. A Marlboro dangled out of the side of her mouth and puffed happily after she spoke.

Bubba looked at her expectantly.

"Sorry I shot you," Tandy said.

"You dint change the bullets, did you?" Bubba asked.

"Of course not," Tandy said. Her face transfixed into a frown. "Is that what the law thinks? That someone did it on purpose? Whoa. Intense. Death by actor. That's like Agatha Christie extreme."

"You dint happen to notice anyone messing around with the guns, did you?" Bubba asked, as if he was discussing the weather or whether or not they would eat pie after lunch.

Tandy puffed furiously. She blew a ring and then another ring that went through the first one. "This have something to do with the DEA?"

Bubba frowned. "Prolly not." He thought of his mother. She might pseudo frame him to get him and the DEA out of her way for the moment, but she wouldn't have messed with a shotgun. Furthermore, she didn't think Bubba getting shot was funny.

"That was H in your truck?"

"Flour," Bubba said succinctly.

"Flour?"

"Self-rising," Bubba said. "Whole wheat, too."

A smile quirked across Tandy's lips. "There's always something going on during filming. So and so sleeps with such and such. So and so got into a fight with such and such. I gave this one actress a black eye once. She was such a bitch, she had it coming. I had to write a check with five zeroes on it. But this place has been making new records for weirdness."

"Pegram County has a way of doin' that," Bubba said. Sadly it was true.

Tandy puffed again. She crossed her arms over her chest and looked at Bubba consideringly. "They don't think you did Kristoph, right? That's why they released you."

Bubba nodded.

"And if that had been H, that much H, then you'd be in jail until the next decade rolled over. Living *la vida loca* with Horace the Biker as your cellie."

Bubba shrugged. He didn't know who Horace the Biker was and he probably had never been arrested in Pegram County.

"So someone tried to kill you on the set," Tandy said. "I thought it was just an accident. That's wicked bad."

Bubba thought of McGeorge. She'd been a little too happy weird after he'd been shot. He hadn't seen the executive assistant around much since he came back to the set. But he'd like to know why she'd thought that him getting a hole was amusing.

"You see McGeorge that day I got shot?"

Tandy puffed as she appeared to think about it.

Bubba looked around them. Most people were busy doing whatever people did on a film set. Risley was talking to the redhead. The redhead had her hand on Risley's shoulder and was gently caressing his deltoid muscle. *Did executive assistants do that? And hadn't the redhead done something similar to Marquita?* And Bubba thought Pegram County was weird.

"She was there," Tandy said. "She was near the weapons, too. As a matter of fact, she shouldn't have been near the weapons." Her pretty mouth opened into a wide O of surprise. "You think the McGeorge did that?"

Bubba didn't reply. Someone had said something about McGeorge working in special effects before becoming Kristoph's executive assistant. What that meant to Bubba was that she had the knowhow to try to do Bubba in. But why?

"The McGeorge had a thing for Kristoph and she was there right after you found his body, so damn, she could have been waiting for you to find him so she could pretend to find you and frame you." Tandy nodded admiringly. "She went all Lucrezia Borgia on you. Except without the poison ring."

It could have happened that way, Bubba acknowledged. But Kristoph hadn't been strangled to death. He hadn't been stabbed to death. Marquita said he was alive when she left. That meant that someone else went into his house before Bubba came back.

A cameraman came past, hauling a large Red One unit over his shoulder.

Bubba had a thought. It was the first time he actually thought that his thought was a good one.

Chapter Twenty-two

Bubba and Oblivious Obfuscation

Thursday, March 14th

It didn't take Bubba long to find the person he was looking for. Mike Holmgreen was lurking around the catering van, chatting up a pretty server, telling her all about his experience in the "film" industry. He waved his compact camcorder around in an effort to impress the lady. "It's a Cannon full HD camcorder. It has 32 gigabytes of internal flash drive." He nodded firmly, emphasizing the coolness of what he was telling the young woman.

Bubba approached with Precious trailing at his heels. She sniffed appreciatively. A blackboard with words scrawled across it sat in front of the van. The "Zombie Special" featured bacon, avocado, and arugula. There was also a vegetarian alternative. The "Zombie Lite" had avocado, arugula, bean sprouts, and mushroom pate.

"Hey, Bubba," Mike said. "You wouldn't believe the footage I got this morning." He leered at the young woman in an apron as she leaned out of the van's window. "I was just telling Clara about it. Marquita and Risley arguing their butts off. I already uploaded it to YouTube. Too bad there wasn't a smack down."

Clara's eyes rolled. "You want something?" she asked Bubba.

Bubba was still in his Farmboy outfit and it was obvious that Clara knew he was one of the so-called actors. (Bubba didn't feel like an actor. He felt like a doofus standing in front of a person with a camera saying

258

a stupid line that didn't even make sense.) He shook his head.

"Mike," he said, "kin I have a word?"

Mike looked mildly alarmed. It was clear that he was going over recent events to see if there was something he had done or hadn't done that would have ticked Bubba off in some manner. Ultimately he must have decided that he was clean for the moment because he nodded and gestured for Bubba to lead the way.

Bubba led Mike far enough away to get out of earshot of the catering van. "You bin filming stuff around here?"

Mike nodded.

"The day that Kristoph died?"

Mike nodded again.

"You over by my house that day?" Bubba hadn't seen Mike but there had been a lot of people wandering all over the estate in the last week. It was a lot more than when people came on the biannual sightseeing tours of the "haunted" estate. His mother was even thinking about adding a Halloween event. (Bubba's heart thundered with joy. Not.)

Mike nodded a third time.

Bubba waited for it.

Finally Mike's eyes got large and round. "I might have captured the killer on film," he breathed. "O.M.G." He tugged his backpack off his shoulder, put the camcorder inside, and pulled out a large tablet all the while muttering, "O.M.G., O.M.G., O.M.G." Bubba noticed it was about the slimmest, most compact computer a fellow could have. Oh the days had changed from the time he had ruined his first clunky computer that would have sunk a ship if it had been used as an anchor.

Mike powered it up and Bubba looked over the younger man's shoulder. Mike found the appropriate

259

website and used his finger to tap on the computer screen. "Here we go. What was the date? The tenth, right? I've got three on the tenth. That was the filming downtown. I got you being fired by that director." He chuckled. "I'm going to have that one recut and have you doing Party Rock Anthem by LMFAO." He looked up at Bubba's face and his smile faded away quickly. "Let's see. The other one was when they were filming at the cemetery again. They weren't there very long on account that Miz Bushyhood got righteously angry that one of them zombies stepped on her husband's grave. I wouldn't have thought a woman that old would have been able to hit that hard." He shook his head sadly.

Mike looked at Bubba again and moved on. "So this must be the last one. I was filming all over the place that day." He stabbed with his finger and a screen appeared. The words "HOLMGREEN PRODUCTIONS" appeared and then it got right into the filming. There was a candid shot of the zombies getting made up. Bubba saw Simone Sheats chattering away to a woman with half of her face dripping down the front of her flowered smock. Mike panned around and got Risley Risto talking to the redhead. Then there was a take where the redhead was talking to Marquita.

Bubba glowered because Mike's work of art was a series of clips that he had filmed throughout his day. There was no rhyme or reason to his activity. Whatever caught his notice was apt to be filmed. If someone had dangled a sparkly spinning lure in front of Mike, he would have filmed it. The camera went past the catering van and focused on Clara. Rather it focused on Clara's cleavage. Then it was on Bubba's house where he caught a moment of Marquita arguing with Kristoph.

260

Bubba perked up. They stood on Bubba's porch and Marquita said, "You should hire the redneck back."

That was okay. Bubba had been called worse names.

Kristoph shuddered. "That damn dog. It's got the droopy red eyes. It's like Snoopy on crack. It's going to give me nightmares."

Marquita shook her head. "It's *just* a dog. Besides Risley got a couple of takes of that dog. Dogs are great for film. People will remember the damn dog. The dog will get more press than some of the actors. Zombie dog."

"It's *my* movie," Kristoph said. "I'm going to do what I want."

"You always do what you want," Marquita said.

Kristoph opened Bubba's front door. "I just want to see if we can use the inside of this house. It's pretty quaint. Visions of D.W. Griffith abounding."

"Jesus, Kristoph," Marquita said, "do you know whose house this is?"

Kristoph said something, but Bubba couldn't make it out. Then the pair went into the house. No less than thirty seconds later, Marquita returned to the door and threw over her shoulder, "You can be *such* a Prima donna!" She stalked off and Mike followed her as she strode away in high heeled boots, muttering, "I *have* to find a bathroom."

Bubba knew that Marquita was probably not the one, given that she had already passed a polygraph test. Kristoph had likely still been alive when she'd stalked off and besides she'd only had about a half minute to do him in. Doable but unlikely. The last thing Bubba noticed was that when Mike turned his camera he'd captured one of the upper windows of the Snoddy Mansion and Pilar had been watching again.

"Shoot," Mike said as the footage stopped. "I dint get anything."

"You cleared Marquita," Bubba said. "She's goin' to like that. Mebe let you on the closed sets, for it."

Mike brightened.

"And I reckon you need to show this to Sheriff John," Bubba added.

Mike's shoulders slumped. "I guess. He looks at me funny ever since I was in jail the last time."

Mike had failed an algebra test in high school and then attempted to burn down the school in order to hide it. He had only scorched one of the walls, but he had gotten himself thrown in jail until he could be tried. His record had been adjudicated on account of all of his community service and reparations but no one was going to forget anytime soon.

"Go on, now," Bubba said with a little push. "Sheriff John needs all that information."

Mike sidled away with a little wave at Clara.

Bubba looked at Precious. "Now I got to go talk to Ma and Pilar."

Precious whined piteously.

•

Bubba had to stop by the makeup tent again in order to get his own clothing and give the film's clothing back to the wardrobe department. Schuler had returned and was issuing orders like a general from the ship off the beach in Normandy. "More blood! More stringiness! More goo! That is so *not* what a zombie is supposed to look like! Are you using crayons? Really?" The purple-haired man ignored Bubba and Bubba ignored him. Bubba couldn't think of anything else to ask him. If Bubba had been framed, it stood to reason that Schuler had probably been framed, as well.

Ain't that odd, though? Bubba asked himself. *Why frame two men? Why not just focus on one?* How could anyone know that Kristoph was going to be in Bubba's house? *Why, the answer ain't difficult. They didn't know. They took advantage of a situation. Hey, look, we're in Bubba Snoddy's house and he's bin accused before. Let's just make it look like he did it. But first, let's make it look like the head makeup artist who hates him, did it.*

Bubba rubbed his head. It was starting to hurt again. He was having to think of too damn many things. He finally wandered back toward the mansion with Precious trotting behind him. He noticed that Ol' Green had reappeared and was parked beside the large house. Someone had taken pity on him and returned it from the impound lot.

Once inside, Bubba made sure his dog had enough water and that no corpses were about. Live ones. Dead ones. Any kind.

Apparently it was clear.

His arm hurt a little and he did a little first aid. Everything looked all right for a bullet wound. Actually it didn't look like a bullet wound. It looked like he'd been peppered with multiple pellets. Then a doctor had taken about an hour to take each and every one out. (Or so Bubba was informed since he had slept through the procedure.) (But he did have a little glass jar full of blackened pellets the size of mouse turds. It jingled in a most interesting manner when he shook it.)

Miz Adelia came into the kitchen just as Bubba was putting his shirt back on. "Be still my heart," she said. She fluttered her hand over her face. "Better cover up all that skin, boy. I might become crazed."

Bubba smiled grimly. "Do you know what my mother did?"

263

"Your mother?" Miz Adelia said innocently.

"Bet you had to buy another ten pounds of flour, dint you?"

"Flour," she said weakly. "I don't think she thought they would keep you so long."

"Where is my mother?" Bubba asked coldly.

"She went to the store with Pilar to get formula and diapers."

"Prolly some flour, too. And dint they get diapers and formula a couple of days ago?"

"Babies go through a lot of formula and diapers," Miz Adelia snapped. "Ifin you had one, you would know." Offense was often the best defense for women like Miz Adelia and Miz Demetrice. "Ifin you're wondering, that is a hint. A man your age should be providing a passel of grandchildren for his mother to play with and spoil."

"Blanca and Carlotta aren't exactly the age to need formula," Bubba said slowly, ignoring the grandchildren issue.

Miz Adelia began to clatter around the kitchen, picking up pots and pans and putting them back into place, as if she was looking for something particular. "There's a special formula for toddlers. Is that the time?" she asked with a pointed look at the clock on a nearby wall. "I got to get things cooking. Them chicken breasts won't wander into the oven all by themselves. Lordy almighty."

Bubba finished buttoning his shirt.

"Was that your wound you was looking at?" Miz Adelia asked. "Mayhap I should take a gander? Make sure it ain't infected?"

"Mebe I kin have the doctor from the prison look at it," Bubba suggested.

"It was *flour*," Miz Adelia snapped. "Ain't nothing illegal about having flour in your truck."

264

"I reckon it might be illegal to make a phone call and tell the DEA that there ain't a bag of flour wrapped up in clear plastic and packing tape under the bench seat." Bubba sighed loudly. Precious decided to hide under the kitchen table. All that could be seen of the canine was her brown and white tushy and the tail that drooped sadly. "I don't believe the DEA arrested me because they thought it was flour. Perty shore they thought it was somethin' else altogether."

"*Self-rising* flour," Miz Adelia said. "Whole wheat," she added for emphasis.

Alfonzo came in, carrying one of his daughters. The other one toddled behind him. "Did you know that those film people don't want me scraping on the front of the mansion until they're done filming? How am I supposed to get this place painted?" he asked, unmindful to the tension in the room.

He saw Bubba and stopped. "*Hola,* Bubba."

"Alfonzo," Bubba said.

"Sorry about the whole DEA mess," Alfonzo said. "I don't know where those people get their ideas from. They think since Pilar and I have been to Mexico, then we must be drug smugglers. Or perhaps we're smuggling something horrible and wretched, like knock-off handbags and football jerseys. They wanted to know if my Cowboys jersey was really from China."

Then what *are you smuggling?* Bubba asked silently. It was probably better that he didn't know. Then he could have plausible deniability later. "I don't know" would be the ultimate excuse and it would be sincere.

The toddling girl wandered to Bubba and lifted her arms expectantly, looking up at him with chocolate brown eyes. Bubba could no more deny her than he could deny a whining puppy with a red ribbon tied around its neck. He carefully picked the small child up in his good arm and propped her on his hip. She pulled at his nose and giggled at his reaction.

Wait. Chocolate brown eyes. Bubba looked up and studied the other child in Alfonzo's arms. *Also brown eyes. Not hazel.* "Dint one of them girls have green eyes?"

Miz Adelia chuckled. "You just got shot and then arrested by the DEA, Bubba. I don't think you're all right in the head."

Bubba shrugged and sat in a kitchen chair. Miz Adelia made a bottle of formula for the one child while the other one got a sippy cup full of milk. Bubba helped with the aim of the sippy cup. "When is my mother apt to return?" he asked politely.

"Oh, you know your mother," Miz Adelia said. "It could be ten minutes. It could be an hour. They might have run up to that Walmart. Better price on diapies. They might have even gone to Sam's Club. Get a crate of diapers."

Bubba gave up after a half hour. He helped Alfonzo with the two little girls until one of them fell asleep in a pile of oversized Mega Bloks and the other one yawned widely. Alfonzo carried one upstairs while Bubba got the other one. The two girls were asleep before they finished tucking in the blankets.

When Bubba slipped outside the door, Alfonzo said, "I really am sorry about the DEA."

"But you cain't tell me what's happening," Bubba said.

Alfonzo shook his head. "People are depending on us."

"I kind of figured that. Ma wouldn't do it otherwise." Bubba sighed loudly. He was prepared to play the martyr. "Don't worry. The DEA will get right tired following me

266

around.   I'll take them down away from the house whenever you need."

"Tonight after six?" Alfonzo asked hopefully.

"Shore," Bubba said. "I'll take them down to the park past Sturgis Creek and park behind one of them ginormous crape myrtle trees. It'll look like I'm waiting for someone. It'll be funny when they search me again." The words were half joking and half bitter. "Mebe there will be a body cavity search. I could back up and wiggle just for a laugh."

"You're sure you want to do this?"

"I'm shore," Bubba said. "It'll be just like I'm the fox and the DEA are the hounds." He knew deep inside, there was something going on that was bigger than he was. It was bigger and more important, and his mother was just one of the organizers. She had briefly thrown him under the bus, but she had done it for a good reason.

It didn't mean Bubba had to like it.

●

Bubba drove down the lane at precisely six p.m. He left Precious at home, locked in the house. The canine hadn't been happy. She had threatened to chew holes in the quilt on his bed. Bubba had promised treats when he returned, but she hadn't been appeased.

So he whistled the theme to *Mission Impossible* while he drove down the lane, at the end of which was the large gate. It was still mangled from someone trying to blow him and it up during the 1st Annual Pegramville Murder Mystery Festival. Bubba had meant to see if he could bend it back into a useable shape, but about a thousand other things had gotten in the way. It remained a testament to the thought logic processes of a twisted murderer who'd had access to chemicals used in demolition.

A hundred feet down the main road sat a plain gray van. It didn't have windows on the sides nor did it have a logo. It did have a man sitting in the front driver's seat, wearing sunglasses and a black jacket. The man watched Bubba assiduously.

Bubba was tempted to wave but he didn't want to be too obvious.

Let's see, he thought. *What does a drug dealer do? I mean, what does an* alleged *drug dealer do?*

Bubba drove downtown in Pegramville, which consisted of Main Street and a few significant crossroads. He found the statue of his distant relative, Colonel Nathanial Snoddy, and parked in the street beside it. Then he went to the statue and tied a piece of yarn around the Colonel's right hand. *What does that mean?*

Bubba did not know. He was winging it. Perhaps he was signaling someone. He could have left a candle lit in his window but no one drove past the caretaker's house on a regular, non-smuggling basis. As he finished the bow on the pink length of yarn, he caught movement out of the corner of his eye. The plain gray van had pulled up to the nearest corner and the nose was just edging out probably so the driver could see what Bubba was doing.

Then he got back in his truck and went to the cross on Haymaker Hill. He walked up to the cross that someone had put up years before and that Jeffrey Carnicon, the town's only atheist, regularly tried to get demolished. He circled it on foot three times and then waved cheerfully to the west.

Good view of the sunset up here, Bubba thought. *Need to bring Willodean on a picnic, ifin I kin figure out what went wrong.*

Bubba followed up the cross circling with a visit to Bufford's Gas and Grocery. He bought a package of Krispy

Kreme Juniors Crullers from Leelah Wagonner and immediately threw them into the garbage outside of the store. It was a perfectly good waste of donuts but the origin of the package was iffy when one considered it was purchased from Bufford's.

Bubba watched with one eye as he drove away from Bufford's. One of the agents dove out of the van and attacked the garbage can, dumping the contents over the pavement. Leelah rushed out of the store brandishing a summer sausage and yelling.

I'm goin' to have to apologize to Leelah later, Bubba thought. Then he went to the manure factory, the Red Door Inn, and City Hall, each in its turn. When he was finished dropping some lead sinkers into one of the cannons on the front lawn of City Hall, he glanced at his watch and decided that enough time had passed for the Garcias to get well enough away from Pegramville.

Bubba went home and gave his dog a treat. Then he went to sleep and dreamed of his mother eating chicken-fried zombie for breakfast.

Chapter Twenty-three

Bubba and the Prevaricating Peoples

Friday, March 15th

Bubba woke up with a shudder. He had been dreaming weird things again. On the end of the bed, Precious woke up with a snort and a grunt. She kicked at Bubba's legs and then slid off the side of the bed in a snit because her sleep had been abruptly disturbed. He heard her claws rattling against the hard wood floors as she went down the hallway, likely to go downstairs and see if her food bowl had magically filled itself.

There was stuff to be done and Bubba didn't want to get up. He wanted to go fishing, where he didn't have to think about anything except the sound of the line as it unfurled itself against a mellow spring breeze. There would be the soothing sound of the bass jig as it hit the top of an unruffled lake surface. It would be followed by the slap of the tail of the fish as it fought to escape the hook. Then there would be the splash of the fish as it was released back into the water.

The phone rang. He ignored it and it kept ringing. Eventually the machine downstairs would pick up; but what if it was Willodean calling?

Bubba groaned and reached for the receiver on the nightstand. "'Lo," he said as he brought it to his ear and mouth.

"BUBBA!" someone cried into the other end. Bubba winced. "What it be like, homes?"

"This here is Bam Bam!" Bam Bam added, although Bubba had already figured it out.

"'Lo," Bubba repeated because coherent thoughts were almost impossible without coffee in his system.

"I got a lead on something very suspicious," Bam Bam said. "I be hoping them DEA agents ain't following you around, so we kin go check it out. Me and David, you remember that fella who used to dress up all in purple? Well, we started talking with film crew people at this great little dive bar ya'll have here. Grubbies? Grubs?"

"Grubbo's," Bubba said.

"Grubbo's," Bam Bam confirmed. "And we found someone who knew somethin' somethin'. We gots to reconnoiter with this fella and see what be up, yo."

"Reconnoiter," Bubba repeated. It was a four syllable word and one that made his head hurt.

"It means check it out," Bam Bam said helpfully.

Bubba rubbed his eyes with his free hand. If memory served him he needed to be on the film set at ten a.m. There was a big showdown scene to be shot. All the zombies would be blown to smithereenies while the hero and heroine flew away into the sunset in a conveniently provided Cessna that the heroine had learned to fly from her long dead father when he hadn't been long dead or a zombie. (The last was an assumption that Bubba made, but he thought it made sense that a zombie wouldn't be giving his daughter flying lessons.)

He didn't have a line in the scene except for the odd grunting zombie moan. But he would have to wear the prosthesis on his face again and those dagnummed white contact lenses.

Then he needed to chat with Pilar about what she'd seen out her window. Bubba had finally decided that it didn't matter what his mother was doing or not doing with the Garcias. It couldn't be that bad in the larger scheme of things, as long as Miz Demetrice would rethink her whole

Let's-Use-Bubba-as-a-Diversion technique. Lastly, but not leastly, there was Willodean Gray. He didn't care if the whole town was watching. He was going to do what he had determined to do weeks ago.

"What is it that this fella thinks is goin' on?" Bubba rumbled.

"I don't know," Bam Bam said. "But it's illegal and wicked whacked. That's what he told me after he had done eight shots of pink pantie droppers."

"Pink pantie droppers," Bubba repeated. He wasn't sure he wanted to know what that was.

"That's gin, white tequila, mixed with a little vanilla ice cream and pink lemonade," Bam Bam said. "That bartender was all like 'Yo, I kin mix a kickin' drink, yo, and you cain't drink *just* one.' And the bitchin' part was that he could and we couldn't. I don't remember how I got back to the hotel last night. Lucky I didn't wake up with a new tattoo."

"Gin, tequila, ice cream, and pink lemonade," Bubba said. It didn't sound good. It sounded like the next morning the guy would be tasting ice cream and pink lemonade until he had thrown it all up. Then he would have pinkish ice cream burps for the rest of the day and he would never, ever, never want to have pink lemonade or vanilla ice cream or tequila again.

"Well, Gus, that's the fella, said he'd clue us in this morning." Bam Bam paused for a moment. "Them DEA fellas ain't there, are they?"

Bubba lifted his head incrementally. He could see out the window but not so much that he could tell who was or wasn't there. "Beats me. They were following me last night."

"Following you," Bam Bam said warily. "I heard tell about them people. They don't give up. You'd best take the back way out this morning."

"They might even have the phone tapped," Bubba suggested slyly, feeling his Wheaties for a moment.

Bam Bam didn't reply for a long moment. "Oh, hell no," he said finally, "I don't know who this is. I dialed the wrong number, yo. My name is Martin Jones from Duncanville, Texas, and I have nothing to do with anything illegal. I paid my taxes on time last week. I renew my car insurance every year on time and early, too. I took my mama to church last Sunday. I tithe. I tithe *eleven* percent!" There was an abrupt sound that indicated that he had disconnected the line.

Bubba smiled sleepily and put the receiver back into the cradle.

●

An hour later, Bubba picked up the phone downstairs to see if he could get in touch with Willodean Gray. That whole thing had been dragging out too long. He was busy but not so busy that he couldn't take a moment to try to mend a fence. Everything else was done. He'd showered, brushed his teeth, fed his dog, and paid his bills. All he had to do was put them in the mailbox on his way out and wave to the DEA agents as he went.

However, the phone was dead.

Bubba stared at the phone. He leaned to the side and saw that it was still plugged into the wall.

Precious bayed at something outside. Bubba frowned at the phone and put it back. He'd have to call the telephone company from the big house if he wanted it repaired. In the meantime, he needed to find his keys, put his bills in the mailbox, and hope that he could find Willodean this morning before she started a shift.

There was a knock on his door and he opened it to find the sun had come out from behind a large black cloud. The sudden bright light almost blinded Bubba. But Willodean stood in front of him. Dressed in blue jeans and a Cowboys jersey, she was clearly not headed for work, and she still looked like a million bucks. *A billion. No, her worth is* undefinable.

The next moment she was kissing him and her arms were wrapped around his neck, not that Bubba minded in the least. He certainly wasn't going to complain about it. Bubba lifted her up and walked her back into the house. Precious continued to bay at something but Bubba pushed that observation to the farthest edge of his thoughts.

When Willodean finally came up for air, they were sitting in his living room, with her on his lap and her arms still wrapped around his neck. "I'm sorry I haven't been around," she said. "How's your arm?"

"It's better," Bubba said, diving into the green depths of her eyes. "You goin' to tell me what the matter is?"

"I'm going to," Willodean said. "I wasn't sure how to say it. I'm still not."

"Okay, just say it," Bubba said, "I reckon you're not breaking up with me on account of all that smooching. I don't think a girl like you would kiss a fella like that ifin you were planning on breaking up with him."

"Break up with you?" she said with evident surprise. "What gave you that idea?"

Bubba grimaced. "Well, you ain't bin around. And you've bin avoiding me."

"Steve Simms came down with a case of shingles and two of the other deputies have some kind of weird swine flu. I had to go to the doctor because I was worried about—" Willodean cut herself off.

"You ain't sick, are you?"

274

"No, I got a shot," Willodean said with a weak smile. "I had to have a special kind of shot. Very special."

"Okay," Bubba said slowly.

"Your phone doesn't work," Willodean said, "or I would have called you."

"It was working an hour ago," Bubba said and gently brushed a lock of her hair away from her forehead. "The whole DEA arresting me thing don't bother you?"

"*Your mother*," Willodean said in explanation. "Miz D is a *bad* girl," she added, but her tone indicated that Miz Demetrice's badness was an acceptable tradeoff for her positive attributes.

"You like her," Bubba accused genially.

"Most people do," Willodean answered. "She isn't mean to people unless they're mean to her first."

"That's getting to be a long list," Bubba said. "And what would you call planting fake evidence in my truck so that no one would be watching her and her two handy people for the moment? That's not mean?"

"Miz D didn't think you'd be hurt," Willodean said. "It's not like you haven't been arrested and put into jail before. Also she knew they'd have to let you go because it wasn't really illegal drugs."

"She tell you that?"

"No. She didn't have to."

"I know, but it doesn't mean that I have to like it. I wouldn't have minded the whole arrested thing but did she have to do it while I was eating lunch with you?" Bubba chuckled. "I dint get to finish my meal or my conversation."

"I ate your dessert," Willodean confessed.

"They make good red velvet cake," Bubba said.

"Better than mine," Willodean said. Bubba knew that he was supposed to fill the moment with an obligatory

"No. Your cooking is fine." But it would have been a big fat lie and he tried hard not to lie. It was always a pain in the ass trying to remember what lies he had told to whom. Besides Willodean couldn't cook. Oh, she could cook but what she made didn't turn out well.

"We need to go back and finish both, unless you'd like to finish the conversation now," Bubba said sincerely.

Willodean nodded. "It's time."

Naturally that was the moment that something interrupted them. Miz Demetrice walked into the front door, saying, "Your truck has flat tires on it, Bubba, and the Garcias need to go out, so could you be a dear, and oh." She stopped as she came around the corner of the living room entrance and looked at the pair of them. "I suppose I should have knocked."

Bubba's eyes rolled. "Your timing is excellent, Ma."

Willodean glowered. Then she climbed off Bubba's lap and stood up. Bubba's shoulders slumped.

"What do you mean my tires are flat?" Bubba asked.

"All four," Miz Demetrice said. "Who did you tick off?"

"You apparently. The fella who tried to frame me for Kristoph's murder." Bubba looked at his fingers and spread them out as if preparing to count them. "Mebe God. I ain't sure. I aim to ask Him the next time I go to church."

"I didn't flatten your tires, dearest," his mother told him. "I wouldn't have stooped so low. Really, my back has been aching this week, picking up and putting down babies."

"You did frame me this week, Ma."

Miz Demetrice tut-tutted, as if framing her own son was something that was done every day of the week. "It was *flour*, for goodness's sake. Can you take the Caddy and dawdle by the front gate for a little while and make sure the DEA get a good look at you, that's a dear."

There was a noise from the door and a toddler came bouncing down the hallway and paused by Miz Demetrice's legs. The little girl reached up and tugged on the bottom of his mother's sun yellow dress.

"Uh-Carlotta!" Pilar's voice came. "She's so busy!"

Pilar stopped behind Miz Demetrice and Carlotta. "*Lo siento.* That child is a barrelful of monkeys. I turned my head for three seconds, I swear. She's like the Flash, you know the comic book man who goes really fast. And you left your front door open."

Bubba glanced at Miz Demetrice meaningfully.

Alfonzo appeared behind the others. He held the other child with one arm and had a diaper bag hung over the opposite shoulder. Blanca waved her hands up and down and wore an expression that indicated that Hurricane Blanca was about to commence. *"¿Qué pasó?"*

Miz Demetrice picked up the child at her hem. She winced as she pulled Carlotta into place. "See. I'm going to have to go see that chiropractor. Bubba, you'd best get moving on that end because I'm not going to be the granny who—"

"Miz D!" Willodean protested and wonder of wonders, his mother shut up abruptly.

Bubba looked around and was mildly surprised that so many people could fit into the small hallway and the miniscule living room.

"While ya'll are here," Bubba started until Blanca let loose a horrendous cry. Her little face contorted into a rictus mask of fury.

"I think," Bubba started again. Blanca paused only to take in a breath. She waved her little chubby arms up and down, demanding something.

Alfonzo murmured to the child, patting her on the back. "I fed her already," he said. "She had a nap, too. This one will not be calm. I don't know what's bothering her."

Pilar asked something in Spanish that Bubba didn't catch.

Bubba stood up. He walked over to Alfonzo. "Hey little girl. What chu all upset about? Ain't nothing but a thing, is it?"

A new face caught Blanca's attention for a moment. She reached for Bubba and Alfonzo let Bubba take the child. "I just think you need a little moment, don't you, princess?" Bubba asked. "And you *are* a little princess, aren't you?"

Blanca gurgled uncertainly.

Pilar glanced at Alfonzo uncertainly.

Willodean stared at Bubba uncertainly.

Miz Demetrice didn't look at anything uncertainly.

Carlotta said, "Hufla maboo!"

Bubba tested the back of Blanca's diaper with a babysitter's expertise. There had been the time when he had been put in charge of five children all under the age of three, and only one had been potty trained. (Although the term "potty trained" didn't mean the same thing to Bubba as it meant to the mother of the allegedly "potty trained" child.) That had been a week where his mother was trying to overturn a series of Texas laws designed to prevent women from...he couldn't remember exactly what. Miz Demetrice had been successful and Bubba had learned the As to Zs about quickly and efficiently changing a diaper. He had also learned that when one child went, the others were apt to follow. Going number two generally had a cascading effect and not in a pretty waterfall sort of way.

Then the smell usually followed. Bubba grimaced. He snagged the diaper bag from Alfonzo's shoulder and went into the living room. He spread out a throw with one arm, glad that the wound on his shoulder was feeling much better, and carefully laid the baby on her back. Blanca waved her arms and kicked.

"I think she did a poopenetta," Bubba said. He tickled Blanca under the arms and she wrinkled her little face. Then he popped the bottom snaps of her onesie. He glanced up and Pilar said quickly, "Let me do that."

Bubba said, "I got it." There was a little amount of wanting to show Willodean that he really *was* good with children and a little bit of knowledge that everyone was suddenly acting a little odd.

Alfonzo said, "Really, maybe I should do it. That's a little messy. Hershey squirts worse."

"Poopie wipes off," Bubba said sagely. He chuckled and added, "Poop happens." He looked down at Blanca and murmured, "Ain't that right, little one? You just got a little case of mookie stinks?"

Blanca kicked again but it was clearly in agreement to what Bubba was saying.

"I don't think no one likes to have dookie drop-drops in their underwear, right, baby?" Bubba asked in a sing-song voice.

Miz Demetrice said, "Bubba, perhaps you should just let—"

Bubba's head came up, he saw that everyone was watching him with horrid anticipation.

What in hellfire and tarnation? Bubba thought. His hand hesitated just a little.

Blanca's tiny face crumpled again. She didn't like the poop in her pantsies anymore than anyone else did.

"It's all right," Bubba said to Blanca. "I kin take care of this business. I bet there's a little baby powder in that bag. We'll just take them diapers off." His fingers efficiently found the tabs at the sides of the disposable diapers. "You remember, Ma. One of them babies had a mama who only used cloth diapers. I must have poked myself with them pins about twenty times before I learned better. Safety pins, hah."

Bubba glanced back at the crowd watching him. He would have thought he was performing an exacting surgery on an infamous patient if he didn't know better. "I like them disposable ones better. You know Jeffrey Carnicon calls them 10,000-year-old-kaka-bombs because he says it takes that long for them to decay in a landfill. That Jeffrey. He shore likes to put his nose into everything. But since when is that a crime for someone who lives in Pegram County?"

Bubba dug in the diaper bag with a free hand while he tickled the little girl under the chin with the other. "Bet ya'll have some wipes in here, and a new diaper, too. Shore you do." He pulled out a folded diaper and a package of baby wipes. Then he extracted a travel size bottle of baby powder. "All prepared, just like I knew you would be."

Then he pulled the diaper away from the baby.

Bubba stared downward, dumbstruck for a long moment. "What the Sam blazes?" he asked finally and glanced back at his observers.

Miz Demetrice clucked disapprovingly.

"Uh," Pilar said.

"Perhaps you should..." Alfonzo started to say and trailed off.

Willodean pointed at the baby. "Bubba," she said and it was too late.

The baby who was known as Blanca and was supposed to be a girl baby, giggled and a stream of urine erupted from him and immediately soaked Bubba down. He might have just made a great big stinky poo poo but he had saved the peeing for when the diaper came off.

Bubba tugged a wipe out and was cleaning his face off when someone else came into the house and said, "I've got a gun and no one moves an inch."

Bubba sighed. "Kin I finish changing the poopy diaper?"

Chapter Twenty-four

Bubba and the Discomposed Denouement

Friday, March 15th

Bubba finished the diaper job with a calm efficiency that, under the circumstances, surprised even himself. Blanca, or whatever his name was, waved his arms cheerfully and gurgled in a pleased note. Everyone had been herded into the living room and was staring at the interloper with the gun.

"Not again," Willodean said. "I cannot believe this. Is every gun-wielding murderer on the face of the planet drifting through Pegram County at any given time?"

"Ixnay on the urderermay amenay," Miz Demetrice said out of the corner of her mouth.

"Where's Brownie when we need him," Bubba muttered. "If ever there was a time for a Taser toting kid to be around, this was it. It ain't like that kid to miss a prime opportunity."

"Shut up," said the person with the gun. "Hands up, everyone!"

"I'm holding a baby," Miz Demetrice protested.

"Then hold the baby's hands up!" the person with the gun said illogically.

Bubba sighed. "I guess we don't need to go looking for the person who done Kristoph in, then."

The person with the gun snarled, "No, we don't, do we?"

Miz Demetrice looked around the room. "You mean the killer's in here?"

282

"Of course," the person with the gun snapped. "Are you all stupid? The killer is right here!" The gun pointed down at the living room floor. Five pairs of adult eyes followed the gun's barrel as it pointed. The two pairs of baby eyes didn't follow because they didn't care much.

"The killer is the living room floor?" Alfonzo asked.

"Shut up!" the person with the gun said again.

Precious came trotting in, holding a T-bone in her mouth. For inundating herself into a dangerous situation, she looked remarkably happy.

"Did you give my dog a steak?" Bubba demanded.

"She was barking at me and it's Angus beef," the person with the gun said. "That piece cost me $11.99. Your dog's eating good."

"Did you flatten my tires?" Bubba asked. "And cut my phone line?"

"I did, and I would do it again!" the person with the gun said.

"That truck dint do nothing to you," Bubba said. He patted Blanca, or maybe it was Blanco, (but no one could do that to a child, could they?) on the belly.

"Miz Adelia will be calling the po-lice right now," Miz Demetrice said firmly.

The person with the gun laughed. "Your housekeeper went to town a half hour ago. She got a call from the hospital about her mother. She won't be back until she finds out that her mother isn't in the hospital."

"Very diabolical," Miz Demetrice approved. "You don't intend on killing all of us, do you?"

"No, not unless I have to," the person said. "All I want is *him*." The gun's barrel directed itself at Bubba.

"What'd I do?"

"Bubba killed Kristoph," McGeorge announced to the group at large, "and I'm going to kill him." They all stared at McGeorge. She was still short with blonde streaked hair that was equally short. Her blue eyes were icy as she stared back. She wore a t-shirt that said "WARNING! If the zombies chase us, I'm tripping you." The gun she held was a large one with a six inch long barrel. *Some kind of .44,* if Bubba knew his mother's weapons. It might have been his mother's gun. McGeorge could have been wandering through both of their houses looking for potential weapons to use in framing other people. In fact, his mother probably gave guns away to wandering homicidal psychopaths because they looked like they might need one.

It was funny that McGeorge didn't really look like a homicidal psychopath. It was even funnier that Bubba had an idea what a homicidal psychopath should look like.

"Wait," Miz Demetrice said, "I thought the killer was *you.*"

McGeorge stared at Miz Demetrice and then she said, "You think *I* killed Kristoph? I *loved* him. I never would have killed him."

"Bubba didn't murder Kristoph," Willodean said.

"You'd say that, you're his girlfriend *and* the police," McGeorge snapped.

"Really, Bubba didn't murder—"

"If you say anything else, I'll shoot you," McGeorge said.

Bubba rose up from the baby. "You might shoot her but a second after that you'll be sorrier than I kin say."

The fury in Bubba's face must have registered with McGeorge because she took a step back. The end of the gun wavered. "I'll shoot you first," she warned. "There's...uh...a bunch of bullets in this gun."

284

"There are six rounds," Miz Demetrice said helpfully. "That's a Colt Anaconda. You should watch out for the kick."

"Ma," Bubba said warningly.

"What?" his mother protested. "A person should know about the gun they're carrying."

"Is that one of yours?" Bubba demanded. "Jesus wept, Ma."

"Yes. Apparently, the young lady was digging around the mansion."

"People around town said you had a lot of guns," McGeorge defended herself, "and I didn't have time to file paperwork and wait two weeks."

"I think we need to get you a gun safe, Ma," Bubba said.

"Shut up," McGeorge said again, glaring at the group of people before her. "Jesus, who smells like pee?"

Someone charged down the hallway and Precious yipped as someone stepped on her paw.

Bam Bam and David Beathard came to a stop just in front of McGeorge and seemed to have their eyes locked on the weapon in McGeorge's hands. McGeorge backed up marginally and turned halfway in order to get them all in her sights at the same time. "Stop!" she screamed but they were already stopped, frozen into place by the sight of a big bang-bang thing.

"I think we be in the wrong house," Bam Bam said conversationally to David. "We'll just head back to—"

"No one's going anywhere!" McGeorge yelled. The end of the gun wavered. Then it went back and forth between Bubba and Bam Bam, who stood next to David.

Bam Bam knew an opportunity to talk himself out of a situation when one arose. "We came in the back way on account that them DEA peeps are—"

"Bam Bam!" Bubba said before Bam Bam could say more. It was possible that the DEA agents would figure out something was amiss and save their collective sets of bacon, but not if Bam Bam spilled the beans. "They dropped the charges."

McGeorge's brows knitted together into a fierce frown.

Bam Bam nodded weakly. "They did. And that fella, Gus, I tole you about, well, his big secret was that illegal cockroach racing after hours. Can you believe that shizz? I couldn't get you on the phone." He glanced at McGeorge. "Say, darling, is that a gun or you just happy to see me?"

"That gun isn't as big as Nancy's .50 caliber Smith and Wesson," David remarked. "Nancy said hers would take down an elephant."

McGeorge glanced down at the revolver. "It's not? I didn't see a .50 caliber Smith and Wesson in the big house. Who's Nancy?"

"He's talking about a gun that belonged to another woman who tried to murder another group of people, dear," Miz Demetrice said accommodatingly.

"So you're planning on shooting Bubba," Alfonzo said, "and *only* Bubba?"

"He murdered Kristoph," McGeorge snarled.

"Kristoph wasn't—" Willodean's mouth slammed shut when McGeorge rotated the gun's barrel in her direction.

"Uh-uh-uh. What did I tell you?" McGeorge said. "No more talking from the deputy who likes to grab a girl's finger."

Willodean sighed.

"Okay, then just leave all these people be, and I'll go with you," Bubba said, "wherever you want to take me. No need to involve them or them babies."

286

McGeorge frowned again. She plainly didn't want to take a suggestion from Bubba. "You are coming with me," she said slowly, "but I can't leave them here. I could tie them up." She took a moment to consider the plan.

"You can't tie up little babies!" Pilar said.

Clearly McGeorge hadn't taken into account the presence of toddlers. Blanca (or was it Blanco?) took the moment to say, "Barfloo!"

"They might suffocate or something," Pilar went on. "I promise I won't call the police. I don't like the police, you know. They always think we're doing something illegal. It's terrible to have *la policía* looking at you funny all the time."

"I can't..." McGeorge said and stopped. "I can't trust you to do that. I'm not that stupid." She brightened suddenly. "I have a company van. Everyone's going. Then when I'm done with Bubba, it doesn't matter. You can tell whomever you want. Tell it to CNN or maybe Joan Rivers."

"You can't have the babies watch!" Miz Demetrice said as if it were fine that McGeorge was going to kill Bubba in front of them, but God forbid she did it in front of small children. Murdering Bubba was okee-dokee, but not in front of the kids.

"Thanks, Ma," Bubba said dryly.

"They won't have to watch," McGeorge promised. She got very serious again, "but you *all* are coming with us."

"Dang, Bubba," Bam Bam said, "don't you know no body who ain't a stone cold killer?"

●

In an uneasy group, they shuffled into the Pegramville High School gymnasium. The film crew had been busy setting up the scene for the day's shooting. Reflective sheets had been set up to maximize the lights in the room.

287

Cameras were in place, along with microphones, boom poles, and rigging equipment. Marks had been made on the floor for the various actors to take their cues from. But no one was around.

Bubba held the door open and said, "The lights are over there." The only thing he had been happy about was that Precious had been left at the caretaker's house, content to chew on the remnants of the T-bone steak. Precious hadn't cottoned to the fact that she was being left behind until the front door had closed and she was on the wrong side.

McGeorge pressed her gun to the back of Willodean's head and had one arm wrapped around the deputy's neck to keep her in place. Willodean looked less happy about the whole thing than Bubba did. Willodean had come to see him out of uniform and her service weapon was likely in her Jeep locked in the safety box in the back of the car, along with her night stick and her handy cans of mace. *Bet she don't do that again.*

"You get those lights on," McGeorge said, "and no funny stuff. Everyone else inside."

"This is what a brotha gets," Bam Bam said, "when he try to be good for a change. All I was trying to do was help Bubba out and get this film on track so I could get my quarter percentage point."

Bubba got the lights on and illuminated the entire gym. The previously prepared equipment lay all over the gym's floor, ready for whatever Risley Risto was going to do on this particular day of filming. The school had been closed in response to the filming and everyone was happy that money was falling into their coffers.

"Oh, my goodness," Miz Demetrice said loudly, "I cain't believe we've been kidnapped and held at the Pegramville High School gymnasium!"

Everyone looked at her oddly for a moment.

McGeorge indicated that Bubba should go to the podium on one side of the gym. When the school had its weekly group meetings, it was in the gym that all the students gathered, and the podium was used by the various people who needed to speak at those functions. It was the podium that Risley was using in the big finale shots. They made their way across the glassy floor, avoiding the various accoutrements of the film industry, until they were next to the podium, waiting for McGeorge's next move.

"Here," McGeorge said. "Kristoph would want it that way," she added solemnly. She wiped a tear away from her eye.

The doors to the gym suddenly banged open and people started flowing inward. Bubba looked up and saw Risley, accompanied by Marquita and the redhead. Then there were some of the actors including Tandy North and Alex Luis. They were followed by Schuler and Simone Sheats. They were all talking at once as they poured in, not even paying attention to what was happening on the other side of the gym.

Risley said loudly, "And then the midget said to the preacher—"

"Well, crap on a popsicle stick," Tandy said just as loudly, looking at McGeorge and accurately taking in the new situation. A cigarette dangled from the side of her mouth and she puffed on it as she stopped.

"No, the midget didn't say that," Risley said. "He said—"

"Crap on a pogo stick?" Alex Luis asked.

"No, he said...is that a gun?"

There was a momentary lapse in conversation.

"That isn't funny, Ris," Marquita said. "Why would a midget say 'Is that a gun?' It doesn't even make sense. The preacher didn't even have a gun."

Risley pointed at McGeorge, who was gaping at the director and the rest of the film crew. "No, *that's* a gun? What are you doing with a gun, McGeorge? I don't remember a .44 from the script? Did we add a .44 in the script? And are these extras?"

"No one move!" McGeorge shrieked.

It finally dawned on Risley that McGeorge was serious. "That's a real gun," he said to Marquita. "McGeorge, what are you doing?"

"I'm going to kill Bubba, the man who killed Kristoph," McGeorge announced into the wide open area of the gym. The words echoed around the room for a long moment. Then she felt compelled to fill in the silence. "I might not have seen it, but he was there and it was his knife. He must have done it!"

"But—" Risley said and then abruptly stopped.

Marquita looked at Bubba. "You said you didn't kill Kristoph."

"I dint kill Kristoph," Bubba said tiredly. He saw Willodean shaking her head and frowned at her. He didn't want her trying to overpower McGeorge and getting shot in the process.

"Move over to the middle of the gym," McGeorge ordered. Risley and the rest moved uncertainly toward the middle of the room.

"Just let the police deal with Bubba," Tandy suggested. "That way you don't have to go to jail, McGeorge. You don't have to go through that agony. I'm pretty sure that Kristoph wouldn't have wanted you to go to jail."

"The police aren't dealing with the problem!" McGeorge shouted. She shook the gun at Willodean. "She's the police! She's his girlfriend! They're covering it up!"

"They're not covering it up," Risley said. "I got a call from the sheriff this morning. They're going to make an announcement about Kristoph's death and it isn't what you think it is." He held up his iPhone and showed it to McGeorge.

McGeorge sputtered indecisively. "What kind of announcement?" Then she perked up and said, "Everyone put their cellphones in the middle of the room! Take them out of your pockets and throw them down! Right now or the deputy gets it!"

Risley threw his on the gym floor and it cracked ominously. It was followed by a few others. Then everyone got into the act. Bam Bam tossed his like he was making a basketball score through a hoop. "I needed a new one, anyway," he said.

Tandy threw an Android down. Then she threw an iPhone down. She followed it with a Blackberry. "What?" she asked, with a quick puff on her cigarette. "I like phones."

"Okay," McGeorge said, looking at Bubba. "No one move. Only Bubba needs to get hurt. He's responsible for Kristoph's death, so he has to pay. Move over by the podium, Bubba. That's where Kristoph would have stood and—"

That was when the DEA broke into the door. Bubba had seen them as he had driven the company van past the entrance to the Snoddy Estate. They had seen him too. McGeorge had made him drive while she held the rest of the people hostage in the back. Bubba had been hoping that he hadn't messed with the DEA agents too much and that they would follow him again. Perhaps they would even think he was up to something new since he was "illicitly" driving a film crew van.

Voila. DEA agents in the thick of things.

Agent Warley Smith variously pointed his weapon at Bubba, Risley, and then Miz Demetrice. He yelled, "NO ONE MOVE! DEA!"

"Could this get any better?" Tandy asked sarcastically.

"No one move, I said!" Smith yelled again.

"Boofarg!" Carlotta yelled although Bubba was wondering if Carlotta was a Carlos.

"There aren't any drugs in here!" Risley shouted. He glanced at Tandy. "Tandy?"

Tandy looked at the ceiling and then at the floor. "Nope," she said, "no H. Not at all."

"What's going on?" Smith yelled.

"She's got a gun on the sheriff's deputy!" Miz Demetrice shouted. "Shoot McGeorge!"

"Who's McGeorge?" Smith asked. He pointed his gun at various females until several people pointed at McGeorge, who was trying to hide behind Willodean. "PUT THE WEAPON DOWN!"

"I will not!" McGeorge screeched. "I'll shoot her if you move! Put YOUR guns down! You're making a mistake!"

"Ma'am, we're the government," Smith said. "We don't back down and we don't make mistakes!"

"Bubba killed Kristoph!" McGeorge screamed. "And he smells like pee! He doesn't deserve to live!"

"I tried to explain that—" Risley said.

"We won't be having any killing in here!" Smith yelled. "Everyone get out who isn't a hostage or a federal agent!"

"NO BODY MOVES!" McGeorge pointed the weapon at Bubba.

But of course, that was when Sheriff John and Big Joe burst into the same doors as the DEA.

"NO ONE MOVE! POLICE!" Big Joe yelled. He swung his cannon sized pistol around at various targets, systematically targeting Special Agent Warley Smith and his men as well as Bubba and McGeorge.

"We got a call from someone with a cellphone," Sheriff John said. "Mary Lou Treadwell said ya'll was being kidnapped and held at the high school gym."

Bubba glanced meaningfully at his mother, who shrugged.

"Shoot the woman with the gun who is STANDING RIGHT BEHIND ME!" Willodean screamed.

"Shut up!" McGeorge said forcefully and poked the end of the revolver into Willodean's neck.

Bubba said, "No, don't shoot Willodean! Shoot me!" He rushed forward and McGeorge pulled back in alarm. The executive assistant wavered in her attempt at homicidal behavior. The barrel of the gun went back and forth between Bubba and Willodean. Bubba stopped about ten feet away and said, "You don't have to shoot her, McGeorge. I dint kill Kristoph but ifin you think I did, then don't punish no one else for it. Just let her go and you kin have me."

Willodean groaned loudly and said, "Oh the hell with this."

Chapter Twenty-five

Bubba and the Equable Ending

Friday, March 15th

McGeorge's gun was pointed toward the floor when Willodean moved and her left arm was wrapped only loosely around Willodean's neck. Willodean simply tugged on McGeorge's left arm and bent forward. It was a smooth uncomplicated undertaking that made it appear as though Willodean was simply turning, tugging, and tossing.

Bubba took a breath. It seemed as though the air moving through his mouth was the only thing he could hear for the longest time. It was half gasp, half protest, and all amazement. McGeorge went right over Willodean's form, sliding over the petite deputy like she was greased up with 15W-40 motor oil. Then McGeorge was doing a flip in the air and the weapon went flying away. Bubba couldn't take his eyes away from what Willodean was almost effortlessly doing to McGeorge, but he heard the crack when the Colt Anaconda hit the bleachers. Then McGeorge's feet were in the air, pointing straight toward heaven. There was another crack when Willodean slammed the other woman into the floor.

McGeorge let a breath escape her mouth and her entire body went limp.

"No one is going to hurt the father of my baby," Willodean snarled, straightening up, and brushed her hands off. Sheriff John walked over and handed Willodean his handcuffs, which Willodean used with a competence that Bubba admired tremendously. She flipped McGeorge over onto the woman's stomach and put the cuffs on her wrists with two loud clicks. The words finally penetrated Bubba's consciousness. His mouth opened and closed. He remembered to breathe again.

Willodean knelt over McGeorge and her lovely head came up as she realized what she had done. Her perfect mouth formed another word. "Oops." The "Oops" echoed in the gymnasium like it was a great empty cathedral.

Big Joe said, "Hey, ya'll are in my jurisdiction now. That's my prisoner, I'll have you know."

"Waffle!" Carlotta yelled. (Carlos?)

"McGeorge kidnapped us outside city limits," Willodean said, not taking her eyes off of Bubba.

"She kill Kristoph, too?" Big Joe asked.

"No," Bubba said, "she dint kill no one. She put the real bullets in the gun that Tandy fired at me, though. Don't reckon she was really trying to kill me. She knew Tandy's a terrible shot."

"Hey," Tandy protested, then shrugged.

"That's a helluva gamble to take," Willodean said and stood up. She nervously crossed her arms over her chest and Bubba's eyes automatically sank to her abdomen.

Bubba was supposed to say something else. He knew it and his tongue tied mouth was messing it up. He was supposed to declare his everlasting love and pledge his troth and he was supposed to make it special. This was a moment in time he would never forget and he was screwing it up.

"What do you mean, she didn't kill Kristoph?" Big Joe asked.

"You killed Kristoph!" McGeorge screamed suddenly, glaring at Bubba. Willodean glanced down and toed the woman in the side.

"Bubba didn't kill Kristoph," Sheriff John said. "What the blazes makes you think that?"

"It was his big-ass knife in Kristoph's back," McGeorge said. "Everyone said so!"

"The knife didn't kill Kristoph," Sheriff John said. "He was dead before that."

McGeorge lifted her head up to stare at Sheriff John.

A new voice spoke up. "Bubba wasn't inside long enough to kill the director man before the girl on the floor showed up." It was Pilar. She pushed forward, holding one of the babies in her arms, and stared determinedly at Sheriff John and then at Big Joe.

"Who's this?" Big Joe asked.

"I'm Pilar Garcia," Pilar said. "We work for Miz Demetrice. I was watching out of the window that day. I saw everyone coming and going from Bubba's little house. Busy house. First, Kristoph and his wife went in." Bubba waited for someone to ask why Pilar had been watching out of her window, but no one thought to ask and Pilar wasn't going to volunteer why they were so paranoid.

"Marquita dint do it," Bubba said. "Mike Holmgreen caught the footage on his camera. She argued with Kristoph but came right back out."

Marquita pushed forward and said, "Kristoph was fine when I left. Grumpy but fine. Lord, he was so grumpy last week. He said he didn't feel too good."

"Well, the person who went inside Bubba's house before Bubba came home was…" Pilar said and pointed.

The crowd around Risley parted. It might have been Moses standing before the Red Sea but Risley wasn't Moses and the people there weren't the Red Sea. Risley said, "I didn't do it. He was *totally* dead before I got there."

"That man was in there a long time," Pilar said indicating Risley. "Fifteen, twenty minutes."

"I admit I found Bubba's bayonet in his room," Risley said, "and I—"

"You stabbed a dead man with a bayonet," Sheriff John said. There was a hint of disgust in his voice.

"Well, I couldn't let, I couldn't let, oh crudcakes, I admit it! I stabbed a dead man with a bayonet," Risley crossed his arms over his chest and shut his mouth, obviously taking an opportunity to utilize his Miranda rights before someone read them to him.

"You tried to frame me," Bubba said to Risley.

"It wouldn't have stuck," Risley said weakly, clearly forgetting about those vexatious Miranda rights. "It hasn't ever stuck before. I read all about you. You're like the Teflon redneck. They arrest you once a week. You must have your own jail cell."

"Is that why I got a role in the movie, because you sorta felt guilty about the whole thing?"

Risley shrugged halfheartedly.

"Why would you do that?" Willodean asked.

"Risley was covering up for someone," Bubba said. "Why else? He thought someone else did it. Mebe he thought Marquita did it and tried to cover up for her. She *is* his sister." There was a moment of silence while everyone considered that.

"Maybe it was for that other woman," Pilar said.

Carlotta said, "Burgopoo!"

"What other woman?" Bubba asked.

"She watched Kristoph and Marquita go in. She watched Marquita go out. She went in. She went right back out. Staggering a little," Pilar said. She tickled the baby. "She went off toward the film's tents. Then she came back about five minutes later holding a necktie."

297

"Scarf," Schuler said. "It was signed by Liza Minnelli and a work of art. It's a *scarf*." He fingered the shimmering red one adorning his neck. "Can't you people just get it right?"

"Then she came back out," Pilar said. "I almost thought they were having a party in there. I had no idea someone was dead or I would have said something before."

"Who was the woman?" Bubba asked.

"Her name is Leigh," Pilar said. "I heard it later when I saw her talking to the other director man." She pointed at Risley again. The toddler liked that, so he/she/it pointed, too.

"Who's Leigh?" Bubba asked.

Every single person from the film crew excepting Risley pointed at the redhead. The redhead winced.

"The redhead killed Kristoph?" Bubba asked.

"I didn't kill Kristoph!" the redhead exclaimed. "He was dead when I went in."

"But you put Schuler's necktie around Kristoph's neck?" Bubba asked. "You were trying to frame Schuler?"

"It's a scarf, dammit!" Schuler said.

"I couldn't let people think Marquita did it," the redhead said.

Bubba remembered when he had witnessed the redhead touching Marquita. "You and Marquita are, uh, together?"

"Marquita!" Risley exclaimed. "*I'm* with Leigh!"

"And he—" Pilar pointed at Risley again "—watched Leigh come out the second time and then he went in and spent all that time in there."

Bubba looked at Marquita and then at Risley. Then he looked at the redhead. "You were having a fling with both of them?"

The redhead shrugged. "I didn't know Ris saw me or I would have told him what I was doing. Kristoph and Schuler hated each other. Better that Schuler go to jail for his murder than Marquita. Poetic justice. Schuler almost got Kristoph fired from the studio."

Bubba sighed with abject confusion. "So I dint kill Kristoph. Risley dint kill Kristoph but stabbed him in the back with my daddy's bayonet. The redhead, er, Leigh, dint kill Kristoph but tried to make it look like Schuler strangled him with his scarf. And Marquita dint kill Kristoph, unless she did it very fast and managed to pass that polygraph test."

"I did not kill Kristoph," Marquita said definitively. She shook her head in emphasis.

Bubba looked at Pilar. "Did someone else come into my house in-between when Marquita left and when the redhead, er, Leigh, went in?"

Pilar shook her head. "You know I would have told *la policía* this, if we hadn't been...otherwise occupied. I didn't know what was at stake. *Lo siento*, Bubba. You've had such a miserable week, *no*?"

Bubba waved her off.

"So who murdered Kristoph?" Bubba asked.

"Well," Sheriff John said in his gravelly voice and scratched the side of his nose, "there's the rub. Doc Goodjoint said this morning that Kristoph had a heart attack. A huge one. Must have happened right after Marquita left your house. That's the announcement I was making today. I couldn't make heads nor tails out of the other stuff such as the fake strangulation and the fake stabbing, so it's nice to have all the answers now. It was just a big confused mess that folks made a bigger mess out of. Kristoph was NOT murdered."

299

"Kristoph wasn't murdered?" McGeorge asked incredulously.

"No," Sheriff John said, "Doc had the Dallas coroner double check it which is why it took so long. Massive, immediate myocardial infarction. Man was probably dead before he fell down on Bubba's floor. Sad but it happens sometimes."

Bubba shouldn't have felt relief, but he did. Then he looked at Willodean and felt something else altogether.

"What about the smuggling?" Agent Smith demanded. "Someone is smuggling something and everyone is acting suspicious!" He pointed at Bubba. "He tied yarn around a statue! He put lead sinkers down the barrel of an old cannon! Someone is smuggling some damn thing!"

"What smuggling?" Bubba asked innocently.

•

As he sat in a recliner, Bubba held a sleeping toddler. The little boy's head was braced against Bubba's shoulder and he rocked him gently back and forth. They all sat in one of the big living rooms of the Snoddy Mansion. His mother was there as was Miz Adelia, the Garcias and the two toddlers, and Willodean sat in a chair as far away as she could get from Bubba without being out of the room. He didn't like that one bit. "Ya'll bin smuggling *babies*," he said. Miz Adelia and Miz Demetrice had referred to them as shipments. It had probably been so that the cat wouldn't have been let out of the bag.

"Orphans," Alfonzo said and rocked the other one. "The fake birth certificates we have said they were two girls, so they had to be girls all the time, or until we got them to their adopted parents. Most people wouldn't have noticed anyway."

"The Central American country they're from is rocked with a civil war," Pilar said, gently touching the toddler.

300

"There were twenty of them. We've found them homes in the United States, but the government was slow to allow them entrance."

"They were in danger," Miz Demetrice said. "We set up a baby super highway. Safe houses. Honest people willing to break the law for a good reason."

"Those trips at night," Bubba said, "you were delivering babies and then getting another set of children. That explains how they were managing to grow and shrink and change eye colors."

"Si," Pilar sighed. "These are the last two. The priest and nuns who ran the orphanage made it out last night. They're all safe."

"And the DEA thought you were smuggling something. They just dint know what," Bubba said. He couldn't complain about that. How could anyone complain about their mother breaking the law to smuggle endangered orphan babies out of a hostile environment? He'd be like Ebenezer Scrooge, Hannibal Lecter, and Charlie Manson all rolled up into one.

"And we'll be moving on tomorrow," Alfonzo said. "Sorry we didn't finish the painting."

"I'll take care of it," Bubba said. "All the homes for the children," he added questioningly, "good homes. Good people? You're certain?"

Willodean said, "I've vetted all of them. That's why I've been so busy. Sheriff John is onto me, but I think he's okay with it. The DEA will get tired of you in a few days, Bubba. Agent Smith will be explaining his mistake for a month. I should feel sorry for him but I don't."

Bubba sighed and silence ensued for a moment. They'd spent a few hours downtown, explaining what had happened and to whom and by whom. Bam Bam and David had snuck off immediately, probably because Bam

Bam had an avid distrust of all things law enforcement. Eventually McGeorge, Risley, and Leigh the redhead were the ones officially and lawfully detained by Big Joe, although Sheriff John wanted to charge McGeorge with kidnapping and attempted murder. Apparently, Sheriff John was feeling magnanimous and let Big Joe have the arrests.

"Let's get these babies to sleep upstairs," Pilar said and reached for the one in Bubba's arms. "We've got a long trip tomorrow and we have to lose the DEA in the morning."

"I'll do that," Bubba said. "I'll skip down the highway singing 'Lucy in the Sky with Diamonds.'"

Alfonzo chuckled. Pilar went out the door with one child and Alfonzo followed with the other one.

Miz Demetrice glanced at Willodean and then at Bubba. "I think I shall go and count lima beans in the kitchen. There's a need to do this, right now."

"And I'll help you," Miz Adelia said. "Some of them beans might get overlooked otherwise."

Willodean continued to sit in her chair and looked steadily at Bubba. When they were alone, she said, "I tried to tell you but I got a little nervous. I think I missed a pill somehow."

Bubba found the little velvet box in his pocket. He'd taken a moment to retrieve it from his house because he knew he was going to need it. He didn't take it out at first. Instead, he said, "When we went to the cemetery last Friday, I was...I had it all planned, I thought that I would—"

"The flowers," Willodean said in apparent understanding. She stood up and took two steps toward him. "You were going to ask me..."

"And when I was in the zombie makeup, I tried to, but the words didn't come out right and there never seemed to be a time where it was right," Bubba tried to explain, but the words were just as jumbled and tied now as they'd been then. He stood up. "I didn't want you to think that it was only because you're pregnant."

Bubba winced. "Did that sound wrong?" He put his hands out wide. "The most important thing is that I love you." He nodded firmly. "I love you and—" he took the ring box out of his pocket and her eyes went very large as he went to his knees, holding the box out with one hand "— would you do me the very great honor of becoming my wife, Willodean Gray?"

Willodean put her hands to her cheeks and started to cry.

There was a large painful moment while no one else said anything. Bubba was uncomfortably aware that he should have flowers ready or doves waiting to be freed from a cage or perhaps fireworks ready to be launched in exhilarating glee of an anticipated moment, but he had none of those things.

Willodean took another step toward him, still crying. Bubba didn't care for the tears. He couldn't recall if he had ever seen Willodean cry and he supposed it could be the hormones, but he never wanted to take her for granted.

But she was nodding and then he was smiling. When Willodean fell into Bubba's open arms, he was waiting. And for one single sliver in time, everything clicked into place and was perfectly right.

It was a while later that Miz Demetrice said loudly, "Willodean. Willodean! You should take Bubba outside! You know, *because.*"

Bubba had his head resting gently on Willodean's abdomen. Willodean reluctantly pulled away from Bubba and admired the ring on her left hand. "Sorry," she said, "everyone got tired of waiting and they, well, they did something. They didn't tell me until earlier today and the timing is horrible. I wasn't sure how you felt about the baby."

"It ain't exactly the way I planned it," Bubba said but he grinned hugely, "but it's the best thing that ever happened to me. Besides meeting you, of course." He kissed Willodean tenderly and she pulled away reluctantly. "How bad could it be?" he asked, almost as an afterthought.

"Now! Willodean! Quick!" Miz Demetrice said and they heard her footsteps going down the hallway and opening the front door.

Willodean dragged Bubba outside and Precious came over to nose at his leg. She barked once and Willodean knelt to scratch her head. "I hope you like babies," she said to the canine.

I love babies, Precious thought. *The baby shall be my slave and bring me doggy biscuits and we shall gnaw them together.*

"Look up," Miz Demetrice hissed as Miz Adelia joined them.

Bubba looked up into the afternoon sky. It had been a long day but it had been productive and his chest no longer felt tight and constricted. He heard the rubber band-like engine of the plane before he saw the smoke coming out of its sides and the curling sweeps that it made in order to get the job done. He had been correct. He should have gone with the sky writer. That was what the townspeople had done.

The words read in tremendous smoke formed letters "SURRENDER, BUBBA!"

The End.

Bubba and the Author's Addendum

I usually add a few things at the end. Probably because I'm slightly OCD and also because it's my book. Thanks to Lauran Strait who edited this book. But she's not responsible for my errors so give her a break. It really is a horrible job to have to fix all the eccentric author's mistakes. She jumped in just when I desperately needed someone to correct my glaring booboos. Thanks to my husband and daughter who always put up with my insanity while I'm writing. ("Don't look at her daddy, she's got her headphones on," my daughter has been known to warn off my husband.) Finally, thanks to all the lovely people who buy my books. It means a great deal to me to have your support. There are so many authors out there who try to get their foot in the door only to have it slammed shut and I count myself as one of the fortunate few who was able to make it work. I appreciate the readers more than you can know.

Sincerely,

Caren

P.S. In case you thought this was the end of Bubba, it's not. There will be other books with Bubba. I *can't* wait to write about the wedding.

About the Author

C.L. Bevill has lived in Virginia, Texas, Arizona, and Oregon. She once was in the U.S. Army and a graphic illustrator. She holds degrees in social psychology and counseling. She is the author of *Bubba and the Dead Woman, Bubba and the 12 Deadly Days of Christmas, Bubba and the Missing Woman, Veiled Eyes, Disembodied Bones*, and *Shadow People*, among others. Presently she lives with her husband and her daughter in Alabama and continues to constantly write. She can be reached at www.clbevill.com or you can read her blog at www.carwoo.blogspot.com

Other Novels by C.L. Bevill

~

Mysteries:
Bubba and the Dead Woman
Bubba and the 12 Deadly Days of Christmas
Bubba and the Missing Woman
Brownie and the Dame
Bubba and the Mysterious Murder Note
The Ransom of Brownie
Bubba and the Zigzaggery Zombies

Bayou Moon
Crimson Bayou

Paranormal Suspense/Romance:
Veiled Eyes (Lake People 1)
Disembodied Bones (Lake People 2)
Arcanorum: A Lake People Novel (Lake People 3)

The Moon Trilogy:
Black Moon (The Moon Trilogy 1)
Amber Moon (The Moon Trilogy 2)
Silver Moon (The Moon Trilogy 3)

Cat Clan Novellas:
Harvest Moon
Blood Moon
Crescent Moon
Hunter's Moon (Coming soon)

Shadow People

Sea of Dreams
Mountains of Dreams (Dreams #2)

Suspense:
The Flight of the Scarlet Tanager

Black Comedy:
The Life and Death of Bayou Billy
Missile Rats

Chicklet:
Dial 'M' For Mascara

~

CPSIA information can be obtained at www.ICGtesting.com
Printed in the USA
LVOW06s1623080715

445461LV00014B/231/P

9 781494 869175